D0761075

8.19 **DATE DUE**

SEP 2 6 2019	
OCT 0 7 2019	
JAN 3 1 2020	

Dear Carolina

Center Point
Large Print

**This Large Print Book carries the
Seal of Approval of N.A.V.H.**

Dear Carolina

KRISTY WOODSON HARVEY

CENTER POINT LARGE PRINT
THORNDIKE, MAINE

This Center Point Large Print edition
is published in the year 2016 by arrangement with
The Berkley Publishing Group,
an imprint of Penguin Publishing Group,
a division of Penguin Random House Company LLC.

The text of this Large Print edition is unabridged.
In other aspects, this book may vary
from the original edition.
Printed in the United States of America
on permanent paper.
Set in 16-point Times New Roman type.

ISBN: 978-1-62899-834-4

Library of Congress Cataloging-in-Publication Data

Names: Woodson Harvey, Kristy.
Title: Dear Carolina / Kristy Woodson Harvey.
Description: Center Point Large Print edition. | Thorndike, Maine :
Center Point Large Print, 2016. | ©2015
Identifiers: LCCN 2015038571 | ISBN 9781628998344
   (hardcover : alk. paper)
Subjects: LCSH: Large type books. | Domestic fiction.
Classification: LCC PS3623.O6785 D43 2016 | DDC 813/.6—dc23
LC record available at http://lccn.loc.gov/2015038571

For my two Wills,
A real-life happy ending

ACKNOWLEDGMENTS

It seems that every time a book is published, there's a little bit of magic involved, a sprinkling of fairy dust. For me, that magic was winning the Women's Fiction division of the Tampa Area Romance Writers contest, which was judged by my editor, Katherine Pelz. Thank you, Katherine, for loving this book, for saying yes, for sharing my vision, and for helping these characters come alive. You have made this process so fun and easy that I didn't get to complain about my editor even once!

And Bob Diforio, my wonderful agent, thank you for orchestrating rewrites and asking for opportunities, for continuously opening doors, and for taking a chance on me. Your voice on the other end of that phone line, telling me that this far-off fairy tale was actually happening to me, will always remain one of the pinnacles of my life.

I am so fortunate to have the opportunity to work with the amazing team at Berkley. Thanks to all of you for everything you did to help this book come together. Thanks especially to copyeditor Amy Schneider for taming my love of commas and polishing this manuscript so well. And thanks to Diana Kolsky for the beautiful cover, and Caitlin Valenziano for helping *Dear Carolina* get out into the world.

The real hero of this story is my husband, Will, who didn't bat an eye when I wanted to quit my job to be a freelance writer, and didn't flinch when, after that, I told him that maybe I'd like to write a novel. When I was frustrated and daunted by depressing publication statistics, I would say, "How long do I do this? When do I throw in the towel?" And he would always respond, "When writing quits making you happy." There really aren't men like you. Your love and support is always the thing that makes me brave enough to take a chance. There's no one else I'd rather navigate this life with.

Thank you to my mom, Beth Woodson, my amazing first reader, who took on so many responsibilities at our blog, Design Chic, and, quite often, also became my personal shopper, party planner, and babysitter so that I could sneak in writing time. Thanks for teaching me to always follow through when I start something and never letting me quit. Thanks to my dad, Paul Woodson, who taught me to always be my best, to always be prepared, and that practice really does make perfect, even if it's just for the church softball game. Thank you both for being such amazing examples and for telling me from the day I was born that I could be and do anything I put my mind to.

My grandfather, Joe Rutledge, when I announced that I was going to go to journalism school, unflinchingly and very seriously said, "Well, someone has to take Barbara Walters's place," and my grandmother, Ola Rutledge, was the voice in my head saying, "This too shall pass," in those moments when those rejection letters clouded my vision of an ultimate happy ending. Thank you to both of you for always cheering me on.

Kate McDermott, Nancy Sanders, Cathy Singer, and Anne O'Berry, my friend and aunts, were the best "editors" a girl could have. Thank you for poring over these pages, asking questions, making suggestions, and, ultimately, loving this novel. Your support made this nerve-wracking time so much easier.

Thank you to my son, Will, for fulfilling the biggest dream of my life. Being your mother has changed me completely, has made me feel more and love in ways I never could have imagined. Thanks for keeping me up all night so I could send all those query letters and for being willing to have your breakfast on my lap while I snuck in a few hundred words. Never forget that you can do anything you put that little mind to, and, of course, that you are loved so unconditionally.

Most of all, thank you to God, who, as always, put these thousands of puzzle pieces together and combined them into this one little book in ways I never could have seen or imagined. Grace is the most astounding miracle every, single day.

There are no words to express the gratitude I feel to all of you who hold this book in your hands, who walk through this world with these characters. That you would take your time to read something I created . . . That, I think, is the real magic.

Dear Carolina

Khaki

SALAD GREENS

I designed a special scrapbook for each of my children. A custom-made blue or pink album with white polka dots and a fat bow tied down the side, the front center proudly displaying a monogram that was given to each of you. I take those books out every now and then. Sometimes I add a new photo or memento. Other times I gaze at the pictures and marvel at how quickly the eyes-closed-to-the-world phase of infancy morphs into the headfirst-plunging alacrity of toddlerhood.

Other times, like tonight, with your book in particular, my sweet Carolina, I sit on the floor of our family room overlooking my favorite field of corn and simply stare at the cover, running my finger across the scrolling monogram. *It's only a name,* we have been reminded since middle school in what has now become perhaps the most cliché of Shakespeare's musings. But, in what is certainly not the first exception to a Shakespearean rule, that name means more than the house your daddy built in this field where we spent so much time falling in love or the sterling silver service that has been in our family for generations.

It means more because that name wasn't always yours. And you weren't always ours.

I was, just like a mother should be, the first person to hold you when you were born. Your birth mother, after thirty hours of labor, fainted when she saw you, perfect and round and red as a fresh-picked apple. I felt like holding you first would be like stealing money from the offering plate. But as soon as the misty-eyed nurse placed you in the nest of my arms, you quit crying, opened your eyes, and locked your gaze with mine. That instant of serendipity was fleeting because it wasn't more than a few seconds that your birth mother was out.

When she came to, and I was there, cuddling this lighter-than-air you that she had grown inside herself for nine long months, I begged for forgiveness. But she said, "I'm glad you got to hold her first. You've been here this whole dern time too."

I had given birth myself before, and that teary first introduction to a new life after a forty-week hormone roller coaster was fresh in my mind, still damp like the coat of paint on the wall in your nursery. But I'd never been on my feet, outside the bed, when four were breathing the air and then, with one tiny cry, there were five. To experience that kind of wonder is like being born again.

Even in that resurrection moment, I couldn't have known that one day, I would get to hold you, swaddled and warm, all the time. But I did swear that I would do everything in my power to protect you, love you, and make sure you grew up good and slow as salad greens.

And so, my love, if you ever look at your book and think maybe it's a little thicker than your sister's and your brother's, it's only because instead of having one mother to save snapshots and write letters and remind you how much she loves you, you have two: the one who brought you into the world and the one who brought you up in it. And if you ever start feeling like maybe you got dealt a bad hand, that having a mother who raised you and a mother who birthed you is too tough, just remember this: You can never have too many people who love you.

Jodi

JAM LEFT ON TOO LONG

Some things in life, they don't even seem right. Like how you can preserve something grown right there in your own backyard and have it sitting on your pantry shelf 'til your kids have kids. And how them women down at the flea mall can write a whole Bible verse on one of them little grains of rice. And then there's the thing I know right good: how ripping-your-finger-off-in-the-combine awful it is for a momma to have to give up her baby.

I think you already got to realizing, looking at me right now, messin' in your momma and daddy's white, shiny kitchen, that I ain't just your daddy's cousin. 'Course, you're still so little now, you cain't know how I grew you in me, how I birthed you, how I loved you and still do. But you give me that same crooked smile my daddy had and squeeze my finger real tight—and it's like you know it all. Whenever I say that to your momma, she says back, "Of course she knows. Babies know everything."

It's a right simple thing to say. And simple is who I am and what I've been knowing my whole life. I cain't say a lot of fancy things, and I don't believe in making excuses as to why I'm not doing your raisin'. So here's the boiled-down-lower-than-jam-left-on-too-long truth: I gave you up 'cause I loved you more than me. I gave you up 'cause I wanted you to have more. I gave you up 'cause, in some, murky way, like that river that runs right through town, my heart knew that it'd take giving you up for us to really be family. I used to tell your momma I was scared that being in your life was gonna hurt you. But then she'd tell me, right simple: You can never have too many people who love you.

Khaki

OTHER PLANS

My favorite interior design clients have always been those who approach me with file folders with magazine clippings seeping over the edges like overfilled cream puffs. They like the feel of this room, the light of this one. They can't live another day without a chaise precisely like that.

I'd always been like one of those clients, totally in touch with what I wanted. So when your daddy Graham and I got married, I knew we'd have lots of babies. I already had your brother, Alex, of course. But when he was born it was different. I was a very young widow living in Manhattan full time, my design business and antiques store taking off. In short, I was busier than a Waffle House waitress when third shift let out.

But once I moved back home to North Carolina and married your daddy Graham, his calming demeanor and being so close to nature soothed my soul like a raw potato on a cooking burn. I wanted to breathe deeply, feel the sun on my face, and watch my children grow.

I was dreaming about Graham and me rocking on the porch watching Alex and his two little sisters—little sisters that he didn't have—play, when I woke up that Sunday morning, my arm tingling numb from being up over my head. I looked down to see Alex nestled in the crook of my body, his arms splayed wide in that unencumbered, worriless sleep of children. He was snoring on one side, Graham snoring on the other, the three of us snuggling like a litter of puppies in the barn hay. I smiled at how the morning sliver of sun peeking through the small opening in the curtains glistened off of my three-year-old's blond strands.

Graham yawned, opened his eyes, and leaned to kiss me. His muscular grip wrapped around me as I shook my practically dead arm, the pins-and-needles feeling burning through me. "Mornin', Khaki," he said.

My name was really Frances, but Graham had changed it nearly two decades earlier when I used to dress in head-to-toe khaki work clothes and ride around the farm with my daddy. It was one of those nicknames that had grown like creeping ivy and been impossible to escape.

I looked back down at Alex's closed eyes, smiled at his legs propped on mine, and whispered to Graham, "Do you have any idea how many times we've had sex in the past two and a half years?"

"Mmmm," he hummed, nuzzling his face into my hair, his unshaven chin pricking my cheek. "I like where this conversation is going."

"No, I'm serious," I said. "Four hundred sixty-two times."

He nodded. "I'm glad to know that someone is keeping track. Are you saying that's too much or not enough?" He grinned that boyish grin at me, his blue eyes flashing, and said, "Because I'd err on the side of not enough, personally."

I rolled my eyes. "Come on, Graham. Why the hell am I not pregnant? I mean, how hard can it be? I wasn't even trying for Alex, and 'bam!' just like that." I snapped my fingers, ignoring the fact that I had been only twenty-six then. I tried to push away the thought of that declining fertility chart the OB-GYN had shown me at my last appointment. He had said, "Well, at your age it just takes a little longer." He'd made Graham and me feel like a couple of forty-eight-year-olds asking for some sort of miracle, not thirty-one-year-olds on a very reasonable quest for their second child.

Graham shrugged and yawned. "Maybe my guys don't want to swim in the winter. Maybe it's too cold. Maybe we should wait until summer."

I crossed my arms, my nostrils flaring. He pulled me in closer and kissed my cheek.

"Oh, come on, pretty girl, you know I'm just teasing you. We're going to have lots more babies and fill this house up."

I looked up at him, my lower lip protruding the slightest bit. He kissed it back in place, leaned his forehead on mine, and whispered, "I promise. I'd never let my girl go 'round not getting something she wanted."

I smiled, my heart feeling that familiar, practically lifelong surge of love for my childhood sweetheart, when Alex rolled over, looked around sleepily, and laid his head on my lap. "Hey, Mommy?" he asked.

"Yeah, sweetie?"

"Can we have bacon for breakfast?"

I laughed and ran my hand through his shaggy hair. "You can take the boy out of the hog farm, but you can't take the hog farm out of the boy." I pulled him up and gave him a firm kiss on the cheek that was still plump and juicy as a ripe tomato.

"I think we might be out of bacon, but I know some grandparents who never run out of pork." I pinched his side and said, "You go brush your teeth, and we'll go over there."

Graham perked up, and, rubbing his tight stomach, said, "I need a big ole Pauline country breakfast."

Pauline had worked for Mother and Daddy my whole life on the farm, and she made the best homemade biscuits and gravy in the world. I shook my head. "I will take Alex to Mother and Daddy's. Then, when I get home, if you impregnate me, you may have a Pauline breakfast as a reward."

He whistled and rubbed his hand down the back of my silk gown. "Oh, baby, I love it when you get so romantic with me."

I slapped his thigh and pointed my finger at him. "I'm not teasing you. I'm getting Alex ready, and you better concentrate on producing some of that fine Jacobs baby-making sperm."

When we pulled up to the end of Mother and Daddy's driveway I took a moment to marvel at how the giant oaks, each of them having been there for centuries longer than the home itself, grew together into a green canopy, the ideal frame for the white plantation home that graced their ending. I had an entirely new feeling about this house now, its white columns of Pantheonic proportion that were so quintessentially Southern.

When I was younger, coming home equated to poorly chosen words and hurtful digs from my mother. Maybe it was becoming a grandmother or the general smoldering of temper fire that comes with aging, but my once impossible-to-please mother—though still a force to be reckoned with—had become much, much more pleasant.

Alex unsnapped his booster, jumped out of the car, and flew through the front door before I could even say, "Hey, wait up!" or wrangle him into his coat.

He always got as excited as a jewelry collector at a Christie's auction to see his grandparents. It was the same way I felt when I saw Daddy, that mixture of love and pride that swirls together like a backroom science project. Mother stepped out onto the front porch, her sassy hair perfectly styled in keeping with the same Chanel suit she'd been wearing for decades. I felt myself unwittingly roll my eyes. She leaned over to hug my son. We still didn't always see eye to eye, but Mother could have slapped some butter on Alex and eaten him right up like one of Pauline's homemade biscuits.

Instead of following Alex through the front door, I walked around to the side, smiling at Pauline's imposing figure turning bacon on the griddle at the opposite side of the blue-and-white tiled kitchen while she hummed "A Mighty Fortress Is Our God." When she heard the screen door slam, Pauline wiped her molasses-colored hands, almost the same size as the eye on the antique stove, on the apron puckering over her thick waist. She wrapped me in a hug and said, "What's wrong with my baby?"

I had a smile on my face and hugged her back as hard as I could, and Pauline still knew something was wrong with me. "I was just wondering why you're back here frying bacon when I tried my damnedest to bust you out."

She laughed heartily and shrugged. "Had to come back. You was the one that introduced me and Benny, after all."

Pauline had met her second husband and late-life love when she, Mother, and Daddy had come to New York to help after Alex was born. They had started their life together there, but, as I knew all too well, you simply can't take the South out of the girl. Much as I would imagine one would want to escape the claws of my momma, not a year later, Pauline was back like a homing pigeon, Benny in tow. When I confronted her, jaw agape, about why she hadn't run far, far away, she said simply, "You know, baby girl: You and Miz Mason and Daddy Mason's my family."

And so we were, which was even more evident when Pauline said, "Come on, baby. You can tell Pauline."

I sat down on the stool beside the range, my lifelong Pauline-talking perch, and said, "I can't get pregnant."

She looked me up and down. " 'Course you cain't."

I crossed my arms. "Why on earth not?"

"Girl like you cain't get pregnant. You ain't nothing but skin and bones."

I looked down at myself. I was naturally thin. But maybe the stress of traveling back and forth to New York for work was getting to me. Or perhaps the vegan diet and yoga kick I'd been on was too much. The hormone-balancing book I read said it would help me conceive. But every month I was more disappointed than the last when that minus sign appeared on the EPT. "You think that's all it is?"

" 'Course," she said. "You was lookin' healthy when you got pregnant with little man."

I nodded, thinking that, who knows, maybe I was just too thin. Pauline might not have been a doctor, but she was always right. Feeling sorry that I was kissing three months of sprouts, flaxseed, and leafy greens good-bye, I grabbed two crispy pieces of bacon off Pauline's drip pan and crunched. I was a hog farmer's daughter, after all. Bacon was my birthright.

"Good girl." She nodded. "Now you get on outta here and come back for some breakfast when you're good and pregnant."

I laughed, and she added, "I'll keep an eye on little man."

Lying in bed an hour later with my legs propped on the headboard—I had read somewhere that elevating your legs helps the sperm find their target—Graham kissed me and said, "I just feel like it took that time, babydoll."

I smiled weakly. "I sure hope so."

He nodded. "I'm going to go get ready for church while you . . ." He paused, circled his finger around where I was lying, and said, "While you do whatever it is that you're doing there."

An hour later, sitting in church, light streaming through stained-glass windows, Graham's arm around me, Daddy beside me, and Alex playing down the dark wood pew, I felt the strongest message from heaven that I had before or since: I was going to be a mother again. Of course, I thought, naturally, that I was pregnant. Turns out, God had other plans.

Jodi

UNDERTOW

Whole grapes is one of the hardest things to put up. You got to seed 'em and stem 'em and, even when your fingers are worked to the quick, all stained and blistered and burning, the end result ain't worth a whole heck of a lot. But try telling that to a regular at the farmer's market who's so crazy about grapes he cain't see straight. He scrunched his nose and said, "Well, I know they won't be perfect, but, hell, can't I just skip all that and can 'em whole anyway?" If you ain't never canned you cain't understand.

It's the same way with drinkin': People who ain't never had a run-in with the bottle don't get what it's like. They squint their eyes, look at you like you've been spoutin' off some kinda calculus formula, and say, "Can't you just stop drinking?" They shake their heads to make you feel the Lord's shame and say, "Can't you see what you're doing is ruining your family?"

But you cain't.

One time when I was coming up, Daddy took me to Atlantic Beach, and, while I was swimming in the ocean, wouldn't you know, that dag dern undertow got me. And it was gonna have its way with me too. I paddled left and kicked right, spewing and choking and coughing, that salt water clogging me all up. Then I figured that the waves is gonna win this fight. So I let go, gave in to that madder-than-hell devil ocean, and let it take me away. Finally, when it was done with me, it carried me to shore.

Same thing when I was drinking. I'd claw and kick and spit all day long not to have that first sip. But it was only just a matter a' time before that bottle'd be calling my name so hard I couldn't do nothing but feel my lips wrapped around its fat, dirty neck.

When Momma was sober one time she said, "Baby, I ain't just gonna stand around here and watch my girl go through this shit."

But my raisin', it had been oil-slick with Momma passed out on the bathroom floor right after she'd gone to an AA meeting. And the other mommas would corral their youngens outta our house like dogs on sheep's heels when they met my word-slurring momma. I remembered all that one morning, while I was fixing to get my head in the toilet and rid of the poison I'd drunk the night before. And I made a promise: I would never put anyone through a raisin' like mine. I would never, ever, I promised my dragon-breathed, dark-circled reflection in the mirror, make a child go to wonderin' every time she walked through the door if she was gonna get the nice sober momma, the short-fused craving-crazed momma, or the angry drunk momma.

Even while my head was pounding like a hammer on a two-by-four, while that black sea of drink was doing the tango with me, I knew I was being like my momma. I could smell that same godforsaken venom on my breath and feel its grip on my body, like one of them pythons in the woods that got Bobby Daniels when I was a girl.

But I couldn't stop.

And so, I lost everything. I had already lost my daddy, which is how I got this whole drinkin' thing started anyhow. Now I was losing my momma. My friends. My job. But I would have rather lived on the street than give up the destroyer that felt like it was the only thing sacrificing itself for me.

I can see now that being with my boyfriend Ricky weren't a good idea no way you look at it. He was as stumbling and slurring and crazy-ass acting as I had ever been. My therapist in rehab—that's what they call it when they lock you up in a hospital with a stranger snoring in the hard twin bed beside you—said that women choose to be with men who belittle them because that was the example they saw during their raisin'. That might be right. 'Cause, the girls I know, we been through more bad men than the slaughterhouse has pigs.

I guess that, even though he could be the meanest son of a bitch you've ever seen, when Ricky was having a good day, he was the guy you wanted to be around. Like the afternoon he practically ran into the garage where I was working, lifted me up in the air, and said, "I got us a house!"

We'd only been courting a few months, and I ain't never heard hide nor hair of us moving in together. I almost told Ricky that. But then I thought about Momma. I mighta been clean and sober, but she was a dirty drunk. Me and Momma, we was like fishin'. One of us's that bobbin and one of us's that weight. One's floating by minding her own business and the other's trying her damnedest to sink 'em down to the bottom of the sea. While I was at my AA meetings, she was fixing to go to the bar.

"This is all your damn fault," she'd slur when she got home. "Having you ruined my life. I coulda been somebody."

I got to looking at her good, that shriveled woman alone in her nicotine-stained single-wide. "Momma," I asked, "who in the hell'd you think you was gonna be? You pushed away every person who ever even figured on helping or loving you."

When I told her I didn't have time to get her

more cigarettes before I left for work that afternoon, she took to yelling. "You're so damn worthless." That vodka was talking for her right good. "Get the hell out and don't come back," she had slurred at me from the couch, cigarette hanging out of her mouth, yelling over the TV.

I looked into Ricky's deep, hazel, bloodshot eyes and kissed him square on his clean shave. Ricky, when he got all clean-shaved it meant he had woke up with one hell of a hangover and decided his drinking, partying, womanizing days was over.

I wished that that cigarette would fall outta Momma's mouth and burn up her vodka-soaked couch with her on it. I got all happy about it for a half second. Then I felt right sorry. It'd been me on that vodka couch not too long ago. And couldn't nobody or nothing save me from drowning neither.

But my momma, she could make me take to drinking again like nothing you've ever seen. So I did what I reckoned I ought to. I said, "Yay! I cain't wait to see it!" I kissed Ricky, he lowered me to the ground, and I asked, "So, where's this house you're so tickled over?"

"Well, it's still on the lot 'til we find a place to put it, but then they're moving it to us free of charge."

I wasn't trying to let Ricky see how disappointed I was. My entire life I'd been clawing my way outta that trailer park like a cat up a tree. "Just you make sure it ain't in the same park as my momma," I said.

Ricky laughed, kissed me, and said, "Love you, babe. Cain't wait to show you when you get offa work."

As he turned to leave, a voice behind me said, "He seems like a nice guy."

I turned and stood right up on my tiptoes to put my arms around my cousin Graham's neck—my oil-stained coveralls and his mud-covered overalls meetin' up. We were people that made it through this life by workin' with our hands. I shrugged and said, "Sure."

My big cousin, he always been watchin' out after me. He and his wife Khaki, they stuck by me even when everybody else turned their backs. I was all looped out and spinning around one afternoon, but I remember Graham scolding Khaki for giving me money when we all knew good and well what I was gonna do with it. Khaki, who was damn near as feisty as crazy old Miss Pat in the trailer down the lot, she looked at Graham and hissed, "I know what it is to lose the most important person in your life. She'll work it out when she's good and ready."

Khaki's first husband died from drugs, keeled over right there on that fancy Wall St. trading floor, just about how I like to have died from drinking.

Graham said, all whispery like, "If she doesn't kill herself first."

Khaki gasped. She hadn't realized yet that me and her husband, we was the same—and she was helping me do what he done. And I loved her for it that day like she was the fireman who rescued my cat from a tree.

Graham got me all outta my head, saying, "Sounds like you need somewhere to park your new home."

I nodded and scrunched my nose. "One of my goals in rehab was to get out of a trailer park once and for all." Tony, who'd been working at this garage practically since it opened, was looking up at me kinda mean. So I said, "No offense."

He shrugged and slid underneath a white 1998 Oldsmobile just like my momma used to drive.

Graham nodded and said, "I've got this patch of land a few acres over from the house that not a damn thing'll grow on. It's all yours if you want it."

I gasped. Me and Ricky could be sitting in lawn chairs, holdin' hands and staring at the trees, grilling out, maybe even having a kid or two sometime. It don't matter that that picture assumed Ricky could act like his nice, human being self for long enough to make it through a meal. "Now don't get to thinkin' I'm being ungrateful. We'll pay you rent and whatnot," I said.

Graham readjusted his cowboy hat and said, "Tell you what. You keep us in Grandmomma's blackberry preserves I love so much, and we'll call it even."

I shook my head, thinking a' my daddy and how he wouldn't never take a handout. "Graham, you been getting into the whiskey again?" I said. "That ain't nowhere near even."

Graham shot me that half smile with the dimple that made all the girls in high school swoon, that made all them hate Khaki for how he chased her like a retriever after a pintail. He said, "You don't know how much jam I eat."

I thought about it and it didn't take too much more convincing to make me say yes. I wondered what it was gonna take for Momma to clean up again, how far that bottle would have to drop her off the balcony before she'd kick it to the curb.

For me, it took a lot. It weren't until I woke up in a trailer park with no shoes, no purse, facedown in a puddle of my own throw-up, not one dag dern clue what I'd got into the night before, that I finally hit rock bottom. Or, near like I was that little girl at the beach again, the undertow released me. And I was carried to shore.

Khaki

RESCUE CREW

One of my favorite rooms I've ever designed was featured in my first coffee table book. It was an awkwardly configured bathroom in which, years before it was popular or I had ever seen it in *Veranda*, I placed a gorgeous, antique claw-foot tub in the middle of the room. It was something I'd never expected.

Adopting a child wasn't something I'd ever expected either. But you can't know how your life is going to turn out until you're living it.

I feel guilty sometimes about the way it all happened, about my participation in your birth mother giving you up. But then I push that thought away because if I hadn't been at the right place at the right time, if I hadn't done what I did, then I wouldn't get to wake up every morning to the sweet sound of cooing through the baby monitor or see you laugh with delight when I walk into the room. And so I know it all turned out like it was supposed to.

But I'll never forget the day that Jodi came to me, head hung down, eyes red-rimmed and puffy, and asked, in the quietest, saddest voice I've ever heard, "Can I borrow some money?"

It sounds terrible now, but, in the moment, I was kind of annoyed. I had planned a call with the head of my design firm, Anna. And I was in the throes of three very demanding design projects, was working on a marketing plan for my new book, had to get a blog post finished, and needed to check in with Daniel, the manager of my antiques store in New York, to see what I needed to buy at the auctions that weekend. And Alex was with Mother and Daddy for only three hours. Needless to say, every moment had been carefully orchestrated.

But, all the same, I brought Jodi through the front door and sat beside her on the couch, holding her hand, looking deep into her watery eyes, my mind going to the first, natural place it would go. "Oh, Jodi, you're not drinking again, are you?"

She shook her head like that simple movement was taking all the strength in her bony body. I looked her over, her mousy hair stringy and greasy, hanging in her face, a tomato-sauce stained sweatshirt over a pair of faded jeans with holes that hadn't been put there ironically. My mind jumped to a vision of poor, sweet Jodi, down on her knees, wearing away at that fabric, praying every minute that God would give her a different life.

"I am happy to lend you money," I began slowly. "And I'm not trying to treat you like a child. But I can't give you cash without knowing what it's for." I thought back to the last time I had helped Jodi out, to the lecture from Graham I was certain would never end. He was usually fairly amused by my antics, my husband, and I craved that way he looked at me like I was the only thing on earth that mattered. He scolded me only when it was serious. And he was serious that I never, ever give money to an alcoholic.

One fat tear fell down Jodi's face, but she wiped it away quickly and said, "I gotta get an abortion. I ain't got the money to do that and make the trailer payment."

I leaned back on the couch and took a deep breath. My first thought was, *Why her and not me?* But I pulled myself together. I knew exactly where she was because I had been there a few years earlier, right after my first husband Alex had died. Of course, I wasn't contemplating an abortion for the same reasons as Jodi. I was just afraid. Afraid of being a widowed mother. Afraid of being alone. Afraid of dying and leaving an orphan. It was the kind of afraid that wakes you up at night and won't let you settle back down, the last wound-up, sugar-crazed girl at the slumber party. Part of me wanted to tell Jodi I was sorry, give her the money, and go on about my day. Part of me knew that, at nineteen and a recovering alcoholic with a minimum-wage job, the future was bleaker for her and that baby than a hospice patient.

But the other part of me knew how having my Alex had erased the gray rain cloud hovering above the black-and-white sketch of my life and replaced it with a full-color blue sky. The other part of me knew that one day, the little girl in front of me shaking like a guitar string in a blues solo might wish she had known all the information before she had made her decision. And so, I found myself wrapping my arm around her and saying, "Honey, I've got to tell you about when I found out I was pregnant with Alex."

I told her about the abortion clinic that rainy day in New York and Jane, the counselor who had helped me realize that I should at least think about my other options. I told her about how I saw Alex jumping inside me for the first time on that ultrasound screen, and I realized that I wasn't just a widow and I wasn't all alone; I was a mother. I told this teenager, whom I didn't know much better than the teller at the bank, my deepest, darkest secret, the horrifying truth that I had shared only with Graham and my best friends Stacey and Charlie.

I poured my soul out onto the living room rug like a can of Carpet Fresh. And I knew from her vacant, listless stare that she was so buried in the ash from the eruption of her life that she couldn't hear me.

So I said, "Jodi, I have to tell you: I was in the worst, deepest, darkest well of my life and that baby was the rescue crew that came to fish me out. I don't know how I would have made it without having him to live for."

Her face shifted. "Ricky left me."

I nodded solemnly, but I was thinking that was probably the best thing that could ever happen to her. But I didn't say that, of course. Instead, I asked quietly, "Did he know about the baby?"

She nodded like she was about to be unhooked from life support and take her final breath. I knew how she felt. I remembered that weariness that seeps through your organs and hides out in your bones, that sadness that takes over your mind and grips you in a way that you don't think you'll ever get back to a place where a smile can dance on your lips or a laugh tickle the back of your throat.

"He seemed like he was all right with the whole thing. But he didn't show up for my doctor appointment yesterday mornin'. And he didn't come home last night. And he ain't been here all day today."

I wanted to say, *Good riddance*. But you can't make someone see how terrible their partner is when they're blinded by love, no matter how ill-advised that love is. "Doesn't he disappear like this from time to time?" I asked.

She finally leaned back on the silk faille-covered sofa, pausing for a second, staring down at her feet. Then she said, her voice cracking, "He's gone for good this time."

I wanted to tell her that *gone for good* meant dead like my husband Alex. Gone for good didn't mean cruising around in the truck that your pregnant girlfriend was paying off with her hard-earned money. It didn't mean chugging beer with one hand on the wheel, throwing empty bottles out the window into the bed—and, if you were really, really lucky, a girl drunk enough that she didn't realize what a no-good bastard you were. But I remembered being nineteen. I remembered that shiny half dollar of love story hope that made you think the beast was going to turn into a prince if you just waited a little longer. Sure, he was an ass, but he was going to *change* for you.

I had bitten my tongue long enough and so, in a way that I hoped seemed encouraging, I said, "Sweetie, I think you're better off raising this baby by yourself than you would have been with him."

She shook her head. "I cain't be trusted with a baby."

I cocked my head and adjusted the books on the mirrored coffee table, catching a glint of my diamond in the reflection.

"I think you'll be an incredible mother. Why couldn't you be trusted with your own baby?" She shook her head again. I added, "I know you're young, but you're smart and ambitious." I leaned back, smiled, and rubbed her arm supportively. "For heaven's sake, you can change a tire faster than a highway patrolman."

I thought that would elicit a smile, but instead, I saw a shiver inch up her spine. "What if I get to drinking again?" she whispered like she was afraid the cloisonné lamps would hear her and tell.

And that was when I realized it: I could try to equate our two situations all I wanted to, but they'd never really be the same. Because addiction is a force that I can read about or listen about or think about, but that, praise Jesus, I'll never truly understand.

Jodi

NOBODY FROM NOWHERE

Asparagus is one back-flipping tricky vegetable. Some people can it, store it, pull it out and eat it like their last meal in the joint before they meet their maker. But I wouldn't give you two grubby cents from the car cup holder for canned asparagus. Now, when I was coming up, I wouldn't touch fresh asparagus with one of them clubs we played trailer park golf with. I didn't like that light green crunch I'm so crazy 'bout now. I'd down that slimy goop straight from the can. But, like them sparkle high-tops the ladies down at the Salvation Army brung to the house one Christmas, I grew outta canned asparagus.

I reckon Ricky and that asparagus was kin; I

grew outta him too. In any sorta crisis, any time you needed your man to stand up, take charge, Ricky, he shriveled up on you like that poor, limp canned asparagus.

When I told your birth daddy that we was having a baby, he looked me up and down, sighed, and said, "I thought you had that shit taken care of." Then he turned and said real low like, though he knew I was in earshot, "Should've known she was too stupid not to get pregnant."

I hope you're wonderin' why I would let a man treat me like a maggot-filled garbage bag. But that's how my momma done my daddy. And I was all wrecked from drinking and not even thinking I deserved Ricky, that flea-bitten dog.

Right straight from rehab and clean raw like an asphalt scrape, I walked outside, sat down in front of all them rich-looking red flowers that Khaki and me planted like we was gonna be happy, and cried. I kicked myself like Mr. Simms done them poor dogs down at the trailer park before the animal control people come in and took 'em away. I sat up real straight and said out loud, "Jodi, you get to leaving that sorry-ass man. Trailer's in your name anyhow on account a' his sorry credit."

But here's the thing about worthless men: They know how to behave right well enough that every time you're right on the verge of scraping 'em off your shoe, they do something that makes you ignore how awful they been.

About that time, that truck I cosigned for come up the road, dirt flying out from bald tires. Ricky scrambled out, holdin' one a' them gas station roses with the baby's breath. He jumped outta the truck and kissed me good and hard. "I'm so sorry I said that, baby. I think I might like to have a youngen."

And damn if I weren't right there again, thinking the devil was a saint. Why I let him pull me in and reel me back out over and over again like a fly rod on a riverbank, I cain't say. I can say it was on account of my age, but I think it was something more like fear. I was nobody from nowhere and didn't have nobody. What decent guy was ever gonna want me?

So I think it was a blessing from heaven when Ricky didn't show up at that ultrasound appointment. I had to stand in line with that Medicaid card, face burning with shame. I had to lay down on that rough, white paper sheet with no one holdin' my hand. I had to see my baby all alone.

Khaki, she had some life-changing moment when she saw Alex for the first time, one of them visions from heaven that gets people to thinkin' they can make it through dern near anything.

But me, I saw a jelly bean, reckoned it didn't look like a person, and decided to take care of it once and for all. Khaki, she tried to talk me out of it, but my mind was made up.

I had carried my friend Marlene to have two

41

abortions already, so I got to figuring she'd be the best person to call. But before I could even pick up the phone, I heard a knock at the door and, lo and behold, wouldn't you know it? There she was.

I know she cain't help it, and, heaven knows, she's my best friend. But some people are just born looking cheap and stay that way 'til the worms get done with 'em. A sorry excuse for a dye job from Antonio's salon right there in the trailer park and makeup done up tall like so much cake frosting weren't good no matter how you looked at 'em. But that weren't it. Khaki could take Marlene on up to New York City and get her plucked and brushed and trimmed and scrubbed and clothed by the fanciest people in the world. But one look right hard and you'd know she'd grown up on the rough side of the trailer park.

"Girl," she said when I opened the door. "You gotta do something to yourself."

I knew my hair was greasier than them fast-food fries my momma was always trying to pass off as home cooked. And wouldn't no amount of makeup cover up them dark circles. But, for Pete's sake, I was fixing to make the biggest decision since rehab. Marlene squinted brown up at me from under blue shadow, and I could smell the Aqua Net holding her curling-ironed ringlets in place.

She cocked her hip and pointed at me, them dark eyes gettin' even squintier. "You been drinking again, Jodi Ann? 'Cause if you been drinkin', you cain't hide it from me of all people."

Watermelon breath flew clear across the trailer, and I could see that wad of gum hiding in the corner of her mouth. I'd been knowing Marlene for sixteen years, since her momma left her daddy and moved into the trailer right beside ours. And I couldn't think up one time I ain't seen gum in her mouth. I asked her 'bout it one time and she said, real cocky like, "It's my diet plan. If I got gum in my mouth I ain't puttin' a brownie in it."

"Ain't being poor our diet plan?" I had said.

That day, I peered back at her. "I ain't drinking again, Marlene."

"Oh good," she said, shimmying past me through the door and plopping down on my couch. " 'Cause I started selling Shaklee, and I think it's gonna go real good. You gotta do it too."

I sighed. Marlene was always climbing up on one moneymaking pyramid or another. She'd get all happy and carryin' on for a week or two, realize she couldn't sell water to a man on fire, and go back to waitressing while figuring how she could get the government to give her more money for community college. She handed me the brochure all official like and said, "See, it's environmentally friendly cleaning products."

I looked at the brochure, and I near about dropped my teeth when I saw that a "starter pack" was getting at $100.

"Who in their right mind's gonna pay more than a day's wages for some Windex?" I asked.

Marlene smacked her gum, twirled a piece of hair around her finger, and rolled her eyes. "Jodi," she said, like I were denser than poor old Mikey that swept the floors at the market. "You don't understand. They're *concentrated*."

"I don't care if they clean the dag dern house. We don't know nobody who can spend a hundred dollars on some cleaning mess."

Marlene wasn't listening, same as usual when I tried to talk her out of these harebrained schemes. First it had been Tupperware. Then Mary Kay. Then prepaid legal. Now this.

"Jodi, I just don't know why you gotta be so negative all the time. All we gotta do is sell to rich people who don't want chemicals in their house."

I leaned back on the couch. "We don't know any rich people."

Marlene shook her head. "You know Graham and Khaki. They can send us on over to all their rich friends, and we can get them hooked on supplements and weight loss products and cleaning supplies." She snapped her fingers. "Before you know it we'll be living in big houses like theirs thinking expensive, fancy cleaning supplies ain't nothing."

My head was hurting good now. "Look," I said, setting the Shaklee pamphlet down beside me, thinking that it sure did look fancy. I sighed. "I'm pregnant."

Marlene squealed. "Yay! A baby!"

Before I could even get to tellin' her that I weren't having the baby, she was going on down the line about streamers we could get from the party supply store and who she was gonna invite to the shower she was throwing and how much fun it was gonna be to have a baby.

"Marlene," I finally broke in. "If you're so in love with babies, why the heck didn't you have the two you got pregnant with?"

Marlene looked at me like I just told her I ain't been washed in the blood after all. "Because, obviously, Jodi, I got a *career* to think about."

Like Marlene was some Erin Brockovich saving the world and I was sitting up here on my ass watching soaps all day. "Well, I'm not sure if you've noticed, but I ain't exactly shining my diamonds over here." I took a sip from the glass of water beside me. "I ain't some pampered house-wife. I gotta work too."

"But you got a man to take care of you," Marlene protested. "Nobody's ever took care of me."

My chin got to quivering, and Marlene was across the room faster than a twin-diesel pickup at a green light. "Oh, sweetie. Where is Ricky?"

I leaned my head onto Marlene's shoulder and sobbed good. "He's gone. He left when he found out about the baby."

Marlene jumped up again and said, "That no-good bastard! How could he leave you all alone like this?"

I shook my head. "That's why I have to have an abortion," I whispered. "There ain't nothing else to do."

Marlene stomped her foot. "No. No, no, no. I'll help you. You always been the smart one. I ain't lettin' you ruin your life over some asshole cain't even make his own damn truck payment."

I hadn't let Marlene talk me into one dern thing before. Not Mary Kay or prepaid legal or any a' that mess. But I got all weepy and girly when Marlene started going on and on about tiny socks and hair bows and having someone to love you no matter what. *Having someone to love me no matter what.*

Now, Marlene cain't sell a tube of lip gloss to her own momma. But she got me all stirred up and believin' that having you was gonna be some great adventure. Having you was gonna be the thing that turned my life around. Sometimes, when we want to believe something bad enough, even a second-rate salesman can close the deal.

Khaki

HAPPY CLAMS

Here's something I know: Homes with small children should forgo white sofas, regardless of how much Scotchgard they have. Here's something else I know: Men don't like fertility clinics. Cups and small rooms and other things that you're too young to hear about are involved. Graham might have been "sure" that that Sunday morning baby-making session had taken, but, a week and another negative test later, I thought I might disintegrate into a puddle of tears on the Stark area rug–covered ground. I reminded myself about a million times a day how lucky I was to have one healthy, beautiful child. But I felt like another baby was the missing piece in our family puzzle.

I had waited as long as I could to broach the subject. As the edge came off the cool and the whole world felt like it was going to burst into bloom on the first warm day, I knew my time had come. I wasn't going to be the only one who hadn't blossomed. So I said, "Honey, I'm making us a doctor's appointment, you know, to make sure everything is okay."

He gave me an Elvis lip and replied, "We're

young and healthy, babydoll. We've just got to keep trying."

I crossed my arms, looking down on him where he was lounging shirtless on the couch, watching *SportsCenter*. His tight, toned abdomen and upper body, sculpted by nothing more than good genes and sweaty, manual labor, almost distracted me enough that I let him win. Almost. I got my wits about me and sighed loudly, and, when he saw my serious expression, he said, "Fine. Make the appointment, and I'll go."

Truth be told, I simply assumed something was wrong with him. I had, after all, success-fully created one offspring with another man. So it shocked the daylights out of me when a doctor who looked young enough to be one of Graham's summer high school farmhands said, "Mrs. Jacobs, I'm so sorry to tell you this, but according to your preliminary tests and ultra-sounds, it appears that you have a condition called endometriosis."

I only half listened to him chattering on about tissue surrounding my ovaries. I was stunned because I hadn't let myself consider that some-thing might actually be wrong with *me*. I think I came back into the space across from the huge, mahogany CEO desk that made my physician look even more like he was playing pretend right about the time he said, "A simple laparoscopic surgery could both diagnose the extent of the disease and clean it up so that it would be easier for you to conceive."

Without so much as thinking, I said, "Great. I'm available tomorrow."

Graham looked at me skeptically and said, "Khaki, let's not be so hasty."

I glared at him and, I must admit, raised my voice a bit. "Hasty? I'm fairly sure that after three years making this decision isn't hasty. I want to be pregnant *now*."

I knew I sounded like a spoiled child, but I didn't care. I turned my raised, worked-up voice to the doctor. "This surgery will mean I'll get pregnant, right?"

He looked a little scared of me, which was logical. I was something to fear.

"Well," he started, "it will certainly increase your odds, but . . ."

I set my hand on the desk and peered at him. "But what? Spit it out. What are you trying to tell me?"

He leaned back farther in his chair, and said, "There's some evidence that women with endometriosis have difficulty carrying a child. Uterine muscle cells lose their ability to expand and contract—"

I inhaled sharply and loudly, cutting him off. "What's the bottom line?" I asked, far too irritated to sit through an hour's worth of medical jibber-jabber.

"The uterus isn't . . ." He rubbed his fingers together, looking for the right word. "Stretchy."

My OB-GYN had just used the word *stretchy* when referring to my uterus, and I might not be able to have a baby. Not the news I had dreamed of. Instead of asking for a Kleenex, I looked at Graham and said, "I am happy to discuss this with you further when we get home." Then I looked back at the doctor and said, "Theoretically, how quickly would I be able to get in for the surgery?"

"Well," he said, and I could tell by his body language that he was fully prepared to put both hands up to cover his face in case I launched a pointy object at him. "Dr. Stinson is one of the foremost experts in the country in this disease, so I would assume you would want him to do the surgery."

"Of course," Graham responded before I had the chance to say that any old resident would be fine with me as long as he or she could un-gunk my ovaries.

"Honestly, you're probably looking at seven to eight months before he can work you in."

I pulled my thick sweater tighter around my waist and practically spat at him, "What!"

I thought about Alex, like I do about every thirty seconds when I'm not with him. Finding out you're pregnant with your dead husband's baby pretty much classifies as a miracle no matter how it happens, so I wasn't one bit above believing that his conception was an act of God. But I asked all the same, "So if I have this condition, why did I have such an easy time getting pregnant and carrying my son?"

The doctor just shook his head. "I wish I had a clear answer to that question."

I wanted to roll my eyes, but I was starting to calm down a bit, realizing how lucky I was to have Alex, how I had taken for granted how simple and natural it had all seemed, like it was my right as a woman to automatically get pregnant.

The doctor continued, "The disease affects every woman differently, so you may have had it all along and it didn't affect your fertility, or it may have started after you already had your son. We may be a little bit clearer on that after the surgery, but there's no way to really know for sure when it began."

I nodded and looked at Graham, wondering how difficult it was for him to look unfazed by all of this. But I wasn't surprised. He was always, always my rock.

I stood up, grabbed my toy- and Goldfish-full Lanvin tote off the floor and said, "Thank you so much, but I think I'll try to find someone who can work me in a little more quickly."

I was already Googling "endometriosis experts NC" on my phone as Graham followed me out the door saying, "Sweetheart, I know you're upset, but let's calm down for a second."

I crossed my arms and huffed, "I don't have time to calm down. I have to find another doctor, and Daniel is coming to town today to help me buy for the store and I have to get a blog post done in the car on the way back to Kinston, and I promised Father John that I'd design the event hall for the church bazaar this weekend." I sighed, let my shoulders fall, and said, "And all I want to do is climb in bed with my little boy and take a nap."

In the midst of that freezing parking lot, my breath billowing around me like the steam I needed to blow off, Graham, as he so often does, wrapped his strong arms around me and rested his chin on top of my head. He was as rock-solid and even-keel as I was crumbling and hysterical.

"It's going to be okay, you know," he said. He kissed the top of my head. "If this is supposed to happen for us, it will." He kissed me again and added, "And if it's just the three of us, I'm happy as a clam." I could feel his jaw shift into a smile as he said, "We'll get a bigger boat." He squeezed me tighter. "Hell, maybe we can even upgrade you to a little larger work apartment in the city."

He was trying to cheer me up, and I didn't want him to know I was crying, so I didn't say anything. I pulled back, turned away quickly so that he wouldn't see me wipe my eyes, and said, "How do we know those clams are even happy?"

He smiled and opened my car door for me. As I stepped up on the running board of the Suburban, I said, "Do you think this is why my stomach hurts so badly all the time?"

Graham shook his head. "Your stomach hurts all the time and you didn't think to have it checked out?"

I shrugged. "I thought maybe it was from having a baby." I leaned my head against the window, the freezing pane soothing my hot head. "Plus, who has the time?"

As I looked out the window, the sky appearing again after the level after level of concrete parking garage, I realized that maybe I had been in denial all this time. Deep down, I knew something was wrong. But considering that I might not be able to have any more children was like considering moving to another country. For some people it might have been just right. For me, it felt completely foreign.

Jodi

DUST AND ALL THAT

I used to feel right sorry for lettuce when I was coming up. You could pickle them winter beets and keep 'em all purple and juicy. And you could throw broccoli in the freezer and keep it all green and crunchy. But poor lettuce. You cain't do one dern thing to save it.

Me and that lettuce, we was the same. 'Cause I was different too. When other youngens was having tea parties with their dolls, I was puttin' together carburetors with Slick Sal and Hard-Time Tony at Al's Body Shop. Momma, she was always serving time for swigging a few and then sneaking Aqua Net or Pond's in her purse. I never had no polished toes or braided hair. I changed oil and rotated tires. And thank the good Lord up above, really. I weren't the kind of girl from the kind of family where people get to talkin' 'bout going to college or bright futures or any of that other hog slop. I was from the kind of family where people got all worked up like you had cured cancer if you got outta high school.

Mrs. Petty, the fancy, thin high school guidance counselor who told me that she put rubber bands through the buttonholes in her pants to make them fit all the way through her pregnancy—good advice once I was pregnant—had called me to her office one day and said, "Jodi, I think you've got a lot of potential. I think if you'd take the SAT one of these Saturday mornings we might get you a college scholarship."

"I work down at the garage Saturday mornings," I had said, looking down at my grease-stained fingernails.

Mrs. Petty, she pinched up her pink-lipsticked

mouth and said, "Surely you could take a morning off." She waited, but I didn't say nothing. "Or maybe we could find another surrounding school that's offering the test in the evenings."

You knew by her look that she couldn't understand where I was coming from any more than I understood her pretty blond children and sweet, faithful, sober husband in one of them white houses up on the hill. I ain't never thought about leaving Kinston or college or nothing else. Nobody ever told me I was worth something or could do nothin'. So I weren't gonna jump up and hug her neck and say, "Wow! I could go away to a college where won't nobody understand or accept me for free?"

Plus, there weren't nobody to take care of Daddy if I weren't home. And I was a darn sight better than Momma at caregiving even if I was only seventeen. Lucky for me, the garage where Daddy worked 'fore he took to bed, where I was working on Saturday mornings, had an opening for me full time. Spark plugs and changing batteries and replacing fan belts—them things I knew. College and other fancy mess was for rich girls.

I was doing right good 'til I started showing up at work drunk. Al called me right there in his office and said, "I'd try to keep you out of respect for your daddy, darlin', but it ain't safe to operate heavy machinery when you're sauced." I nodded and hung my head, but by that point, I didn't care 'bout nothing but my next drink. So I sure as hell wasn't worried 'bout keeping my job. "Get yourself cleaned up and you always got a job with me," Al had said.

And Al, he's a man as good as his word. Once I quit smelling like Jack, my job was all mine again. The thing is, them greasy, hard-living, missing-teethed men didn't get all hot and bothered over an addiction. But they couldn't near look at me when they found out I was pregnant. Al bit down on the toothpick hanging outta his mouth and said, "How the hell you gonna fit underneath a car when you look like you swallowed a watermelon?"

"Al, your damn belly's twice as big as mine'll ever hope to be." I smiled like my grandmomma taught me, crossin' my fingers and toes.

He laughed, but no dice. "Honey, you're better to look at than all these other jackasses around here, but I can't see having some knocked-up chick running around my garage. It seems like it'd look irresponsible, be bad for business."

I got canned the day after I decided for sure I's gonna have you. I found an old tube a' Momma's red lipstick crammed between my car seats, bought a newspaper, and circled anything I could right near understand. I got interviews for being a fry chef, Walmart greeter, store clerk, bakery manager, dry cleaner, Laundromat attendant, housekeeper, yard mower, and coffee maker.

Turns out, I ain't got one real skill apart from mending cars. 'Course, I could plant an old leather shoe and make it grow into something beautiful and cook it up into something right near delicious. Grandma, she'd made sure of that.

I was just laying in my bed in the trailer, looking up at the ceiling, turnin' my eyes down every few minutes at how my belly was just bowing out the tiniest bit, like a crescent moon half sneaking out of the sky. I didn't want 'em to, but them tears escaped down my cheeks, thinking about my grandma, all them days I spent on an old upturned bucket rolling out biscuits or putting up all them sweet peas she loved so much.

I closed my eyes, and I was five years old again, the warm near-spring wind blowing, the tall grass of that field tickling my bare feet and pushing that long, unkempt hair right in my face so I could get a whiff a' that smell from Momma smoking right beside me on the couch.

Grandma, looking back, she was too old to be kneeling over that plot of dirt like she was, getting her hands all dirty kneading down in the earth. But she motioned to me, the wind catching her short silver hair too. "Come here, darlin'," she'd said. "Let me show you somethin'."

I kneeled right down beside her, and she handed me a seed. One round, perfect, smooth seed. I'll never forget how it felt in my fingers, how it gave energy to my whole body. I looked up at her, her eyes too blue and glowin' for somebody who'd lived hard on this farm, those deep lines in her face that hadn't ever seen so much as a stitch of makeup. I smiled. And she smiled a knowing smile right back.

"That love of the land, that living right near it and on it and in it, that understandin' how it all works, it's in your blood, Jodi. No matter what happens in your life, no matter how much people let you down, you can count on the land. It won't never let you down."

The sun was starting to set as I pushed that single seed into the straight row of fresh, tilled dirt. And I don't know how I knew, I's so little. But it was like when you wake up and it's still dark and the birds ain't chirping but you just know that if you look out your window the sun is gonna be risin'. I just knew that that little seed was gonna take hold and grow up tall and make me feel like God remembered me out here in the sticks after all.

That was the first year I helped Grandma plant them little dirt rows. And I did it every year after that too. Every year for eleven more years, me and Grandma planted seeds until we was worked right to the quick. The day that last crop was ready to harvest, not a month before Daddy got the pancreatic cancer, I found Grandma, laid up over them sweet peas, deader than a doornail. I just sat there with her a long time, hummed her a lullaby with my arms around her. Me and Daddy had her cremated and scattered her all around that field. Felt like the right thing to do for somebody that loved the land like my grandma. Ashes to ashes and dust to dust and all that.

Grandma, she's the only real momma I ever had, only one in my whole life 'sides Daddy who ever cared about me or thought I was worth teaching something. The only thing that made losing her even tolerable was that she didn't have to watch Daddy, that boy she loved so much, suffer so.

'Course, the worst part a' all of it, the worst one a' them deaths, was letting go a' that field, the only place on God's green earth that my little-girl dreams could run wild and free, the only place I knew I's worth something and could make something beautiful grow.

I sighed long and low, swallowing them tears away, putting my hands on my little sprout. "Grandma," I said out loud, my stomach growling, saying it knew right good I hadn't had nothing fitting to eat in near about a week. "I cain't very well make a living offa talking to them plants the way we used to. So what in the hell am I gonna do?"

I don't know if it was Grandma or God or that hungry ache in my stomach that made the answer seem right clear. But I knew what I had to do. Daddy woulda whooped me good if he thought I was one of them people standing in line for a handout, living off the government. But my daddy, he weren't never at a real dead end like me. When every dag dern door was slamming hard and fast in my face, that check was the window God opened.

Khaki

YANKEES DO HAVE MANNERS

Unless they have a severe aversion to the color, I always paint my clients' offices a shade of green. Green helps focus the brain and hold attention. That day, I was wishing I had a little green because all I could think of, driving from that Chapel Hill doctor's office to the Raleigh airport to pick up Daniel, was pink and blue.

Daniel was a fellow designer who had been working at my antiques store in New York for years and became manager right around the time I became a bi-state commuter. He had taste as flawless as a Tiffany diamond, but I had yet to let him help me with the buying for the store. Graham says it's because I'm a control freak. I say it's because I'm particular.

When we pulled into the cigarette haze also known as baggage claim, Daniel was already waiting with his roller suitcase, looking freshly pressed as always, like he hadn't even been on a plane. We didn't get out to greet him because the terminal was a mess of uniformed officers and blowing whistles and buses.

"Hey, y'all," Daniel said, sliding into the backseat of the Suburban. Graham and I looked at each other and laughed, exactly what we needed to break our baby-fueled tenseness.

"What?" Daniel asked.

"Oh, nothing," Graham said. "It's just interesting to hear 'y'all' with a Queens accent."

"No good?"

I looked back and said, "Dan, you need to put your seat belt on."

He looked around, confused and said, "Seat belt? I'm in the backseat. You don't have to wear a seat belt in the backseat."

Graham snorted like Daniel was going to be sorrier than if he'd renounced the Republican Party to my daddy.

"Oh, sure," I huffed. "No problem. Leave your seat belt off. Then when you come flying through the windshield in a wreck, you won't only kill yourself. You'll hit Graham and me, snap our necks, and kill us too." I turned around to look at him again, and he was already buckling as I said, "We wear our seat belts in this family."

"Geez," he said. "I'm buckling. I might even wear my seat belt in cabs after that lecture."

Graham patted my leg reassuringly. He knew

61

that I was more wound up than usual because, while I was jabbering on to Daniel about seat belts, all I could think was: *What if I never get to buckle another baby seat into the back?*

Daniel rubbed his hands together and said, "Well, so far, the Raleigh airport is one of the nicest I've been to. Is the rest of North Carolina that great?"

"Sure," I said, thinking about how backwoods and undeveloped Kinston would look to someone from Manhattan. But the slow pace and quiet moments were what we loved most about our little map dot. And our farm, no matter where you were from, was something to be proud of.

"Hey, Dan," I said, "I'm just reminding you that if you had flown into Greenville or New Bern this ride home would only have been thirty minutes."

"Yeah," he said. "But then I would have had to switch planes and risk my life during two flights."

Graham winked, and I shook my head.

An hour and a half later we turned up the tree-lined driveway to the double wraparound front porches that had recently graced the pages of *Southern Living*.

Daniel whistled. "Wow . . . I see why you ditched New York for this place. It's amazing."

"Wait 'til you see the inside," Graham said. "I didn't know how bad I was living 'til this little lady spruced me right on up."

Graham was always complimentary, but I knew

he was trying to make me feel better after my heartbreaking morning. I didn't know how I was possibly going to get through the next two days with Daniel, shopping and chatting and acting like everything was normal.

Fortunately, I wouldn't have to do much talking that night because we were having family dinner at Mother and Daddy's—a big, gracious, country "welcome" for my city friend. Daniel politely kissed Mother, shook Daddy's hand, returned Pauline's bear hug, and nodded to my sister, Virginia, and her husband, Allen. But when they had turned their backs to go to the table, he said, "Holy hell. Is this place going to be in your next book?"

I looked around the entrance hall, with the grand double-branched staircase, the intricate woodwork seeming slightly less formal and definitely freshened for a new decade by the sisal runner. The casually covered, French-framed love seat and chairs in the foyer had been almost a harder sell than getting rid of the dark Oriental and Persian rugs that, to me, made somewhere cavernously huge seem dark and stuffy.

I nodded to Daniel and said, "It only took me a decade to convince Mother to let me get my hands on it."

"It was worth the wait." He smiled, letting me walk before him to the living room, proving that, no matter what my daddy told me, Yankees do have manners. My brother-in-law Allen, on the other hand, a native Southerner, showed over dinner that it doesn't matter how many grits you ate growing up; some people simply have no class.

I assume the half-dozen beers he had before dinner contributed to his foul mouth that night. But why he would think it was appropriate to tell the story he did I'll never know. As we sat down across from him, my sister's husband was saying, "So that stripper was as butt-ass ugly as you've ever seen—"

I could feel the table vibrating from Virginia kicking Allen, and Graham interrupted him saying, "So, Mrs. Mason, did Rider's arrange these gorgeous flowers for you?"

It was a clear ploy to get Allen to stop talking. He was either too dense or too drunk to get the hint. "Man, I'm telling a story here," he said, slurring slightly. "So, one of my friends went upstairs, found her purse, and stole all her money." He banged his hand on the table, making the crystal water glasses spill over onto the linen place mats. He snorted and said, "Isn't that the best damn thing you've ever heard?"

Mother pulled her chair back from the table and walked into the kitchen. The rest of us just sat there, a stunned silence filling the room like the smell of frying chicken. I raised my eyebrows at Daddy, who rolled his eyes and shrugged. Virginia was looking down at her hands, her face the color of the pickled beets Pauline was whisking through the door.

"So, Daniel," Daddy said. "Tell us the truth. How is it working with my Khaki?"

Daniel said behind his hand, "Does he know your name is Frances?" Everyone laughed, breaking the tension in the room.

Graham rubbed my shoulder and said, "A little nickname for a little farm girl."

Daniel nodded, put his arm around me, and said, "You know, I owe everything to your daughter. She's taught me all the tricks of the trade. I love her like family."

I leaned my head on Daniel's shoulder and said, "Aw, thanks, sweetie." Then I picked my head up, looked at him, and said, "But I already told you, you aren't getting my office."

Mother reappeared, apparently having composed herself from Allen's totally inappropriate story time, and said, "Virginia, I think your children need you at home."

Virginia looked at me helplessly, but I didn't rush to her defense. I loved her, sure, but I couldn't stomach Allen. I remembered how happy Mother and Daddy had been when he proposed to Virginia. Allen was Daddy's right-hand man on the farm, so it was one of those great Southern alliances from which everyone could benefit. But I wasn't fooled for a second. I'd always found him to be crass, mannerless, and unfit for my sister.

Tonight was no different. "If it's a kid thing, you're the woman," he said. "You go. I'm having a good time."

"I think you better go on home with your wife, Allen," Daddy said gently.

When I complained about Allen, Graham used to tell me that I would never think anyone was good enough for my family. He didn't say that anymore. As it turned out, I had been as right about Allen as I had about cornice boards. They were both fine as long as they weren't in *my* house.

As the front door slammed, Momma said, "Daniel, I am so very sorry for my son-in-law's behavior. There's no excuse, and I hope you weren't uncomfortable."

Daniel, fortunately, had a quick wit and a way of making others feel at ease. "No problem. I ride the subway. Strippers are nothing compared to my morning commute."

Graham raised his glass and said, "I'd like to propose a toast. However we create them, here's to our families."

We clinked glasses, and, though Graham might not have known it at the time, that toast was more of a mouthful than any of us would ever have believed.

I snuggled into Graham when we got home,

66

amazed at how just the smell of him could still render me spellbound all these years later. I sat awake in bed thinking about that poor stripper who was probably a single mom with two kids at home just trying to make ends meet, being robbed by one of Allen's idiot friends.

That night, I made love to my husband for the first time in a long time where I wasn't thinking about the end result, about the baby I hoped and prayed we'd made. In those moments we shared I thanked him for not being like Allen, for not being like Ricky, but, most of all, for being like him. I told him that he was the rock in my life, that his steadiness and steadfastness, the way he had loved me without question for decades, was the only thing real and true in my life.

It's a puzzling dichotomy, but, though I can write all day long about duvet covers and contemporary art, expressing my feelings to the people I truly love eludes me like a golf ball on a dark fairway. While other men in my life have pushed me for that reassurance, Graham never has. And that's the magic of our relationship, the fairy dust unraveling from the wand. I say to him what needs to be said through my body, not my mind. And it's a language he always understands.

Jodi

NEARLY STARVED IN THE YARD

Coming up, I used to eat so many carrots my skin turned right orange. I'd run on out into the field behind Grandma's, yank one of them green stems, and crunch away. Then, one day, I got to where I no more liked eatin' carrots than my momma liked cleanin' the trailer. Crunchin' on 'em hurt my teeth, the taste turned my stomach inside out, and that fresh-from-the-ground craving quit real quick.

The same thing when I was pregnant with you, only, praise the Lord Jesus, it were booze I quit wantin' so hard. That psycho lady the state made me go talk at once a week said, "Jodi, you don't want to drink because drinking is the coping mechanism you use when you want to run away. Somewhere, deep down inside yourself, you don't want to run away from this pregnancy."

More like not craving that drink deep down in my soul was the bone God finally threw me even though He'd kept me right thirsty and nearly starved in the yard for years.

When you're poor like me and you come up in a small town like Kinston, people, they want to help you. The church Momma got herself to when she was sober—the one that been praying hard for her all along—they brung over a whole mess a' stuff for you.

That sweet old pastor, I wouldn't never in a million years have taken a handout from him. So it was Buddy, who been working on the farm for Graham long as I known him, that came a-knockin' at my door with two big black trash bags flung over his shoulders.

"Who is it?" I hollered.

In the ignition crank before he answered back, I thought the damn craziest thing: It was Ricky. He was comin' to wrap me up sweet and kiss me hard and tell me the only thing a girl wants to hear: "Baby, I've changed. Let's make things right for our youngen."

And, oh my Lord, I had longed for him to come back like a farm boy pines for his first hunting puppy. But I wouldn't let on. No. I'd act like maybe I'd be a little interested.

When the voice said, "It's Buddy," I was still going on in my head like it were Ricky gonna be answering me. The mind is one tricky vehicle when it gets going good down a dirt road with a dead end.

I hauled myself up off the couch where I'd been napping all day. I still got to feeling every now and then like I should be working. But it's like how that old oak tree at the trailer park must've felt like the swing wrapped around its branches had always been there. We all just got to learn to adjust.

Buddy dumped them giant black yard bags on the floor between the kitchen and family room with a thud like a pair a' work boots going off over the side of the bed.

"What's that?"

He shrugged. "Just a bunch a' old junk the church sent over. I brought it in trash bags 'cause half of it will probably be going straight to the Dumpster anyhow."

I sat down on my knees. My mind wandered to this yoga lady I flipped by on the TV earlier that mornin'. She said this sittin' on your knees'll make you be able to digest so good you can eat rocks. I said to the TV, like she could hear me, "I don't care how thick a accent you got, lady, I ain't buyin' that nobody can eat rocks."

I got to pulling things outta that bag, and I wasn't trying to look happy or nothing, but I held a beautiful soft white cotton dress with a tiny pink bow right to my chest like it were a baby its own self.

I kept on pulling mess out, and I got to realizing that them clothes, they were all new. I wadded them all back in the bag, scooted it across the floor, and stood up, wiping my hands on my maternity leggings.

"I don't need no handout from your church."

Buddy crossed his arms. "You got some sort of baby fund stored up?"

I peered right hard at Buddy, knowing that he was as straight a shooter as I'd ever run across.

I went to get a glass of water and said, "I don't think that's any of your dern business."

Buddy knew well as he knew how to drive a cotton picker I didn't have no baby money stashed away.

He followed me into the kitchen and said, "I think it would be nice if you would offer me a cold cup of water too."

"This one's for you," I said, shoving it at him all annoyed like. I darn near forgot about my condition for a minute, feeling that heat rising up my spine when our hands met. That was one damn fine-looking cowboy on my green linoleum.

"So how's you giving me a cup a' water that you don't need any different than the church folks giving you some old stuff they don't need."

I didn't realize Buddy was talkin' 'bout scripture or I would've acted nicer. "I ain't taking no hand-out even if I do think it's a nice thing them people's doin'."

Buddy sat down on the couch and said, "Instead of being so self-righteous and acting like you don't need nobody, why don't you write a thank-you note and call it a day?" He pointed over at them bags. "I'm sure as hell not carrying all that stuff back over there, and I doubt you can do it in your condition."

I looked down at my belly, remembering that we

71

wasn't just flirting here. I was knocked up, poor, and all alone.

"Fine," I said. "Motherhood's making me soft," I muttered.

Buddy laughed.

I was giving up pretty easy mostly 'cause any fool could see I worried about how I was gonna get all that baby stuff all day long.

"You know you can come to church any time you want to," he said. "It's a nice group a' folks, and we'd sure be happy to have you."

I nodded. But it was one of them times that life had got me down so hard I weren't sure God even remembered my name. "So that why you came over here?" I asked. "You trying to get somebody new in your church?"

I was baiting, but that Buddy, he weren't biting, not one bit.

"If you ever want to come," he said, "just let Graham or Khaki know." He tipped his hat before turning around. "They'll get word to me."

I couldn't keep from watching his tight back-side in a pair of worn Levi's stroll out my door. Much as I thought Jesus had forgotten about me, sometimes a slow smile from a real cowboy is all it takes to make a girl a believer.

Khaki

A YELLOW JACKET ON A CAN OF CHEERWINE

One thing I always steer my clients away from is any preconceived notion about design. Maybe they think they hate pattern, but pattern is what a room needs to enliven it. Perhaps they think wood floors feel cold, but they would make the room feel grounded and sophisticated. They think black is morbid, but just a touch would make the other colors in the palette come alive as if illuminated by a spotlight.

That's not to say, of course, that I don't believe in preconceived notions about other things. If you've never been to North Carolina, for instance, you've never had proper barbecue. There's a big debate in our state about whose barbecue is better, the western part or the eastern. But it's not much of a competition. Anyone can slop a thick, syrupy sauce over meat. When you can make a pork butt fall off the bone and melt in your mouth with proper seasoning, perfect cooking, and a little vinegar, then you know you've got talent.

I was telling Daniel all about that controversy that was as big a part of Southern politics as the War of Northern Aggression as we sat across from each other at a red-and-white checked table-cloth in the middle of the lunch rush at King's Barbecue. He put down his slaw- and barbecue-filled bun and asked, "What's the matter, Fran?"

I stopped my hush puppy, almost tasting the crispy, golden fried batter, right before it got to my mouth and said, "What do you mean? I'm great."

I was lying, of course. I'd hardly been able to raise my paddle that morning at the furniture auction we'd gone to in nearby Wilson; my head was so full of the information I'd stayed up all night reading. As it turns out, surgery for this condition I had was somewhat controversial, some saying it actually made it spread faster. I had read heartbreaking tales of women who had gone through surgery after surgery and in vitro after in vitro only to never have a baby of their own. On the other hand, I'd read about women whose doctors had discovered the disease had ravaged their insides only when they were performing a C-section for third or even fourth children. I knew already that life was unexpected, and, as I lay in bed beside my husband, iPad with tab after open tab, I made a command decision: It would hurt and it would be hard, but I was going to be thankful for my child and refuse to let what I didn't have overshadow what I did.

That's not to say I would give up; I simply promised myself that I wouldn't let a struggle for another baby define Graham and me. I thought back to that Doogie Howser doctor patting my shoulder and saying, "Don't worry, Mrs. Jacobs. We'll get you pregnant."

"*They'll* get you pregnant," Graham had snickered on his way out of the office. "*I'll* get you pregnant." Then he muttered under his breath, "Arrogant ass."

I thought I might as well tell Daniel what was going on; he would find out sooner or later. But before I could detail my encounter at the doctor the day before, my phone rang. Graham, breathless as a boy in a game of touch football, said, "I have to talk to you."

I mouthed *Sorry* to Daniel, and he grabbed the check and went around the corner to stand in front of the same cash register that had been in the lobby of King's since I was a little girl. I leaned back in my wooden-slatted chair and said, "What are you so excited about?"

"It's fate," was all he said.

"What's fate?"

"I just ran into Amy Perkinson at the farmer's market. You know, from Cowlick Farms?"

I laughed every time I heard the name Cowlick Farms because I thought their slogan was so cute: "No hormones. No drugs. Our cows don't miss a lick."

But this time, I was too anticipatory to even laugh.

"I was asking her about the new baby, and, out of the blue, she started telling me about how she had endometriosis. She and Bill had tried for years to have kids when she got referred to an herbalist by a friend."

My mind flashed back to Virginia making me go see a psychic with her one time. I felt pretty sure that going to an herbalist would be about the same thing. But Graham was so excited that I didn't want to pop his balloon.

"This is it," Graham said, using the same voice he used when he wanted to get Alex pumped up to go grocery shopping or something equally boring. "This is a sign, and this herbalist is going to be the one that helps us get our baby."

I was skeptical at best. I could feel the tears of failure and frustration gathering in my eyes as I hung up, and Daniel, with a fresh sweet tea, said, "There's no way anybody in this town could keep their weight under control knowing there's a Pig in a Puppy right around the corner." When he saw my face he paused. "Oh, I didn't mean you, Fran. You're a fox."

I smiled a little, and he put his hand on my arm and said, "See. I knew something was wrong with you."

I sighed and stood up, picking up my bag as I did to keep the chair from toppling over. "I'm having a hard time getting pregnant."

"Ohhhh." He nodded. "I'm so sorry, shug."

"Shug. Y'all. We better get you home before you turn into a full-blown Southerner."

Daniel led me toward the door saying, "I read an article in the *Times* about how popular Indian surrogates are right now." He took another sip of his tea. "But that would never work for you."

"Why not?"

"Fran, you can barely let me, a trained professional, pick out a piece of furniture by myself. No way you could let some woman you've never met carry your baby without being there to criticize everything she ate and make sure she was following your strict rules."

He was teasing me, of course. But it made me realize that I needed to let go a little. Flying back and forth between Kinston and New York had seemed fun at first, but with a child, a working farm, a household to run, aging parents, an antiques store, a design business, volunteer projects, blogging, and a new coffee table book on the way, sometimes the bi-state schedule felt daunting. The idea that I needed to unload something from my very full life, simplify a bit, lingered like a yellow jacket on a can of Cheerwine. I caught myself thinking, *After all, I am about to be a mother again*. And, for the first time in a while, I realized that I trusted my gut feeling more than what I read on WebMD.

Jodi

LETTING GO TOO EASY

My whole life has been about putting up food and keeping it good and not wasting nothing. So it ain't some big surprise that I'm not real big on change. When I heard some smart people at the garage talking about our "vanishing Americana," it got me worrying. All them special things about America, like a roadside general store and an old Lucky Strike sign. A tobacco barn older than anyone livin' and an album full of black-and-whites. All them stores is always updating, and I don't think it's right. We don't have them fancy cathedrals and monuments or Stonehenge or nothing, but we're letting our history run right down the tubes.

"Seems to me like we need to hold on to our past," I was telling Graham. We were sitting beside each other on the sofa, me all embarrassed because he and Khaki threw me a surprise shower.

Graham patted me on the arm. "I remember Khaki's friend Stacey telling me that when she was pregnant she wanted to start a campaign to keep the polar ice caps from melting. And Khaki's sister decided that she would raise the money to ensure that every person in the world had clean drinking water."

"So?"

"So," he said, "I think it's normal when you're creating the next generation to start thinking about what you're going to do to make the world a better place."

Marlene, she slutted over with that teased, brassy head of hers and interrupted, smiling at Graham like she'd just as soon eat him as look at him.

"You sure are looking good today," she said, wiggling her fingers on Graham's shoulder. He looked at her like she oughta be locked up and walked away. I swatted Marlene's skinny leg and said, "My cousin is married, you tramp."

Her finger was working a poppy seed outta her teeth. "You don't know if they're happy."

That Marlene was always looking out for herself even if it meant killing you and then using your dead body to save hers.

"Hey," she said. "I know it was a long time ago, but have you given any more thought to selling that Shaklee mess?"

I pointed to my stomach. "No. I've sorta had this going on."

"Okay," she said. "Well, that's good 'cause I think I've found something even better for us to do."

Jesus must've sent Buddy over right about then;

79

He must've known I couldn't stomach an hour of Marlene's scheming.

"Well, hey there," she said to Buddy, scooting closer to him on the sofa.

"Marlene," I said, "could you please go get me some punch?"

"Oh, I can get it," Buddy said.

"Oh, that's okay," I said. "Marlene really wants to."

I didn't want Marlene sitting beside Buddy, sinking them long red nails into his thigh and putting ideas in his head. My belly might've reached dern near to Tennessee when I faced west, but that didn't mean that I couldn't think a boy was cute. I might not've been in man-catching shape, but I still didn't want *her* to have him.

"That friend of yours is something," Buddy said.

My heart fell all the way to South Carolina. He musta liked Marlene with her push-up bras and cheap extensions.

But then he added, "I bet she's the kind of girl men get restraining orders against."

I laughed, putting my pink polka-dot napkin up to keep the cake in my teeth from showin'.

"I know we don't know each other real well," Buddy said, "but I'm happy to help you out any way I can before the baby gets here or after."

I could feel that heat rising on up through me again. Buddy's cheeks got a little pink, and I sure was hoping he was feeling that same thing.

He cleared his throat and said, "You know, you being Graham's cousin and me owing him so much."

Maybe it's 'cause I was still right young and all, and I didn't have the confidence I do now. But I couldn't decide right then if Buddy might be being sweet to me over more than just him feeling loyal to Graham.

"Buddy, you been nothing but nice to me through all this, and I think it's a fine person who would treat a girl so good for no reason. You're the kind of man my daddy woulda loved."

Thinking about my daddy like that made my head all woozy and my feet get to feeling numb and tingly. Ever since I been a youngen, when I get too scared or sad or worked up all my blood drains right outta my head and I like to keel over right there on the coffee table.

"I didn't know your daddy, but I knew Graham's real good. And if those two brothers were anything alike, your daddy was a damn fine man."

They were more alike than collards and kale. Stubborn and hardheaded and prouder than one of them old Confederate soldiers. When Graham's daddy started farming he begged my daddy to go into business with him. But Daddy wanted to make something of his own self. When the bank took back Daddy's garage and he was back to being just a mechanic again while Graham's daddy's farm got all busy and moneymaking, that's when it got bad between them brothers.

Graham's daddy begged my daddy to partner up with him on the farm. And my daddy quit talking to Graham's daddy. I remember him stomping around outside the trailer, stem of wheat just a-going in his mouth. "Son of a bitch thinks he's better than me now 'cause he's made all this money and I ain't. I'll show him."

When my uncle died of a heart attack right there in his own field it damn near killed my daddy. I don't have no business knowing why or how people get cancer. But I'd bet my last unemployment check that Daddy was so eat up with never making up with his big brother that it gave him the tumors. Holding in all that pain, keeping it bottled up like fizz in Pepsi, it'll eat you alive just like the cancer did.

That ain't the kinda thing you say at a baby shower to some cute cowboy that's got you dreaming of being thin again. But when Buddy looked at me sideways like, I knew I didn't have to say nothing for him to understand.

About that time, Marlene come back, smacking that gum, saying, "Sorry, I got caught up by the sweet potato ham biscuits."

Buddy, he patted my shoulder and said, "Just remember what I said," and walked away to get food his own self.

He like to have gotten down on one knee and asked me to marry him for how that hand felt.

While a rainbow of Skittles with ponies jumping through it danced in my head, Marlene said, "So, Jo, I was thinking with you being pregnant and all that we should start a baby store."

I was still so lit up from talking to Buddy that I was right more patient than usual with Marlene. So I said, real sweet like, "Marlene, why don't we talk about this later."

It was her worst damn idea yet. We couldn't make hide nor hair of a bunch of numbers and, last time I checked, businesses had to have something we didn't have one damn bit of: money.

"I'm dating this new guy," Marlene said, "and he's gonna give us the first couple months' rent for free while we get on our feet."

Marlene's new man would be running around on her or smacking her up before I had time to even get to thinking on the idea of a store.

So like she ain't said nothing at all, I said, "Marlene, you think any man's ever gonna love me now that I'm gonna have a kid and everything?"

Crazy as she is, Marlene comes through every now and again with a little bit of wisdom. "Oh, honey," she said. "If he's as good a man as you deserve, he'll see that little baby as a bonus."

Khaki

EVERYONE ELSE'S BUSINESS

When I went off to college, practically every person in Kinston told me that I should rethink my interior design major. "If she wants to learn how to move furniture around, you just send Khaki on down to the shop," I remember one of my daddy's friends chuckling.

If you aren't from a small town, you might not know how everyone is all up in everyone else's business every minute of the day. So you have to have a thick skin. I loved design and persevered through the insults and snarky comments. But that small-town cynicism must have gotten in anyhow because I am one of the world's most skeptical people. I believe in Jesus, but that's about it. Ghosts: fake. Bigfoot: no way. The Loch Ness Monster: biggest crock of all. So going to see an herbalist whose "office" was a garage with a few braided throw rugs lying around, old floral bedsheets draped along the walls, and a ratty tan corduroy sofa that would have seemed more at home in your daddy's old dorm room didn't seem like an ace in the hole to me.

We drove way out into the country—I mean,

Graham and I live in the country, but this was the *country*—to a 1900s farmhouse that needed painting a decade ago with a condemned house with fourteen rusted-out cars as a neighbor. I looked at Graham and said, "Thanks, but no thanks. I think I'll take the knife."

He took my hand calmly and said, "Let's just try it. If you get freaked out, we'll leave. We have nothing to lose."

"Except our lives," I muttered under my breath. He rolled his eyes. But, I mean, really, he set himself up for that response, didn't he?

So, the garage wasn't Duke University's Integrative Medicine Center, but it was at least clean. And Esther reminded me of Pauline—if Pauline wore floral-print tribal garb and talked with a thick Trinidadian accent. Esther's warm smile, comforting Dove chocolate hands, and acknowledgment that "I know this isn't what you're used to, but give it time" softened me a touch.

She helped me up onto a massage table that was soft, warm, and comfortable. I figured that, worst case, I'd at least get to rest for an hour or so.

The soft, tinkling music, candlelight, and Esther's waves-crashing-to-the-shore accent did make me feel a bit like I'd been to the islands. She wanted to "read my feet" first thing. As soon as she raised the sheet to check them out, the strangest thing happened.

I rose up on my elbows, looked at Graham, then at Esther, and said, "Is it weird that I taste pickles? Am I having a stroke or something?"

Esther laughed, the beads in her hair tinkling and said, "I put dill oil on the point on your feet that leads to your mouth." She winked at me. "I wanted to show you that the points in the feet correspond to the organs of the body."

Graham smiled at me supportively, and I lowered back down as Esther continued the "foot treatment" that was definitely more deep tissue and less Swedish. "Less time at the computer," she instructed as she kneaded away at my big toe, my body writhing in pain.

So, yeah, I spent a lot of time at the computer, like every other person in the developed world. She moved on from that poor mangled toe and said, "Ah. I feel here that you had a lot of strep throat as a child. Many antibiotics can leave the door open for sickness."

She had her eyes closed as her fingers padded up and down the balls of my feet. "Your lungs weren't fully developed when you were born, and your breathing has been difficult ever since," she stated. "A thyme and honey syrup will help you when it's cold out."

I was starting to feel a bit like that time I went to the psychic with my sister. Graham cleared his throat and, when I looked at him, he made a face like he was impressed.

Esther opened her eyes and said, "Do you have pain in your thighs?"

"Yes!" Graham exclaimed.

I cut my eyes at him. Then I looked back at Esther. "Does that mean something's wrong?"

She nodded slowly and said, "Ah, yes. I feel some stagnation of the liver here."

That was all well and good, and I'm as into my health as the next person, but, honestly, I was here to get pregnant, plain and simple. If my liver was sad and my thyroid was slow, so be it. I wanted a baby. So, I said, "What does this have to do with my endometriosis?"

Then Esther said something that made so much sense I couldn't believe I hadn't thought of it on my own.

"Ah, sweetness," she said. "In our mind and in our body, either we're sick or we're well."

Jodi

PREGNANT-GETTING HORMONES

After you've picked corn, you got two hours to freeze, can, or pickle it before its sweet sugar gets right starchy. Khaki and me, we wore ourselves down to the quick that year putting away cans for the winter. It come fast, too. It don't matter what the temperature is or what the Farmer's Almanac say. When the corn turns good and brown, you can bet your best boots it's fall. And we wasn't wasting any a' that yellow goodness.

I craved that corn we canned like booze when I was carrying you. I weren't working, so I'd cook stews, sauces, and dips all day, and, before I even got it all cleaned up good, it'd be darn near dark outside.

I walked in Khaki's house that day, setting my sights on the pantry and that corn. But I didn't get real far 'fore my stomach right near turned over. "Oh, my Lord," I said out loud.

Alex ran through the foyer and said, "Momma's cooking some sticks and leaves."

I nodded. "She's cooking something unnatural, all right."

It was like she mixed cinnamon and mushrooms and burned the pot on up. But then I saw Pauline. Khaki, now she couldn't cook a lick. But Pauline, I'd dare say, mighta been the best cook in the county—'sides me, of course. I heard Khaki complaining right loud, "I can't imagine that this is right."

I held my nose. *I ain't been sick this whole dern pregnancy.* My time might be coming.

"What the woman say exactly, baby?" I heard Pauline ask.

Khaki stood right up on her tiptoes and peeked in over that witch's pot on the stove and said, "She said, 'Your body will tell you what's right. You make your own medicine.'" She put her hands on her hips. "What is that supposed to mean? I mean, honestly, just give me a piece of paper with some instructions on it, and I'll boil it up and drink the amount you tell me to. I can't go with the flow like this."

Pauline shrugged. "Maybe that's the point, baby."

Khaki lifted the ladle out of the pot, held it to Pauline, and said, "I mean, could you drink this?"

"I couldn't," I said, by way of lettin' 'em know I was standing there.

"Oh, thank God," Khaki exhaled. "Jodi, please come over here and rub some of your good, pregnant-getting hormones on me so I can stop all this nonsense."

I laughed and Pauline said, "I just never heard of no Trinidadian woman practicing Chinese medicine. Don't make no sense."

Khaki shook her head. "She doesn't only practice Chinese medicine. She does like every-thing. Indian medicine, Ayurvedic medicine, yoga therapy. She's studied all over the world. She's super brilliant." Khaki paused to hug me. "She felt like this herb concoction was what my body was telling her it needed."

"Your who said what?" I said.

Khaki shook her head. "I know. It's insane."

I looked over into that brew on the stove and

saw all sorts of ungodly sticks and leaves and whatnot just floating around in there. "I think you got taken," I whispered. "That lady give you what the yard men didn't get off the street."

"That's what I thought," Khaki said, turning the stove on.

"What you doing, baby?" Pauline asked.

"My body *feels* like this slop needs to boil down more."

My ankles and hips got to groanin' and cracklin' as I climbed up onto the stool at the counter. "What is that godforsaken potion?" I asked. It mighta looked like yard clippings, but it smelled worse than a plastic pie pan meltin' in the oven.

"It's *herbs*."

"Herbs? Don't them things come in a pill or something?"

Khaki pointed at me like I hit the nail on the head and let her hand slap back on her skinny thigh. "Exactly."

Pauline laughed and leaned right on over beside me.

"Looks like that baby be coming any minute," she said.

I nodded. "I darn sure hope so. My feet and ankles get much bigger and they're gonna bust all over the kitchen."

Khaki made a face. "That's even grosser than this."

I felt my face getting right red, looked down

at the white marble counter and then back up at Khaki. "I'm real sorry that I'm pregnant and you ain't. It kind of makes me feel like bragging, struttin' around here with my big belly."

"Don't be silly," Khaki said, waving her hand.

To be downright honest, it didn't feel all that bad. I ain't never had much to brag about, growing up like I did. I never had a new car or the fancy shoes or even the best backpack. So, to have something that somebody else wanted. Well, it was kinda like gettin' even in a way.

But a baby ain't the same kinda dream as a promotion at work or a string a' pearls all your own. It ain't the kinda thing you can just pull yourself up by your bootstraps, dust off your overalls, and earn. If you ask me, it seems like a lotta the time the people who should have the youngens cain't get pregnant and the ones who don't have no business raising nobody pop 'em out like candy corn at Halloween.

"So what's up with the princess?" Khaki asked.

I smiled and said, "Well, I went to the doctor today, and he said that now that I'm thirty-seven weeks, I'm full term. She'll be comin' any time." I weren't scared when I said it. I knew childbirth was gonna hurt right fierce. But cain't nobody tell you what it's like to bring a baby home all alone, to be the only person responsible for another person's raisin'. All I knew was that my back was achin', my feet was swollen, I couldn't get near a good night's sleep, and I was as ready to pop as a chick pecking through an eggshell.

But now I know: There's being ready, and there's being *ready*. When you're nineteen, you don't know the damn difference.

Khaki

HOLES

One of the ways I knew that I would be a good designer is that when I walk into a room, I always feel like it's telling me something. It needs another piece of furniture, the addition of color— sometimes all the room is missing is a little more uncluttered space.

Like our rooms, we are so often missing something, walking around with some sort of gap that won't close. I can't see that there will ever be a day that a hole shaped like Alex's daddy won't live in my soul. And, in an even larger way, I'm sure that a miniature version of you will always be cut out of your mom. If you look around, most people have some kind of wound that never stitched itself up. An unrequited love. The one that got away. Losing a momma or a daddy. An irreplaceable family pet. I'd bet the last strawberry bushel of the season that every person you meet wakes up in the morning missing something.

Jodi and I've never talked about this, but I know she's braver than I am on the outside whether she is on the inside or not. She handled having you like nothing I've ever seen. I like to make myself feel better by justifying that she was so calm, composed and, most important, *quiet* because she had the sense to have an epidural and I had my friend Stacey in my ear talking me out of it. But the truth of the matter is, some people simply have more inner strength, more ability to internalize pain.

She told me after you were born that once you're in it you don't have any choice but to get through so you may as well do it keeping as much of your dignity intact as possible. I guess after all the hard knocks that girl has lived through, having a baby just seemed like the hurdle God put out for her to jump over that day.

We hadn't planned for me to be in the room when you were born. I had been with Jodi most of the day, ran home for a quick shower, and came back to the hospital to bring some Popsicles and some thick, plush washcloths for your birth mother's head.

Jodi smiled at me weakly and said, "Cherry flavor would be real nice."

She winced in pain, blew her breath out, and I said, "Bad contraction?"

She nodded. "This is real embarrassing," she whispered. "I gotta go to the bathroom, but I cain't get up 'cause I cain't feel my legs."

"Oh my gosh!" I leaned over and mashed that nurse button about a million times. The head nurse came over the intercom, and said, "May I help you?"

"Yes!" I practically screamed. "I don't know the first damn thing about delivering a baby, and she's feeling like she needs to push!"

It wasn't a heartbeat later that two nurses came rushing in and, as the door slammed, a doctor charged in right behind. I held Jodi's hand and wiped her pale, sweaty face with one of those cold rags while the doctor checked her. "Ten centimeters!" he exclaimed, snapping his glove.

I patted Jodi's hand, and neither of us said a word, but the look on her face told me that she was terrified and could I please stay. So, of course, I did. In the moment, you aren't thinking about how you're seeing someone's parts that should be reserved for husbands and bedrooms. You're thinking about how God's greatest miracle since creation is happening and you get to witness it. That's what I was thinking, anyway.

She closed her eyes in the calmest, smoothest way I've ever seen, and I swear it wasn't ten minutes later you were born. When you watch people on TV give birth it's always screaming and hustling around and doctors directing nurses. But it wasn't like that when you were born. It was peaceful. It was so still and quiet in there, church on a summer day when almost everybody's at the beach. Maybe that's why you didn't make one peep when you were born. You just came out, your little eyes open and looking around, taking it all in for a few moments before you showed us what those tiny pipes could do.

And it wasn't until I laughed, tears in my eyes, and looked back at your mom to say, "You did it!" that I even noticed she had passed out. I gasped and said, "Nurse!" which is when she handed you to me.

My mind was racing because, even though I knew your birth mom was prone to fainting, there are still those incredibly rare cases where childbirth doesn't go well. But the panic alarm in my head quieted when I saw your beautiful face. Puckered little lips and big blue eyes. I shouldn't actually admit this anywhere but in my mind, but, for a breath, I thought that if Jodi didn't wake up I'd take the best care of you in the world. It wasn't like I didn't *want* her to wake up. But, you know, you have to prepare for the worst case.

But then she opened her eyes, and I handed you to her. It was such a moment of pure, unadulterated love between a mother and her child that I didn't even feel sorry it wasn't happening to me. I relished the glow of it all. With me contemplating surgery and fertility drugs and in vitro and other words I never thought would be a part of my vocabulary, I thought that seeing

Jodi hold you might hurt just a little, give me the slightest pang of envy for the motherhood journey that she was embarking on and leaving me behind. And that's how I know for sure that what Pauline always told me was true: God gives you the grace you need for even the toughest moments.

Jodi

LOVE AIN'T ENOUGH

Some vegetables, they like to be crammed up in the jar, juice squirting and getting all good and marinated. Butter beans, they ain't like that. They gotta have their space. They get to absorbin' all the liquid, and if you don't leave enough room for them to expand, they explode just like that.

Having a baby's near like being one of them butter beans that ain't got enough room. There's not one spare squidgen a' space in your life for nothing save feeding, changing, bathing, holding, and then startin' all over again. I've met some girls that handle it like ain't nothing much changed in their life and waking up every two hours all night long to feed and change a baby ain't nothing to get excited about. But I was like them crowded butter beans: fixin' to explode.

I cain't say nothing 'bout other alcoholics and what makes them want to drink, seeing as how

I'm just me. But being tired is like inviting ants to a picnic. That soft voice that whispers real sweet and slow in the back of my mind gets louder. That feeling I can push on outta here, the wind kissing a sail on a calm day, 'fore I know it it's a hundred-knot gale.

But here's the thing, baby girl: I loved you like I didn't know I could love nothing. That tiny voice crying out ripped through me like a machete on a tree branch. I wanted to wrap you up and hold you tight as a tick into me and not let nobody hurt you. But you know what they say: Sometimes, love just ain't enough.

I weren't nowhere near prepared for what it was gonna be like to try to raise a baby on my own. I saw them babies on Gerber commercials and thought it was real sweet to have one of them little people all to yourself.

Maybe it's 'cause there weren't nobody to help me, but the whole dern thing kinda felt like playing the same song over and over on repeat 'til you thought you'd die if you didn't snap that CD clear in two. You would wake up screaming every two hours on the hour, day and night. And that sweet little pansy mouth felt like a hot poker lighting me on fire every time you ate.

But then I'd get to wishing for that hot poker because sometimes you'd rear that head back and get to screaming like I was pinching them skinny legs underneath your hand-me-down lace daygown. Trying to get your little mouth to make them fish lips would have me in a sweat worse than cutting asparagus all day. We'd both finally get all quiet and relaxed and dang if we weren't at the whole thing again an hour later.

You weren't one a' them sleeping babies you see on the TV neither. You'd wake up and want me to tote you around for a while. If I thought about sittin', you'd scream that little head off.

Even the standing and walking didn't help for 'bout three hours every afternoon. You'd be all changed and fed and comfy and you'd just work out them little lungs anyhow. They told me at the doctor's they call it something like the purple period. Felt more like black to me.

All that crying, it'd get me to feeling like walking out the door of the trailer, hobblin' as best I could to the nearest ABC store and using my fake ID to get so good and lit up I wouldn't care 'bout no crying. I liked to think if my sponsor hadn't fallen off the wagon and died of a cocaine-fueled booze binge that she might coulda helped me. But I wouldn't have called her noway.

And what you got to know is there wasn't one single thing wrong with you. You are the most perfect youngen I ever seen. But, being a momma, it's all brand-new, and being all alone with my head not on quite right, it was all a lot for me to take.

I guess I could say that feeling like I was driving

through one of them long, black tunnels with no end in sight was what made me feel like I needed a cold, stiff drink. But if I learned one thing in all that rehab I went to, it's that I wanted to drink on account of me being an alcoholic. Lord knows, Jesus got me through my drinking patch and clear on out the other side. But I was too ashamed to ask for His help now. I shoulda been thankin' Him and singin' His praises so hard and high the angels was dancing. But I didn't feel thankful. So I didn't say nothing.

When you were two weeks old I'd got all sick—fever, headache, vomiting, you name it. You weren't sleeping none, day or night, meaning I hadn't slept none either. We were just dozin' on the couch when I heard a knock at the door.

"Come in," I called, feelin' too lazy to get up and answer it.

Marlene just come busting in saying, "It's Aunty Marlene here to bring you a present!"

She scooped you up off the couch, and I was real grateful for the company. Then she handed me a container of formula with a ribbon tied around it. "What's this?"

She looked up at me like I weren't quite right. "It's formula. What the hell you think?"

"Marlene, I told you 'bout a million times I'm breast-feeding."

She shivered. "Girl, ain't no man ever gonna want you once you ruined yourself like that. We both grew up on formula and look how good we turned out."

I raised my eyebrows, and we both got to laughing. That might not've been the best argument she coulda used. But I was real glad to see Marlene. I needed some company, and I was feeling right warm toward her. She's the one that named you, after all.

I was sitting in that hospital bed, Marlene up there helping me get you home. She was holdin' you and we was just talkin' like it was normal. That nurse come in and said, "Miss Jodi, you aren't going a place until you name that baby." Then she walked on out quick as she'd come.

"Marlene, I don't know what to name no baby."

"Why don't you name her after your grandma?"

We both busted out laughing. My grandma, she's the best woman I ever known. But don't nobody want to be named Ollie Bell.

Marlene, she got out her phone, and music started pourin' out that little speaker. She got to looking through baby names, that finger just a goin'. "How 'bout Marlene?"

I smirked.

"Maggie?"

"Nah."

"Madison?"

"You got any names on there that don't start with *M?*"

Marlene glared at me and then said, "Oh, yeah.

Now this here's a good song!" She clicked the button on the side of her phone, turnin' up that volume so I could hear, "You're so fine, girl you're one of a kind, sweet Carolina girl."

That song, it was my daddy's favorite. We'd ride around in the truck, just him and me, on Sunday afternoons, listening to Steve Hardy's Original Beach Party on the radio. And when that song would come up, we'd turn it up even louder, toes tapping on the floorboard.

Marlene cooed down at you, rubbing her finger on your tiny cheek, "You're a sweet Carolina girl."

Then she looked up at me, and we both said, "Carolina," right at the same time. It was the first name that seemed right.

That day in the trailer, the phone in the kitchen got to ringing. I thought it was gonna be Khaki saying she'd pop on by.

But it was some man saying, "Jodi?"

"Yes, sir?"

"This is Richard Phillips from Sunny Daze Dry Cleaners."

My heart got to pounding and my palms got to sweating. I smiled and give you and Marlene a thumbs-up like maybe you knew this could be a big break for us.

"Oh, hi, Mr. Phillips," I said, hoping I didn't sound nervous. "How you doin'?"

"I promised you I'd call if I got an opening," he

101

said. "And I need a new counter girl starting next week. It pays ten dollars an hour, eight to five, Monday through Friday."

"All right," I said.

I was as excited as a kid on Christmas morning to be busting outta here. I was damn close to figuring what was the day and what was the night again. But then it hit me: What on earth was I gonna do with you?

"You get thirty minutes for lunch, two fifteen-minute breaks, a week's paid vacation, and three days sick leave."

"All right, Mr. Phillips. That all sounds real good. I'll be there at eight sharp."

"Fantastic, Jodi. I'll look forward to working with you."

"Woo-hoo!" I said.

"What's that?" Marlene asked.

But I put my finger up, 'cause I was thinking. Working again, being busy, it was the best thing for shutting up that voice in my head that was dying for a drink. I thought that with three breaks a day I could use the breast pump the WIC people give me. Good thing. Weren't no way I could afford formula, no matter what Marlene said.

I did some quick figuring in my head. Eighty dollars a day was $400 a week, $1,600 a month, $1,300 after taxes. The trailer payment was $400, that damn truck that I cosigned for Ricky, that I could just spit about, was $300, the bills were

$200, and I could probably get by on $200 of groceries, $150 if I cut out meat and packaged snacks. Then there was $60 a month for car insurance. That left $190 for diapers, wipes, and baby clothes, $270 if I canceled the cable. I looked up at the TV and dern near got to crying. It had been my main talking company those past two weeks, and I sure did hate to see it go. There weren't no money for health insurance, but that weren't nothing new.

"Thank the good Lord for Medicaid," I said out loud.

"What are you talking 'bout, girl?" Marlene asked.

I told her about the job, but then I got to realizing it. "Daycare's gonna run me four hundred a month. Ain't no way on God's green earth I can pay it."

Marlene and me, our eyes met and she said, "I know what you're thinking, but don't you do it, Jodi. You know you cain't."

I shrugged. "I don't have no choice. I'm gonna have to ask my momma to keep Carolina."

I corralled your diapers, wipes, burp cloth, pacifier, outfit, and extra blanket in the old purse Marlene give me that was so worn out the strap was about to break clean off. That nausea almost got me again as I cranked the engine of that old Ford.

And it got me good as I started driving through

the trailer park where I grew up. I could see Momma's droopy eyes, her shouting at Daddy, "You're so damn stupid. Cain't even make enough money to keep decent food on the table."

But Daddy needed Momma right near as much as the crops need the rain. 'Cause even though she drank too much and treated him like something she'd stepped in and spent every dime she could get her hands on, someone was there when I got home from school so he could work.

I could almost smell the kerosene seepin' outta the door of that rusting bucket I'd come up in. I waved at Mr. Jackson, sitting in a plastic lawn chair like always. "Just keeping an eye on things," he'd say. All them people in the trailer park, they were the best people I'd ever known, always looking out for me, making sure I had a home-cooked meal. Well, all except my momma.

I scooped you up in my arms. Just like when I was little, I didn't know which Momma I'd get. Last time I'd seen her had been at my intervention. She was all sober and sweeter than the last maraschino cherry in the jar. But when she got to drinking . . . Well, there weren't nothing sweet about that Momma.

I knocked real loud and Momma hollered, "I'm coming, I'm coming."

The door flew open, and there she was in all her glory. Cigarette balancing on her lip, ratty nightgown still on, curlers in the gray hair stained yellow in spots from the smoke cloud she lived in. She stood real still, like she seen a ghost. We hadn't seen hide nor hair of each other in a year. I was hoping she was getting all excited that she was a grandma. But that rough, crackling old voice came out.

"What in the hell have you done now?"

She didn't have to say nothing else. I knew then she were soaking in vodka like a pickle in vinegar. I walked away so you wouldn't have to hear her, but she kept on yelling. "How the hell you expect to take care of a baby when you cain't even stay sober? I know you're not coming 'round here wanting my help after all the shit you put me through."

I whispered down at you, "Don't you worry, baby. I'll happily stand in line for welfare 'fore I'll let you be raised by my momma." That was it too. There weren't no way I was taking care a' that woman in her old age. They could just dump her right on in the home.

My hands, they was shaking like a leaf on a tree on that steering wheel, my head pounding like I's standing too close to the speaker down at the Dugout. It was like my whole body was switching, the insides trying to get out, banging on my skin. "Just one drink!" they was begging. "A few drinks and we could solve all them problems."

This trailer park was the ocean. And here I was again, caught in the undertow.

• • •

Just like when you're plantin' seeds, when you're raisin' a youngen, there are just some things that ain't all right to do. Like, I knew good and dang well there weren't no way I'd ever leave you in the car by yourself. But dern if I didn't after I pulled outta that trailer park. I pulled into the gas station, locked you in the car, and paid for a forty with the change in my cup holder. It was cheaper and easier than Marlene in high school—God bless her soul—and I almost took a swig right then and there.

I wanted to get on down that dusty road to our trailer, the one I had been so excited over when Ricky was acting like a decent man. I was gonna strap you all up in the bouncy seat and get you working right good on the paci, so I could chug that bottle and feel that warm relief wash over me. But then your little feet got to tapping, catching my eye in the rearview, and my heart flooded with love for you like Hurricane Irene done downtown Kinston.

As I got down the dirt road a ways, I could see Alex and Khaki blowing bubbles on the upstairs porch. It was funny how, even from the outside, you just knew that in there, ain't nobody yellin' or cussin'. I thought that maybe I could borrow some of that for us. And maybe it'd keep me from drinking. I opened the door and Khaki hollered, "Hang on, Jodi! We're coming right down."

Before I even had you outta the car seat good, Alex was saying, "I want to see the baby! I want to see the baby!"

Khaki took you from me, and, surrounded by the love of our family like we were, it took my mind off that forty under my car seat for two shakes of a lamb's tail.

Khaki said, "Why don't you let Alex and me take Carolina for a little while, and you go on in there and have a chat with your favorite cousin." She winked at me and patted my back real sweet like. She didn't have to say nothing at all for me to know that she knew right where I was. Not long ago, she'd been knowing that same tired that brings you to your knees and frustration over not being able to do nothing to stop the cryin' and being so scared you like to faint from remembering that this little baby—all she's got in the whole wide world is you. But she didn't know near nothing 'bout addiction. And that was the difference.

Me and Graham, we went into his sunny kitchen, lemon smell off a' honey-colored hardwoods so strong you could right near see it. Walking into Khaki and Graham's was kin to a summer day at the river when you're a youngen. Just free and easy.

"How you doing?" Graham asked.

I nodded. I couldn't think straight I were so busy looking around figuring on where they keep the booze. I'd like to tell you I wouldn't never steal from somebody I love. But I wrote more than a few "sorry" letters to people I loved during them twelve steps.

"Well, Graham, I got me a job."

I could tell he was getting all excited and carrying on, so I put my hand up to stop him.

"But there just ain't no way. 'Tween bills and that damn truck payment and not being able to find Ricky I cain't near afford daycare." I sighed. "I don't have no choice but to get on welfare. I cain't figure no other way around it."

When I was done, Graham said, "You don't need to give up, and you aren't all alone."

I snorted. "Daddy's dead, I ain't got no brothers and sisters, and I intended on askin' Momma's help, but she's drunk again."

He leaned across the table, took my hand, and smiled warmer than the hot sun on a lizard's back. "You have us, Jodi. You and Carolina have Khaki and Alex and me." He leaned back and sat up a little straighter, like he was the one in charge now. "You let me take care of the truck situation, and we'll keep Carolina while you go to work."

"But, Graham, I—"

He put up his hands to stop me just like I done him not a minute before. "I'm not hearing another word about it. That's what's happening."

I cut my eyes at him skinnier than the lemon

slices we liked in our sweet tea. "I ain't taking a handout from you, Graham. Not happening."

He laughed. "Jodi, come on. You know good as I do that it's not a handout when it's family."

I nodded. I guessed that was true. "Well, I ain't volunteering Khaki to take care a' my baby all day, every day. She's got responsibilities her own self."

Graham leaned in closer to me and whispered, "Khaki wants another baby so bad it's all she can talk about. I think it might make her feel a little better."

All them muscles—the ones that'd been clenched tighter than a hose around a spigot—just like that, they got all warm and wobbly again. "Well, you at least gotta let me pay you."

Graham shook his head. "If you're so hell-bent on doing your part, then I'll tell you what: Khaki goes on and on about how great it is to can with you, so if you'll help her put up the extra vegetables from the garden on the weekends then we'll be even." He winked at me. "But that's only if you promise to take enough home for you and Carolina."

I hugged Graham. "Nobody ever been nice to me or cared about me, Graham. I don't want to be too much trouble, but there's a time you realize that it ain't just about you anymore and that pride is less important than your baby."

He looked back at me all teary-eyed and

emotional and said, "It's a big day when you realize that you love your child so much you'd swallow your pain to do the right thing for her."

I thought about that forty tucked under my front seat, and it crossed my mind that, much as I loved you, baby girl, maybe swallowing my pain was exactly what I needed to do.

Khaki

THAT'S A MAN FOR YOU

I know plenty of designers who are enamored of the "rules." They religiously hang every picture's center at sixty inches, leave exactly twelve inches of space around all sides of a rug, and hang every chandelier thirty-three inches from the dining room table. Me, I'm not so concerned with the rules—whether they're for a design project or raising my kids.

Most people around here start their children in preschool at eighteen months old. I thought about it, decided against it, and vowed to try to let Alex go at two. That came and went. So did two and a half. So, when Alex got to be three, I knew that I had to buck up and send him to school whether I liked it or not. The morning of that first day I was more nervous than a blue marlin during the Big Rock Tournament. I had spent an hour the night before getting everything organized. Alex's little frog backpack was by the door. I had made him his favorite pumpkin bread to go with strawberries and bananas for snack time. I had baked during his nap that day, trying to do a phone interview about the new book and finish the layout for a design project I was working on for Bunny, one of my friends and biggest clients in New York.

Graham told me that since the other kids would have a Fruit Roll-Up for snack time that maybe I shouldn't put so much pressure on myself. I'll admit that he probably would have been okay if I hadn't freshly juiced the apple-pear medley in his thermos. But I wanted him to feel as at home as possible in his new school.

Before I got into bed that night, I tiptoed into Alex's room and brushed the hair away from his face. The moonlight shone through his window, and it took my breath away how much he looked like his biological daddy. I was trying my hardest to hold it together, but I couldn't help but cry. I missed my late husband Alex every day, but I mainly shed those tears out of sadness that he didn't get to see how amazing our son was. And, even though Alex didn't know any other daddy than Graham, I still cried for my son that he never got to know his birth father and see how much he would have adored him too.

I kissed his soft cheek and went back down the hall, where I climbed into bed with Graham, whose eyes were closed. Without opening them, he pulled me in close and said, "It's going to be okay, babydoll."

"But he's my baby," I sobbed. "How can I leave him like that?"

Graham kissed my forehead and, looking down at me, said, "You're not leaving him, darlin'. He's going to school. He's going to make friends and learn new things." He kissed me again. "It will be amazing. You'll see."

I wiped my eyes with my hand and said, "But I'm going to miss him so much."

Graham scratched my back and said sleepily, "I'm not trying to be insensitive, but I want to remind you that it's three hours, two days a week."

Then he rolled over and said, "Plus, I have a surprise for you that I think will help ease your pain."

I only assumed it was jewelry since that was Graham's general answer to healing my pain. I could already feel those icy carats in my ears—the studs that I'd been hinting at for a few months. I sat up, wiped my eyes, and said, "Graham . . ." with that slightly scolding tone I use when he spoils me silly, but I'm secretly thrilled about it.

He looked a little nervous. "Well," he said, "I may have told Jodi that we would keep Carolina while she went back to work."

My sadness was rapidly replaced by irritation. "Graham," I said, crossing my arms, "how on earth could you volunteer me to raise someone else's child? Do you have any idea how much I have on my plate?"

He nodded. "I know, and I'm sorry. But she was so sad and scared, and I had to do something to help her."

I love my husband dearly, and his endless compassion and desire to problem-solve are two of his best qualities. The only issue with those great qualities is that, somehow, they always seem to involve me getting a new task or project. I shook my head. "Helping her would have been finding a babysitter or paying for daycare, not volunteering your wife to raise an infant."

He shook his head. "You're right. Let's give her the money for daycare."

I sighed, picturing you, precious, sweet thing. You were so soft and warm and felt so good in my arms. And you were still so tiny . . . "Damn it," I said under my breath. "You know good and well I can't pass up the chance to cuddle and hold her all the time."

I could tell Graham was trying to hide a smile. He pulled me in tight and said, "You want a baby so badly, and I can't give you one." He paused. "I thought this would be good." His face was so earnest that I believed he was trying to help me.

"Honey," I said, "that's so sweet. But I want to be a mother, not a babysitter."

I hate to admit it, but the only thing that got me

through sending my boy to his first day of school was the confusion of getting you, tiny, sleeping bundle that you were, out of the car and juggling you while telling Alex good-bye. He kissed me without an ounce of apprehension, ran right into the classroom like he'd been going there his whole life, and was gone.

The independence of my firstborn made my heart surge like the cable box in a power flash. I looked down at you, tears shining in my eyes, and said, "Not one single tear for the mother who has devoted her life to you? That's a man for you."

As I snapped your car seat back in its base, I marveled at how quickly the minutiae of raising a baby come back to you. And as I glanced at your serene, sleeping face in the backseat baby mirror, I thought that, as is so often the case, maybe my husband was right: Keeping you could be exactly what I needed.

Jodi

THE LIGHT

Putting up herbs ain't like putting up other things. You gotta get to 'em quick—when they've just started buddin'. Once they blossom, it's too dang late.

The day I took the job at that dry cleaners, I was

just like that herb that had blossomed: It was too dang late for me too. I was still so dag dern sore I couldn't half walk straight, and being up all night, every night, had near killed me.

But workin' in a dry cleaners, it ain't the worst thing I ever done. You don't get all dirty like in the garage. I was the person people complained to, but that weren't nothing new. Other than that, I just had to take people's clothes, write 'em up on a piece a' paper, type it in the computer, and staple a little tag to the back.

All in all, I liked it right good. The stapler made a nice click on the clothes and an easy tap back on the counter. It got to be right soothing, good for taking my mind off a' drinkin'. A whole lot of the time I would daydream, wishing I was holding and cuddling my girl. But us girls, we gotta eat, I'd remind myself.

Mr. Phillips, he was all right. I mean, something'd go wrong and he'd fly right off the handle, get to yelling and cussing. But he weren't nothing compared to my momma. So, while the other girls, they'd get all hot and bothered 'bout it, I'd just keep my head down and look busy.

Only, it weren't long until I couldn't hide no more. Mr. Phillips flew outta his office door at me and said, "Jodi, I need to speak with you."

"Can I do something for you, Mr. Phillips?" I asked. I was hoping his anger'd cool on down if I acted real sweet.

"Yes, Jodi. Yes, you may do something for me," he practically spat. "You can tell me if, when the manager of Burger King came in, you quoted her the price to clean her pants and shirts."

"Well, I . . . Yes, sir I did tell her," I stuttered.

"Did you tell her it would be eight ninety-five?"

I nodded, but I weren't real sure why I'd be in trouble for that.

"Are you an idiot?" he exploded, his face getting all red like them Hot Tamales Daddy used to bring me from the gas station.

I leaned back on the counter, feeling Connie's eyes looking right through the back a' my head. Connie was from my part of the county, tougher than nails and bigger than Mr. Phillips. If she thought I was in trouble, she'd pounce on him like a hungry cat on a baby bird, job in a bad economy be damned.

I didn't answer Mr. Phillips straight that day, but, let me tell you right now that, no, I ain't an idiot. Khaki and me, we were talking about smarts one day.

"Honey," she said, "we all have our own kind of genius, and it's almost never the kind that's measured by a test score." Khaki, she's one a' the smartest people I know so I figure, if she says it, it must be true.

"Those pants and shirts are a *uniform*. A *uniform* is only four ninety-five. Do you realize that you just lost me the cleaning for twenty uniforms? Do you realize that that's almost a hundred dollars?"

I wanted to ask Mr. Phillips if he realized that he was gettin' this bent outta shape about a hundred dollars when he drove a BMW to work one day and a Mercedes the next. It took near all the strength I had in my sore, worn-out old body not to ask him if he thought he were acting rational in the least. But I just said, "I'd be real happy to call her and tell her 'bout the mistake."

"I have," he interrupted. "But she's already taken this week's load to another cleaners." He pointed his finger into my face. "So this week's will be taken out of *your* check."

Then he smoothed that shirt, all starched and pressed, and got to marchin' to the back of the plant, probably to take away part of the week's earnings from the presser who'd ironed it.

I felt near like I were a robber who'd got the gun turned around on her. Connie put her arm around me, all fleshy and momma like. "You okay, honey? My man's working two jobs now, so I can lend you that money if you need."

I shook my head and looked down at my feet, trying to keep them tears from coming down my cheeks. I didn't want Connie to think I was a baby. I didn't want her to know how I was feelin' all panicked and yearning right at the same time.

The panic was how I would ever make them ends meet without that hundred dollars. The yearning—baby girl, I wish it was for you. But all I could think about was the dulling, numbing novocaine of a cheap bottle of vodka.

I remember one year when I was coming up, rain ruined them strawberries one month and then the drought killed off all that dern corn the next. And that's how I got to learnin' that when it rains it pours—or not.

You know, it does right often seem like all the worst things happen on the same days. And I guess it's good. That way, your good days ain't all cluttered up with patches of mess going bad. And your bad days—well—you know they cain't be more'n twenty-four hours.

That evening, I was shaking like a worm on a hook from being dern near attacked by the boss that everybody talked about being such a good man. I learned years later that he had a secret pain pill addiction, which, Lord knows, I knew all about. At the making amends part a' his recovery, he sent me a real nice note with a hundred-dollar bill in it. And I needed that hundred real bad right then too.

I thought that coming home to get you would be salve on the poison ivy. I could feed you and rock you and cuddle you, and that would make things all right. Only, 'fore I even got outta the car good, I could hear you screaming at the top of them little lungs. I ran to the front door, feeling all panicky that you were hurt or sick or somethin'.

"She has been doing this for three solid hours," Khaki said. "I fed her, changed her, tried to get her down for a nap, put her in a new outfit, walked, rode, sang, and even called the doctor." She paused to catch her breath. "I don't want to tell you this, but he says he thinks it's just colic."

Colic. My heart was racing. Them horses down at the stable where I used to help out after school was always dying of that. "Oh my Lord!" I could feel my knees getting all weak and wobbly, them tears springing up hard. "She gonna be okay? Is there something we can give her?"

Khaki put her hand on my shoulder and squeezed to calm me down. "She's going to be fine. Colic in babies means that they cry for hours on end with no real reason. It's you I'm worried about."

She didn't say it, but you could tell right clear from her face that she was worried I was gonna start drinking again. I thought about that forty still rolled in its paper bag underneath my seat and my hands got to shakin' right good.

"Why don't you stay here with us tonight?" Khaki smiled. "We'll let Graham take a shift too."

I shoulda said, *Okay*. But you were mine and it weren't nobody else's job to take care of you.

So I said, "Gosh, Khaki, I'm real sorry you had to deal with this all day. We're gonna get home and outta your hair."

"But it would be great if you would stay—"

I interrupted her. "There ain't nothing to worry about," I lied.

I knew that my nerves, bloodshot eyes, and shaking hands from Mr. Phillips that morning weren't gonna do real good with a night of a screaming baby.

I took you from Khaki and whispered in your ear, "It's okay, baby girl. Momma's here."

But it didn't do nothing. I strapped you in your car seat and got to riding down that dusty road to the trailer, feeling like I was marching to the executioner's block.

I give you a bath, walked you around outside, and tried singing and bouncing and rocking. After what seemed like damn near forever, I finally got you to eat. I was just holding my breath the whole time, praying you wouldn't start squalling again.

Them little eyelids got to flutterin' and closed, your breathing getting slow and steady and that tiny mouth falling open, milk dribblin' out the side like a stream of rain down the window pane. The forty in my car, it was calling me so loud I couldn't near think. *That one little drink wouldn't be no big deal. I could still take care of Carolina no problem. It would just make me feel better.*

It was like having that angel and devil perched right there on my shoulder. The devil was saying, "Go on, take a drink. You deserve it!"

The angel was saying, "No, no, no!" Once I

stepped off that high dive I'd keep going down 'til I hit bottom. But you play tricks on yourself.

I held you to me a long time, breathing real slow and deep and rememberin' what it was like when I was all drunk and miserable. I convinced myself I could make it through without a drink, looked at you real hard, reminding myself that I's all you got in this whole wide, green earth. I put you in the crib, sighing with relief when you stayed sleeping hard and breathy like a puppy. I walked by the door real slow, not letting myself even look near the car, and heated up my beans and rice. When you're short another hundred bucks, beans and rice is as good as it's gonna get.

The microwave was humming and groaning, and it right near sounded like somebody coming in the door—but I knew I'd locked it. I pulled my bowl outta the microwave, turned around, and screamed so loud you got to cryin' all over again. Your no-good, soap-scum-ring-around-the-tub daddy was standing there. He didn't have to say nothing for me to know he was good and drunk. You could tell he hadn't slept in near forever and that broken bottle in his hand—well, it meant I was in real deep trouble.

"So, I hear you been going around town making up shit about me, you slut," he slurred, leaning in right close, so I could see the bits of tobacco stuck between his teeth. As he came closer to me, spitting, he said, "You been telling everybody I abandoned you and my youngen? That the shit you been making up?"

It took more strength not to yell in his face, *That's the truth, you bastard!* than it had for me to keep away from that forty. But I heard them tiny cries and I got to remembering that I had to keep him away from you. Weren't nobody close enough to hear me screaming if I got to it. And me shaking and scared would just give him what he wanted.

So I got all sweet and soothin' just like at the dry cleaners. "I would never say any such thing about you. You know, sometimes a man's gotta do what a man's gotta do. Raisin' babies is a woman's place anyhow."

You and me, we both know real good that raisin' youngens is about a village, it's about a family and having somebody there to support you no matter what. What a *man* does when his girlfriend gets pregnant is loves her and provides for his family. But I woulda told him he were king of the world to keep that bottle away from my baby.

He was looking at me all cockeyed, and I could tell I was a little blurry to him. He stumbled toward me again and yelled, "You ruined my life, you bitch!"

I couldn't imagine how *I* had ruined *his* life.

Ricky lunged at me with that jagged bottle in his hand and, without even thinking, I smashed my bowl over his head, beans and rice flying everywhere, looking like the insides of his brain. He fell, moanin' and carryin' on in pain, and I knew it wouldn't take him long to be up again and even madder. I ran on in that bedroom, where you was still wailing, grabbed Grandma's old pistol off the floor a' my closet and locked the door from the inside. It weren't much, but he was so drunk maybe it would take him longer to get to you. Ricky was stumblin' to his feet again. I pressed that revolver flat on his temple and cocked the hammer so he could hear that I was serious. I said, real low and mean like, "Get the hell outta here. If you ever come back I'll shoot you dead so many times nobody in this county'll be able to identify the body."

He sorta slithered along the floor and out the door darn near like the snake he was, and I could feel the panicked tears coming down my face. My head was all full and throbbing and scared from my crying and your crying and life feeling like being caught in a trap with no way out. I got myself out to the car, feeling a little woozy, pulled the bottle from under my car seat, and went back inside. And, wouldn't you know it, thunder crashed through the sky and lightning struck. A big old explosion like a whole mess a' fireworks lit through the stars and the darn lights went out.

My hands was trembling so bad around that paper bag I near couldn't pop that bedroom lock with a pen. I got in there, and you was still screaming bloody murder, but you were okay. I couldn't stand it all one damn more second. I sat down at that there kitchen table, twisted the cap off of that hot alcohol, and cried. 'Cause I knew right well where I was going.

In the middle a' that pitch-black night, my mouth on that bottle, 'bout to burst like a full storm cloud to take my first sip of alcohol in more than a year, my door flung wide open. That full moon, it shone right on them walls that seemed to be closing in. And I realized that what they say is true: Sometimes you got to be blinded by the darkness 'fore you can see the light.

Khaki

FAITH RESTORED

When I'm in the midst of a project, I get completely lost in the design board. I dive into the colors, swim in the fabrics, immerse myself in every texture and detail to not only be able to see the room but also to *feel* how it will be to experience it. That doesn't make me unique. Musicians lose themselves in the notes, and hours fly by in minutes when a writer is lost in a verse of poetry.

That night, after your birth mother pulled out of the house, I hate to tell you that I didn't give the two of you more than a fleeting thought. I was drowning in the renovation of an oddly shaped living room whose perfect floor plan had finally come to me.

I had no idea Jodi was thinking about drinking again, so I had planned to come check on y'all after I packed for New York. After nearly three years of redecorating, writing, photographing, and editing, my new coffee table book on Mother and Daddy's house was ready to be released. I had already had one book published, but it's still nerve-racking to prepare for such a pivotal moment. I had just put Alex in bed thinking how I would run down to give your birth mother a reprieve if you were still squalling like a gale-force wind when an actual gale-force wind swept through—and the power went out.

"Great," I said to your daddy. "How on earth am I going to get ready now?"

I ran upstairs to get Alex from his room, where he was calling, "Mommy, I can't see Thomas the Train," while Graham ran downstairs to find flashlights. My eyes were adjusting to the dark as I put Alex on my hip and heard Buddy's voice meandering up the stairs. I assumed something was wrong on the farm. When I heard your daddy say, "Don't you worry, Jodi, Buddy and me'll make sure you and Carolina are safe," I froze. Then I started running.

I could only make out Jodi's figure in the darkness, but even still you could tell that she was trembling like a Chihuahua in the cold. I gave her a hug and said, "What's happened?" quietly, handing Alex to Graham and taking you from Buddy, holding you close to me. You were quiet finally, but I held you extra tight so you would know you were safe.

"I wish I had killed that bastard," was all Jodi could say over and over again.

I put my arm around her. "Sweetie, I don't know what's going on, but you did the right thing coming here. You're gonna be just fine."

She rested her head on my shoulder, and I could feel her hot tears on my bare shoulder. It amazed me how noiselessly she could cry. "I can't do it, Khaki," she said, her voice finally breaking. "I love her so much, but I cain't take it without a drink."

I looked down at you, swaddled and sleeping, and an intense panic shot through me. But I didn't let on. The last thing Jodi needed was anyone doubting her. "How about we get out of town?" I whispered to Jodi. "We'll just get you and Carolina on our flight tomorrow and—"

Buddy interjected, as softly and evenly as I'd ever heard him, "Jodi, if you just need a few days to yourself, I'll stay here with you."

I started to step in, feeling that panic again, knowing that, as a mother, if anyone had tried to take my baby away from me I would have turned on him like a rabid dog. But this was Jodi's battle, not mine. So I kept my mouth shut.

"No way," Graham said. "Jodi needs to get out of town until we can get a restraining order in place."

I felt those tears again on my shoulder and Jodi whispered, "Khaki, I'm real sorry, but you were wrong. I cain't do it. I just cain't take care of her and keep from drinking."

I rubbed her arm, and Graham's eyes met mine. It was as if he'd said out loud, *What in the hell do we do now?*

"Sweetie," I said to Jodi. "It's going to be okay. Do you want Graham and me to take Carolina for a couple of days so that you can get some sleep?"

I remembered the irrationality of sleep deprivation, the way your emotions ran so wild and thick and right off the tracks. I could feel Jodi's head nodding and she said again, "I'm so sorry, Khaki. I'm just real sorry."

I pulled back from her and held her shoulder with the free hand that wasn't holding you. And I looked her straight in the eye. "Jodi, you don't need to be sorry. We're family, right? And we stick together. So, whatever you need—" I cleared my throat. "Whatever you and Carolina need. That's what we're going to do."

She nodded, swallowing and breathing deeply and standing up straighter. "I'm so sorry, but I think I just need a few days alone to rest and get myself back together."

"Well, you sure aren't staying here," Graham chimed in.

"I know," I said. "Why don't you and Buddy go down to Atlantic Beach to Momma and Daddy's house. Then you can relax and rest, but you don't have to be scared that Ricky will find you, and Buddy will be there just in case."

Those sad little doe eyes looked back up at me from the floor again. "You think your momma and daddy'd go for that? I mean, I don't wanna be no trouble."

I put my finger under her chin and smiled my most confident smile even though I felt like I couldn't breathe. "Family, Jodi. Remember?"

She nodded.

"Graham and I can just keep the kids here, and then if you change your mind you can turn right back around. Carolina will only be a little over an hour away."

Jodi shook her head. "You go on to New York, Khaki. You don't have no choice. It'll just be a few days."

That's when I knew that the situation was more dire than I had expected. I cried for an hour when Alex was a baby and I had to leave him to go across town. I looked up at Graham again, and he raised his eyebrow.

"So what happened?" I whispered.

"Well, he just come in all drunk and staggerin' with this broken bottle in his hand and got to lunging at me—"

She didn't get any further in her story because I

was so mad I couldn't stand there any longer. Without even thinking I handed you back to Buddy, stomped down the steps, fat drops of rain falling from the sky, and got in my car with Graham yelling, "Frances Mason Jacobs, you get your tail back in this house!"

When I get on a mission, though, there's no stopping me. I ran to Mother and Daddy's front porch, getting soaking wet, and Pauline met me at the door. "Good Lord, chile. What you thinkin' coming out in weather like this?"

I didn't even answer her. "Daddy!" I yelled at the top of my lungs. If I had only stomped my foot I could have been two years old again. He appeared from the corner. He kissed me and said, "What's the matter, baby girl?"

"I need you to find that bastard Ricky and make sure he doesn't ever come around Jodi and Carolina again."

I could see Daddy's chest puffing up, like it did when he was hell-bent on making me proud. To me, Daddy was as gentle as an Easter lamb, but cross him, and that six-foot-five, 270 pounds of temperamental beast would come out. He never told me the story himself, but I've heard through the grapevine that Daddy gathered the sheriff, his deputy, three members of the police force, his three biggest, meanest farmhands, and four of the scariest German shepherds you've ever seen to go on a manhunt for Ricky. Legend has it that

Daddy put his pistol up to Ricky's head and said, real low, with the dogs growling and foaming at the mouth and pulling on their leashes, "If I ever hear of you getting around Jodi or Carolina again I'm not going to do you the courtesy of shooting you. I'm going to let these here dogs loose to have you for supper."

I don't know if it's true, but I've heard that Ricky was whimpering and actually wet his pants on the way to the truck that they were still trying to find so your birth mother could be cleared of her responsibility for the debt. He tried to get in with that gun still aimed at him, and Daddy said, "Not so fast, bud. I believe that truck belongs to a young lady down the road."

So Ricky took off on foot and kept on running. And Ricky was right to be scared too. Daddy is a man of his word. If he says he'll let his dog eat you for supper, he'll let his dog eat you for supper. I know what you're thinking, and, yes, those are the same dogs that follow you and Alex around the yard and let you pull their tails and lie on them. What can I say? Dogs know what's what.

When I pulled back into my driveway, Graham was sitting on the front porch, and I could tell he was relieved. He shook his head. "You can't do that to me, Khak. You scare the living daylights out of me running off like that." He put his head in his hands. "What if something happened to you? What would I do?"

I sat in his lap and kissed his head. "Sorry, sweetheart. I just got Daddy to work on taking care of that sorry excuse for a man." I kissed him on the lips and smiled, but I could tell he was upset.

"What's the matter?"

"I'm just worried because when Buddy found Jodi she was about to take a drink." He sighed heavily. "She swears she didn't and she hasn't, but I'm worried that the stress of Ricky and Carolina and making ends meet is getting to her. What if she starts drinking again and something happens to that baby girl?"

The thought of it made my blood run cold. I was so in love with you. Those days that you stayed with me when your birth mother was at work I sat and rocked you Alex's entire nap, breathing that perfect, warm baby smell and rubbing my finger on your soft cheek.

"I know for sure that addiction is an illness because Jodi would never, ever do anything to put that sweet girl in harm's way."

In that moment, that tiny part of me that still blamed my husband Alex for leaving a pregnant widow finally conceded the fight. I had been so close to him that, despite my rational knowledge, my heart had perceived his drug addiction as a choice. But sometimes, no matter how hard you run from them, those inner demons catch up.

Graham nodded. "It's such a shame, and I don't know how to help her. She's going to go to some AA meetings and try to get her head back together." Graham looked up at me. "Do you think it's inappropriate for Buddy to go down there to the beach with her?"

I sighed heavily, feeling years of hard work float on past me, a wispy and thin cirrus cloud. I'd already said it once, but I'd say it again. "We should just stay home and take care of Carolina and Jodi."

I fully expected Graham to agree with me, but he shook his head. "No way. You've worked too hard for this. You deserve it. Giving her a little break from responsibility is all she needs."

"I hate to take her baby." I fiddled with the belt loop on my jeans, thinking how it would have torn my heart out of my chest to be away from Alex when he was that small. "But we'll talk it over with Jodi again, and if she really thinks this is what's best, then you know I'm on board." I sighed. "Oh, no. And she finally got that job and was back on her feet and so proud."

Graham raised his eyebrows. "There's another son of a bitch for your daddy's hit list."

I shook my head. "It makes me sad to see someone treated so poorly. It takes away some of your faith in humanity, you know?"

Graham kissed my cheek. "You want it restored?"

He took my hand and led me upstairs with the flashlight. By the light of the moon peeking through the open windows, Alex was sound asleep. And there, nestled in the crook of his arm, was you.

Jodi

THE SAME DAMNED PLACE YOU STARTED

Parsnips and salsify is the only vegetables that you ought to just leave alone. They're tough as nails, and it don't matter how cold it is. My daddy, he used to call me his little parsnip. But I'd bet dollars to doughnuts he didn't get the comparison. A momma who didn't want me, always scraping by. I could survive damn near anything. But, coming up, I didn't know we were poor. All them rich kids got packed up and sent off to private school. In a room chock-full a' free lunch cards, that dollar I took may as well have been a gold medal. If it weren't for Momma bein' so damn sorry, me and Daddy coulda lived in one of them pretty white houses with the red tin roof out in the country that I dreamed about.

Who you spend your life with, that's everything, let me tell you. My daddy and Graham's daddy grew up pretty much the same. They always had enough, but there weren't a whole lotta extras. The thing that made my grandmomma so proud was that both her boys were smart as whips and worked harder than the plow horses.

They were gonna be somebody, Grandma

always used to say. They would grow up to be landowners. Weren't nothing better to my grandma and grandpa. And that's why they scrimped and saved and got them boys through high school. Daddy, he would've been all right, just like Graham's daddy—if it weren't for Momma.

Graham's momma was sweet and lovin', the woman behind the man. She cleaned his house, raised his youngens, clipped coupons, picked vegetables, and built him up taller than the old bank building in the center of town. And that's why Graham's daddy did so good and my daddy couldn't never get ahead.

My raisin' is chockablock full of wakin' up in the middle of the night, Daddy trying to be all calm and civil when Momma come home drunk. And he'd realize right quick she'd blown his stash of savings to get that way.

"I'm trying to make a better life for Jodi!" he'd holler.

"We ain't never getting out of this shit hole," she'd slur.

She'd pass out, and they'd make up in the mornin'. But one wonderful night, he yelled, "I've had it! Get out. Get outta here and don't you ever come back! And you stay the hell away from my girl!"

I threw my arms clean around Daddy's neck. "Please, Daddy, please, no matter how hard she begs you, promise me you won't take her back."

He kissed my cheek and said, "I'm done with her, baby girl. I promise."

"I'm done with her too." I wiped my hands on my pants like getting her liquored breath off my skin.

Only, I weren't done with her. Daddy neither. They didn't even get their separation legal 'fore Daddy got the pancreatic cancer. They may as well've told me I was dying for how I felt. Daddy worked as long as he could, and I took care of him 'til hospice come in.

That's when that drink took ahold a' me. I was out blowing off steam with Marlene and a group of cute boys I was trying to impress when I had my first sip a' whiskey. I hated the way it tasted, that nauseating flavor, the way it burned when it ran down my throat. But I got to sipping. And the sipping turned to gulping. And the minutes turned to hours. And I was free. What I didn't know yet is that when addiction runs as thick and blue in your veins as blood, that drink becomes its own kind a' jailer.

Daddy's face, 'bout near done in with the cancer, I remember it looking up at me, his mouth saying as best he could, all weak and dyin', "Please promise me you won't drink, Jodi. Please tell me that I don't need to worry about that on top of everything else."

I promised all sideways. But we both knew good

as green Listerine what I'd been swigging. After he died, I didn't have no choice but to drink. It was the only way I'd forget that I had caused my poor, sick, dying Daddy even more distress during his last days.

I didn't know Buddy any better than the clerk down at the Piggly Wiggly, so I cain't tell you why I thought it was all right to tell him all that on the ride from Kinston to Atlantic Beach. When them silences get thick and lingerin' like the smell of a pig cooking on a humid day, I get to chattering on.

"I'm real sorry, Buddy. I just gotta talk myself into not doing all that again."

He patted my hand.

"I mean, bein' away from Carolina hurts like the mischief, but I just knew I was gonna start drinking and acting like my momma if I didn't get away. I don't never want that sweet girl to be around nobody near like my momma." I tried right hard to ignore that voice in my head that said, *Like you.*

My momma, much as I hated a lot of things she did, the worst by far was her always telling me that I was gonna grow up to be just like her. The fear that maybe she weren't wrong was stronger than feeling so dern guilty just sending you off. I didn't want you to think I'd left you or to ruin Khaki's big moment. But I didn't have nobody else. And I still had my wits about me enough to know that you would be safe with Graham and Khaki but you might not be with me.

"I ain't trying to step on your toes," Buddy said. " 'Cause I know we don't know each other too good." I looked out the window. Buddy, he was gonna be just like all the rest. He didn't know being an addict from a hole in the ground, but he was gonna say, *Cain't you just stop drinking?*

"If I were a betting man," he said, "I'd say you don't give yourself enough credit. I bet you was raised with your momma telling you that you were gonna grow up to be like her. You mighta fought her on it, but, all the same, you started feeling like there weren't no hope of being nothing better."

I won't never be nothing but same as my momma. My tongue got all dry and my palms all sweaty. I looked at Buddy, not even believin' that he could be in my head like that. That tanned skin and three-day beard, cowboy hat and soulful brown eyes, Buddy wasn't just good looking. He was wise. But the good Lord knows you cain't say that to a man, so I asked, "What makes you think that?"

He packed a dip in his lip before he answered. "My momma, she always used to tell me I was exactly like my daddy. I was no good and gonna be in and out of jail all the time just like him."

"And?"

He shrugged. "And, I went to jail for stealing somebody's TV once. I was just sitting there in the slammer, and I got to figurin' I was better than that." He took his eyes off the road long enough to look me over, make me feel the weight of what he's saying. "Just because somebody tells you something 'bout yourself don't mean you have to prove them right."

"I reckon I never thought of that."

For the first time in weeks, I thought I might make it on through the rough waters without one red sip of booze and get to sailing smooth on the other side. We had to get some gas, but I didn't go in just in case. Sneakin' a bottle in your bra or up your pant leg ain't nothing to somebody like me. And I couldn't start drinking again. I had a baby to look after now.

Buddy got back in the truck, sighing hard. "You ain't gonna believe this. I missed my turn."

"What? How?"

He shook his head. "I was thinking on our conversation and went right on past the Atlantic Beach bridge."

I crossed my arms. "What kinda man are you anyhow?"

He twisted the cap off a' his Mountain Dew like he was wringing its neck. "I don't know," he said sarcastically. "I ain't tried to kill you yet this trip so I'm a darn sight better than the last man you were with."

I laughed. "I meant 'cause you asked for directions."

"Oh." Buddy's link-sausage smirk melted right into a buttery grin. "Sorry."

Ten minutes and dern if we weren't back to the same gas station. Buddy said one of the truest things I've ever heard. "Now I know why so many gas station workers get shot."

"Why's that?"

"Because they give you directions and you end up back in the same damned place you started."

We dissolved in laughter, all bubbly and sparklin' like Alka Seltzer. We dug out Buddy's old paper map, and I wasn't one bit sorry it took us so long to get there.

"Hey, Buddy," I asked. "Seeing as how you know everything, do you think that once you've let everybody down they write you off? Or do people take a chance on you again?"

Buddy spit that dip into his empty Mountain Dew bottle and said, "Well, all I can tell you is that I went to high school with Graham, and he was the only person I knew that would have enough cash to bail me outta jail. He picked me up, give me a job, and hasn't looked at me cross-wise since. That was ten years ago."

I hoped that spending all that time with Graham would rub off on you some. That you'd get to realizing what a man should act like, that you wouldn't never have to be tough like your

139

momma, that you wouldn't never have to survive the cold. I hoped against hope that you, my sweet Carolina girl, would get to be something softer and sweeter than one a' them little parsnips.

Khaki

SHE ISN'T YOUR CHILD

Even though many of the day-in, day-out aspects of being a designer are wonderful, there's nothing that makes my heart race like my twice-yearly visits to the High Point Furniture Market. New trends, ten million square feet of merchandise, and spotting the who's who of the design world make me feel as giddy and anxious as a teenager in the backseat with her first love.

I realized that morning when we touched down at LaGuardia that landing there still makes me feel a little like I'm walking into the double doors of High Point's Interhall. Don't get me wrong; I love nothing more than a glass of pink lemonade and a slow, Southern summer night. But the rush of packing up my designer labels, hearing my heels click on the sidewalk, my eyes shaded by enormous frames that I would never wear on the farm . . . The energy pulsing through Manhattan is like a jumper cable to my creativity and my zest for life. I feel like I'm a part of something, a vertebra on the backbone of the city that, in large part, made America what it is today.

I didn't think the city could ever get better for me, but I feel even more chic pushing the stroller where you're all dolled up, holding Alex's hand, his cool, city-guy sunglasses on backward (on purpose) and half-untucked shirttail (not on purpose) ready for taking on the city that never sleeps. I am instantly one of those glamorous, "I can have it all" women.

Only, that day I landed at LaGuardia, I wasn't pushing you in the stroller. I was holding Alex's hand, prancing through the airport in my new Louboutin booties—gray with black trim—and a black, fur-trimmed cape that makes me feel a little like a runway model, swishing as I step. Graham was meeting us in the car, as we discovered that taking a three-week-old baby's eardrums on an airplane is a no-no.

Kristin, Alex's nanny when he was a baby, met us in the airport because she can't wait one second longer than necessary to see your brother. Alex's grip broke free from mine the minute he caught her eye, and he sprinted to her like Usain Bolt to a finish line. I had the most vivid flashback of him as a freshly baked baby, swaddled in her arms, and it took my breath away how quickly the time passes. I felt that familiar tug around my middle, that yearning for another baby to love.

Kristin gasped. "You look just like Kate Middleton."

She was referring to my new, dark brown hair, a far departure from the pale blond it had been since I was a toddler. I slapped her arm and gave her a kiss on the cheek. "I do not, but you're getting a raise."

She held Alex's hand on one side, squeezed mine on the other, and whispered, "So, any news?"

I made a disappointed face, and she said, "Well, all I know is that I had a dream last night that you were pregnant."

I pushed my sunglasses on top of my head and hailed a taxi. As we all slid in, Alex bouncing up and down on the seat, Kristin turned to him and said, "I need you to buckle up, please."

I said, "No offense, Kristin, but I have a dream I'm pregnant like every night."

She shook her head emphatically. "I have had three dreams in my whole life that someone was pregnant, and the other two people were." She crossed her legs and sang, "Your turn!"

"Well, you know Graham and I would be thrilled," I said. "But it's not looking good."

She turned to Alex, pulled a plastic car out of her purse, and said, "Look what I found for my favorite boy!"

Turning back to me, she whispered, "Have you talked to your doctor about fertility treatments?

Maybe you could go to someone in the city since you're here so much."

I shrugged. "I'm not sure I want to go that route, you know?" I scrunched my nose. "Not yet anyway." I smiled, thinking about Pauline. "Pauline says all I need is a little bacon grease, and I'll be fertile in no time." I paused to reapply my lip gloss. I considered mentioning my trip to Esther the healer, but decided I'd rather not get into it despite the fact that her crazy potions had me feeling amazing.

Kristin ruffled Alex's shaggy hair and said, "I don't know much about bacon, but, worst case, there are always plenty of kids out there that need a good home."

You crossed my mind. But you already had a mother, I reminded myself.

I was dying to get to my pristine apartment, but we had a photo shoot for the new book first. Alex and Kristin played cars while I got my hair and makeup done, and, toward the end of the shoot, Graham surprised me, showing up with you in his arms. He looked exhausted. I ran to kiss him and said, "So, how was it?"

He sighed and handed you to me. I covered your little face in kisses, and I know they say three-week-old babies can't smile, but you did. I'm telling you, you did. "Well," Graham started, "traveling alone with a tiny baby is a little like clearing brush for a deer stand."

I made a face. Clearing brush was rough. "How could it be bad with this beautiful girl?" I cooed to you. Jaunts to New York might have ignited me, but they certainly dimmed Graham's flame. Give him a Budweiser and an open field any day. He'd leave the wine and concrete to the investment bankers.

The director of the shoot called to me, "Hey, Frances, why don't we get a family shot?"

"Oh, no," your daddy protested, but I insisted. To me, he was never sexier than in jeans and cowboy boots with a two-day beard.

Kristin said, "I'll hold Carolina."

I shook my head. I wasn't letting you go.

"Khaki . . ." Graham said warningly, sensing the tiny change in the air around us, the slightest drop in barometric pressure.

I looked at him and said, "He said family, and Carolina is our family." Graham squinted at me, and I said, my voice getting higher, "She's going to be in this picture, so let's not make a scene."

"Look at the beautiful dress your aunt Khaki got you," I cooed, freeing you from your swaddle and fluffing the pink dress with tiny bunnies smocked around the collar I had given your mom at her baby shower.

As we all posed together, Graham's arm around me, me holding you in one arm and Alex's hand in the other, I mused that with my new hair, you looked more like my baby than Alex did. His hair was whiter than the fleece of the baby lambs on the farm, just like mine had been when I was his age.

"Beautiful family," the photographer said as he snapped. A few minutes later he called, "That's a wrap," and everyone clapped.

"Frances, you have to come look at these," the shoot director called a minute later.

The family pictures were amazing, and I loved the look of it: me all dolled up, Graham looking like he was straight off the farm, and you and Alex tying us together somehow. It was one of those perfect moments like finishing a Lego pirate ship. You realize that even though you never think you'll get all the pieces together, somewhere along the way you created something whole.

"I love it!" I proclaimed. "I think that's the one."

Out of the side of his mouth, Graham said, "You realize that everyone is going to think Carolina is our daughter."

"I don't care what people think," I snapped, feeling immediately guilty, squeezing his hand.

I kissed the crew and thanked them profusely for a wonderful shoot, requesting copies of those fabulous photos. Kristin took you and Alex and said, "I thought maybe I'd take the big guy for his favorite burger while you and hubby have a date?"

I winked at Kristin. She knew I was up to something. "That sounds divine." I kissed you both, took Graham's hand, and said, "Shall we?"

I wanted to get straight to dinner—and champagne—but your daddy insisted that we go to the apartment and let him get cleaned up first. We made small talk about the drive and how nice it was to be in New York—I was telling the truth; Graham was lying. But as soon as the door to the apartment was closed behind us, Graham let me know that he knew what I was up to good as Pauline used to.

"Khaki, you can't just take someone's baby," he said, gently.

I crossed my arms. "I'm not just taking someone's baby." I smiled. "*We're* taking someone's baby."

Graham sighed and shook his head. "Jodi is her mother, babydoll. You are not Carolina's mother, and if this is going to be too hard for you, I'll take her on back home."

I pursed my lips, something your daddy has informed me I always do when I'm about to argue with him, and said, "Jodi is a child. We can help her as much as we can, but she might agree that us adopting Carolina is the best thing for everyone."

Your daddy almost never argues with me. He's the cool, calm snow cone to my jalapeño hot chocolate. I simply assumed that he would hear my reasoning and be on my side. Instead, he stood up, put his hands on my shoulders, looked down into my eyes, and said, "Baby, I know you love Carolina, but she isn't your child."

146

I opened my mouth, and he put his finger on my lips. "She isn't your child," he repeated again very slowly.

I lowered my head and turned toward our bedroom. I could feel the tears stinging my eyes, but I couldn't understand what had me so worked up. I thought of how, even at such a young age, you and Alex had taken to each other like crabs to sand. When your daddy came into our bedroom, where I was sitting cross-legged on the floor of my closet, I said, "I just can't stand the thought of Alex and Carolina not being together. The way he cuddles her up and she coos at him."

Your daddy sat down beside me, and I leaned on his shoulder. He kissed my head and said, "I know you're coming from a good place, baby-doll. But just because something is in your heart doesn't mean it's necessarily the right thing."

I closed my eyes, wondering how I could have one such unfathomably wonderful child but still feel like I needed something—and someone—more. Alex's daddy passed through my mind, and I reasoned that I needed lots of love around me to fill the void of losing my first husband.

But now I know that isn't it. It's just that, even before time itself, written in the stars was the truth that you were born to be my baby. And I was born to be your momma.

Jodi

THE ANSWERS

When you been gardenin' your whole life like me, you get this way of feeling right connected with your plants. Them little seedlings you loved and cared for, you want to know how they're doing real bad, but, even still, you've got enough sense to leave 'em be, not go digging them up to check or nothing.

When you was in New York and I was in Atlantic Beach, it was kinda the same way. I knew I weren't near being the momma you needed right then. But I felt like our hearts were connected with a real long string all the same.

But, Buddy. Well, the good Lord knows what we need even when we don't, and ain't no question He gave me Buddy right then to pull me outta the dark I been in. That situation, it was more awkward than a pimply-faced, too-tall girl at the middle school dance. But, somehow, we made it feel right near normal all the same.

We was just sitting at the porch table, all bundled up in our coats, eatin' dinner, watching the water kiss the shore, the sunset dancing orange and pink in front of us. "Hey, Buddy?"

"Yeah, Jodi."

"Do you think people can change?"

I ain't sure who I was asking about changing, anyway. Me, for sure. Momma, maybe. Maybe even Ricky. Damn if I didn't have this dream that he was gonna come back, turned as them fall leaves, begging to marry me, to make us the family we shoulda been.

"All I know is that a good many of us waste too much damn time wishin' people would change. We cain't do nothing but take 'em for how they are. Or not."

All my life, I'd been hearing people whining and complaining over somebody they wish would change. I cain't tell you how many nights I had heard my friend Marlene say, "Well, Danny says he's gonna change. This time he ain't gonna run around on me."

And guess what? Every time she let him back in that door it weren't no time before he was getting some on the side all over again. Wouldn't nothing be different with me and Ricky. He could say all he wanted that he would treat me better this time, stop drinking and spending our savings on lottery tickets. But there weren't no good way for me to know if he really would or could. And this time, with the jagged bottle and the crazy eyes, he'd scared me so bad it might not even matter if he changed. All in all, like Buddy said, why would I waste my time trying to figure it out?

Buddy looked down into his spaghetti long and

hard like them noodles was gonna do a little dance to spell him an answer. When he looked back up at me his face was dern near as red as the sauce on the plate.

"I wasn't trying to say you couldn't change. I just meant that drinking ain't who you are." He wiped his mouth and, looking down again, said, "Who you are is amazing."

Now, ain't nobody in my entire life ever said I was amazing. And it was just about the best feeling I ever had.

Buddy said, "But I know what it's like, wishing somebody would be different and then them disappointing you all over again."

"You do?"

He shrugged. "Sure. I cain't tell you how many times I took my old girlfriend back. She'd get a better offer, run off, and then two weeks later when it all went south, she'd come crawling back." Buddy squinted out at the settin' sun and took another bite. "But then I realized, all that unhappiness I was living with for so long, that's on me. Can't nobody make you any happier than you can your own self." Then, like we'd been talking about it the whole time, he said, "I heard Graham telling somebody the other day that he and Khaki been trying real hard to have another youngen."

I'm not sure if he saw me roll my eyes. But I surely did. And it hung there between us like that last organ chord in church that I should give my baby to Graham and Khaki 'cause they want one. And I ain't real sure what I want.

Then I felt kinda bad on account a' him being so nice to me and giving me such good answers to all my questions. So I said, "It's real nice a' you to take all this time to come down here with me. Ricky scared the pants offa me, and I don't know what I'd do if he found me all alone again."

Buddy laughed, kinda devious like. "Oh, I wouldn't worry too much about Ricky no more. Rumor has it that Khaki's daddy put the fear of the Holy Trinity in him."

My heart got all mushy and my eyes all weepy just thinkin' about a man so good he'd protect me like I's his own daughter. I thought about my crazy momma and your sorry excuse for a daddy, feeling real sad that they were the only real family you got. Then I got to thinking about Graham and Khaki and their cozy, eating-dinner-together families. And that made me feel right good.

After dinner, I flipped through one of them magazines in the basket by the sofa. It was a *Town & Country*, all fresh and glossy, with a picture of a woman in pearls so big they looked like the whole damn oyster shell. Flipping through them pages, I hadn't never even heard of half the stuff or the places they was talking about like it was normal. And it mighta been the first time I realized that my life wasn't just hard. It was small.

Then I saw a picture that damn near made my heart stop. A family. A husband, wife, son, and daughter standing all proud and grinnin' in front of their farmhouse. They talked on and on about how nice it was to grow your own food and be raised with a place to roam and good, hard thinking time. I thought about the trailer and how your life would be one struggle after another after another. No daddy, a momma who could barely keep the lights on. Maybe even that free lunch card. I could love you all right. But that love wasn't gonna change you being a latchkey kid. Love wasn't gonna make it easier when your momma was gone all the time working two jobs and you was heating up your own macaroni and your back ain't been washed good in a week. Weren't no way around it: You'd get hard inside just like your momma.

I looked down at that smiling family on the page again, and I thought something I'd never thought in a million years I would. I wished you could be part of a family like that.

Khaki

AFTER PICTURES

My favorite part of the design process is the very beginning. I adore putting pen to paper, my desk a mess with pictures and swatches and samples galore. That's the time I get to dream, to create, to imagine how something could be. But you can't bottle that feeling and that process, and you can't show it to anyone. So, instead, we share those "after" pictures with the world like they're the best part.

That's why releasing a new book of my work can become all-consuming; it's how I share my passion. When I was younger and worked harder, I traveled the country cramming in every interview and local TV show and signing I possibly could. Even if three people showed, I considered the day a victory. This time, I didn't think it was fair to drag Graham and Alex all over the country, so I had scheduled different appearances in different cities over months, not all in one swoop.

Usually, doing press in New York was my favorite part of the process, and I savored every second like a Ladurée macaron. But this time, I was as impatient as a child who sees his dessert right out of the corner of his eye and doesn't want to wait for dinner to be over. I looked at my watch obsessively, even during interviews, and one time, I even caught myself saying, "Sorry, guys, we have to wrap. I have to get home to feed my little girl."

Of course, you weren't mine.

Graham was keeping a close eye on me, sensing how attached I was becoming so quickly. When I burst into the apartment, that bottle inches from your mouth, and yelled, "No, no! I want to feed her," he just sighed and handed you over.

When I insisted that we take you along in the baby seat when we went to dinner with Stacey and Joe, our best friends in New York, he shot me a warning: "Khaki . . ."

When we got back to the apartment and I said, "Isn't it amazing how your children can be so different from one another?" he crossed his arms, looked me in the eye, and said, "I will take her back to Kinston tomorrow if you don't stop this delusional behavior."

I waved him away with my hand and gave you a kiss. It *was* amazing how different children could be, though. Alex barely slept more than a twenty-minute stretch his first year of life, and even getting him down for that took an hour. You would drift off anywhere, any time, any place like a narcoleptic old man. And, from the moment you were born, you babbled and chattered like a sorority girl during rush. Alex, on the other hand, didn't make one noise until he started piling out with full sentences. In fact, I was so worried about his lack of speech that I took him to the doctor to be assessed. He was sitting on top of the brown pleather doctor's table, wheeling his car across the white, crackly paper sheet. When the doctor burst into the room, it must have startled him because the car went sailing to the ground. He looked down and, much to my embarrassment, exclaimed, "Damn it!"

The doctor and I both laughed because what else is there to do, really? I said, "I don't know where on earth he got that," but I'm sure to this day our pediatrician thinks I have a truck driver's mouth.

He patted my shoulder, grabbed Alex's chart, and said, "Sounds to me like his vocabulary is developing fine."

I laughed about that memory as I was walking down Fifth Avenue that chilly afternoon, daydreaming about the off possibility that maybe, just maybe, Jodi was having the same tug on her heart that I was. I knew that the chances were slim, but I was having such a wonderful time that I didn't let the thought get me down.

Getting to go out for fancy nights with the husband I loved and having two beautiful babies by my side was heaven. Plus, the book was selling out all over the place, and I was feeling swanky, sassy, and invincible sashaying around Bergdorf with my new crisp, leather Saint Laurent bag over my forearm. I was searching for Scott, my longtime personal shopper turned cherished friend, thinking that all these people glancing at me as I passed by must be admiring my innate chicness, when a voice from behind said, "Excuse me, ma'am."

It was Scott. I squealed like I hadn't seen him in months and gave him a big kiss, even though we'd had dinner together the night before.

He put his hand on his hip, looking bored, and reached for the bottom of my bag. "Is this one of your new accessories?" he asked sarcastically. "Because I certainly didn't send it."

I gasped and put my hand over my mouth. All day long I had been walking around thinking I was the finest thing since Limoges with a dirty diaper hanging off the bottom of my purse. I mean, really, you couldn't help but laugh.

I hugged Scott and said, "This is God's way of reminding me that I'm not nearly as fabulous as I think I am."

Scott took my hand and pulled me toward the nook filled with gorgeous coffee table books. He, no doubt, had been the one to set up a massive display of my new release on top of the stacks in the center island. He ran his finger across the cover and said, "You might not be quite as fabulous as you think you are, but you're pretty fab all the same."

It made me feel a little better. He pointed to a book he had opened to a page with a picture of Mother, dressed to the nines in head-to-toe Chanel and dripping with jewels. "Now that," he said, "is what fabulous is all about."

I smiled. "Yup. That's my momma."

Scott gasped. "You're pregnant!"

I gave him an annoyed look. "No, I'm not. But thanks for rubbing it in."

He shook his head. "I swear you are. I knew before you even told me that you were having Alex. Don't push away my innate psychic wisdom so easily."

Perhaps it was a scrambled signal. "I'm not pregnant," I said again. "But you know how Graham and I have Carolina?"

Scott nodded.

"Graham is scolding me because I'm dying to adopt her."

I told Scott about Jodi, and he said, "Franny, you can't just take someone's baby because you think you'd do a better job with her."

I stood up straighter, trying to win my case, and said, "I didn't say I would do a better job with her. But you know sometimes how you can *feel* in your gut when something is right?"

"Speaking of," he said, putting his fingers up to his lips to hide his smile, "I've been trying to wait until we were all together to tell you, but I can't hold it in one more minute." He inhaled deeply.

"Clive and I are finally doing it. We're getting married!"

I squealed, and we jumped up and down. Scott and Clive had been dating for years, and I always felt like, though they were a bit on-again, off-again, Clive was the only man who could settle Scott down. "Have you made any plans yet?" I asked, breathlessly. "Have you set a date?"

He nodded. "We didn't want to do anything crazy over-the-top, so we're going to get married with just our families and then have a big party at the Waldorf later on."

I could feel tears coming to my eyes. I thought of your daddy and how happy I was with him. I was glad that Scott had found his other half too. "I'm sorry I won't get to see the wedding, but I'll be the first one on the dance floor."

Scott looked confused. "Won't see the wedding? Of course you'll see the wedding."

"I thought you said it was only family."

And then he made me feel all over again like I hadn't spent the day walking around with a diaper stuck to my purse.

"Honey, you *are* family."

I hugged him. "You'll have to find me something fabulous to wear," I said.

He took my hand and led me to the elevator, saying, "This isn't for you, but I have to show you the most absurdly adorable thing I've ever seen for your new maybe daughter."

I sighed. "She isn't going to be my daughter, so I have to get that thought out of my head. I know realistically no one is just going to give me their baby."

Scott led me over to the display of Gucci bags, and I assumed it was because a new bag is always my celebration purchase for a big career move. But right in the middle was a double *G* monogrammed pint-sized purse with a pink pig face. I knew it was an absurd purchase. But it wasn't just a bag; it was my way of digging those trenches, preparing for that manna to fall right from heaven. I had to do it. Scott packaged it up, and that tiny Gucci Zoo bag hid, wrapped and waiting, underneath the bed in our New York apartment, waiting for Graham and me to have a daughter to claim it.

Jodi
ENOUGH

People think that quinces are near the most useless fruit. They're hard and tangy, and you cain't even eat them just how they are. Them quinces, though, they make some of the most delicious jam ever passed over your lips. And I guess that's what God was thinking when He made 'em in the first place.

I didn't have one clue why God had made me

that week. I felt worse than one a' them quinces, like I was just in everybody's way. My head got to aching and pounding, my mouth watering and my hands shaking on account of me wanting to drink so bad. And my heart was sick and sad 'cause I needed to be with my girl. Pictures is just pictures. There ain't nothing as sweet as holding your baby's cheek right next to yours.

That bottle kept coming up in my mind, and I was just flipping through the TV, trying to ignore it. The phone started ringing, and, much as I thought it weren't my place to answer somebody else's phone, I thought I'd rip it clean out the wall if I had to listen to it anymore.

"Jodi." Khaki exhaled, all outta breath. Soon as I heard her, all frantic, I got to thinking about SIDS and babies getting dropped and all kinds a' awful mess.

"What's wrong?"

"Well . . ." Khaki's voice was all speeding and swerving like a car on the freeway. "Graham and I were wondering if you had given any thought to having Ricky sign away his rights to Carolina."

"Um. Khaki, I don't have one dern clue what that means." I wrapped the cord around my finger and bit my bottom lip.

"Oh, well, of course you don't," Khaki said back. "You're nineteen. How would you know?"

I looked out the window and saw Buddy sitting

right there on the porch. And, even though I was right nervous, I felt my mouth smiling.

Everything okay? he mouthed. I nodded. 'Cause, looking at him looking at me, I sorta felt like maybe it was.

Khaki was still running on. "Fathers have a legal right to their children whether they're a part of their lives or not, which means he can come back any time—even if it's fifteen years from now and he hasn't so much as sent her a birthday card—and try to fight for his rights to custody."

I gasped. "But no court in near their right mind would give Ricky my baby!"

Khaki didn't say nothing back. That pounding, panicking steel drum in my brain got to going again. She said, "Let's get him to sign his rights away and then you won't have to worry about it."

I shouldn't even tell you this, but I wasn't sure. When I closed my eyes real tight, laying in bed at night, I could still think that Ricky was gonna come back, clean up, apologize, and we were gonna be that family I had always wanted. Lord in heaven knows women are ridiculous fools when it comes to love. The man had damn near tried to kill me, and I was still giving him second chances in my mind. But then I got to thinkin': What if he'd tried to take you that night? What if I didn't knock him out good and he got my girl? The pounding stopped, and I got real brave. Weren't no choice.

"What do I got to do?" I asked.

"Not one thing but sit that sweet fanny in a rocking chair and breathe and relax and get feeling better." She paused. "Well, and sign a couple of papers. And Carolina is doing great and Graham or I are here with her every minute, so don't worry one second about her either."

That Khaki, she could always get me believin' that it was all gonna be okay. You know what? I think it's 'cause she really believed it would be.

I walked out to the front porch and sat down real close beside Buddy, realizing I was fightin' right hard not to sit down square in his lap and put my head on his shoulder. Somehow I felt like a pair a' strong arms could really turn things around.

"So what was that all about?" he asked, looking like he was on the verge of a nap.

"Something about Ricky signing his rights away."

Buddy laughed.

"What's so funny?"

He patted my hand. "That just means that poor old Ricky's gonna have the piss scared outta him again by some private detective hired to track him down and manhandle him into signing a form saying he can't get ahold of his child."

"Well, there ain't no way I could afford that. What on earth would I do if I didn't have Graham and Khaki raisin' me?" I smiled.

Buddy smiled back and shrugged. "I don't

162

know," he said, "but they're about the finest people." Then he took my hand and squeezed it. "You know what I do know?"

"What?"

"Getting to come down here with you is the best week's work I've ever done." He winked, kinda flirtatious like.

I could feel my cheeks getting all hot and red. "You're probably just thanking the Lord you hadn't made as many mistakes as me."

Buddy leaned over, squeezed my hand again, and whispered, "We all make mistakes, darlin'. It's how we learn."

Speaking of mistakes, my momma crossed my mind. She'd made 'em all. That fear took ahold a' me, making my face feel all tingly and faintish, that maybe I'd be like my momma. "I don't want Carolina to grow up like me."

"Why not?"

"I don't want her to ever get to wondering where her next meal is coming from. I don't want her to be scared of her momma or grow up with a satellite dish as a babysitter and not one soul to help her with her homework."

It weren't too hard for me to be right back in that dirty trailer, dishes piled in the sink, laundry piled all over the floor, the lights off and TV blaring, praying that Daddy would come home from work before Momma came stumbling in from wherever she been. My momma, she'd always say, "I'm doing my part on account of me bein' on disability." To this day I cain't figure what her disability was—besides being a crazy bitch.

"If I start drinkin', won't nobody know it. Carolina won't be taken care of good. And then she'll have to grow up like her screwed-up momma."

"We're all afraid of something, Jodi."

"Nuh-uh. What are you afraid of?"

"Being alone forever."

Most a' the men I know, they're more afraid of somebody tying them down than being alone. And that's when I knew that me and Buddy, we was the same. He might be all Marlboro cowboy on the outside, but inside, he were dern near soft and scared as me.

A boat come up right where we could see it good and floated on by. I wondered what that might be like, being away from everything and getting your head all clear in the fresh air and waves.

"Do you know," Buddy said, "that I ain't never had an entire week's vacation in my life?"

I nodded. "Me neither." I looked around at the matching teak furniture on the front porch and said, "And I ain't never been to a place like this." I got to sippin' on my lemonade thinking how lemonade without vodka is near as useless as a tractor without a field. "I cain't even figure on what it'd be like to have all this money."

Buddy looked at me for the first time in a while

and shrugged. "Rich or poor, we all gotta find a way to be happy."

I cain't imagine that having a bunch a' money don't make you happy. But, then, I always been poor. My whole life has been saving a penny here, living on right near nothing to get some money up in the bank. And every damn time some man like Ricky took it or some emergency come up, and I'd be startin' all over. I sighed, feeling right sad and low thinking of my trailer back home and how I was gonna get to looking for work again and try to keep me and you fed. Maybe old Al'd forgive me now that I weren't pregnant—long as I could keep from drinking on the job. It made me feel tired.

"I ain't disagreeing with you," I finally said to Buddy, "but it sure seems nice not to have to worry 'bout where your next meal and rent check's coming from all the time." I looked down at my scraggly fingernails and could feel myself getting right mad. "Damn that Ricky!"

If I coulda just got pregnant by a decent guy who had a job and woulda stuck by me and paid his child support like he's s'posed to, then we'd be all right. And you, my poor girl growing up without no daddy, 'specially after how much I loved mine.

"Don't you think it's sad for a little girl to grow up without a daddy?" I asked Buddy.

He looked at me real hard in the eyes, making

me want to turn away. "What are you really asking me, Jo?"

I bit my lip and looked right out over the dark water. I couldn't near believe what I was gonna say out loud, even though I hadn't even said it to myself. "Is the best thing giving her up?" I whispered, feeling like I might get sick all over the porch. "How do you even find the right people for something like that?"

Them goose bumps spread up the back a' my neck as Buddy said, "Sooner or later, God drops the people we need the most right into our lives."

Khaki

PUSH THE PLAY BUTTON

When you've been doing my job as long as I have, you become a master at avoiding the things that you don't want to accept. When a client says she'd like to do her room in a red floral pattern, for example, I avoid hearing her until I've found another fabric she falls in love with. When a man tells me he won't part with the green plaid sofa he's had since college that reeks of dog and has duct tape on the corners, I avoid it until I've found something that's such a great deal he can't pass it up.

So maybe that's why it was so easy for me that

last night we were in New York to avoid the truth that I was going to have to take you home the next day. Graham and I piled up pillows in our king bed to watch a family movie. Alex curled up beside me and promptly fell asleep, and, as soon as Graham gave you your bottle, you were out too.

Graham reached over and took my hand, looking at the sleeping figures beside us. He smiled and winked at me, and, though I knew he would scold me, I said, "You have to admit that this feels right."

He shocked the living daylights out of me, saying, "You know, babydoll, I have to agree that it does." He sighed and said, "I'm sorry we haven't been able to have the baby you want."

I shook my head. "That's not what I mean, really. It's not only that I think we need another member of our family. It's that, more and more, I think Carolina is who makes it feel complete."

He held you closer to him, staring into your dreamy face. "Khaki, one of the things I love about you is that you've got more spunk than a whole nest of baby chicks. And I know I can't stop you from doing what you want any more than I can stop the winds from coming in hard and ruining the corn." He leaned over and kissed me softly. "If you want to talk to Jodi, then that's your prerogative. But don't be all disappointed if she says no. And know that you're probably going to offend the pants off her."

I felt like he was asking me to marry him all over again, that excited, out-of-breath, tingling-toed joy that people don't get to experience enough. "You're kidding."

He shrugged. "If you want to talk to her about it, you can. But you have to know that you're running the risk of pushing her away."

I thought of Jodi, sweet, docile little thing, living in that trailer, scraping by God only knew how. She always seemed so easygoing and relaxed, but to push the play button on that bottle like she did, she certainly had some wounds to heal. I looked over at your peaceful face, perfect lips pursed with dreaming, downy hair illuminated by the sliver of light pouring in from the street. I couldn't imagine how anyone, even if she wasn't in her right mind, could give up something so undeniably perfect.

"You do think it's the right thing to do, right?" I asked. "I mean, that night after Ricky tried to attack her when she just kept saying, 'I can't do this, Khaki. I can't do this . . .'" I trailed off, tears of guilt filling my eyes. Because I had played a large part in your birth mother keeping you. I had been the one to convince her that she could do it. But I hadn't known her alcoholism would take hold of her so strongly again. And I hadn't realized that she would feel so all alone in the world or lose her job or be under such a monumental amount of stress.

"Or maybe we could just take them both in and try to help her that way."

Graham shook his head. "I don't think that'd work. It's inconsistent for Carolina and it doesn't help Jodi take control of her own life." He smiled. "I hate to take a page from your daddy, but it seems like a temporary solution to a permanent problem."

"Yeah. Maybe."

Graham said, "You know, she's had such a hard life and she's been through so much that I think I forget sometimes that the girl is only nineteen. I mean, at nineteen she's responsible for a child, a house, a job, keeping them fed and the bills paid . . . She's trying to stay sober on top of all of it." He shrugged. "It's so hard to even think about giving up your child, but, on some level, I have to wonder if this wasn't God's plan for our family all along."

I nodded and smiled through my tears. "I have no idea what she's thinking, if she's feeling strong and better and ready to do this. But if she's that same girl she was a few nights ago, then I think us asking to adopt Carolina might come as somewhat of a relief."

I looked over at the television lights flickering on your and Alex's cherubic faces. "We just have to remember that it makes sense to us," Graham said, "but that doesn't mean that it's going to make sense to Jodi."

I raised my lip and whispered, "Do you think we can change her name?"

Graham laughed. "No, we can't change her name! I love it."

"You don't think it's weird? I mean, Carolina from North Carolina?"

Graham raised his eyebrow.

I sighed. "Well, maybe we could pronounce it Caroleena, you know, like Carolina Herrera."

Graham rolled his eyes and laughed again. "No way, babe." He leaned over and kissed me. "I think it's great," he whispered, his forehead resting on mine. "Now I have two sweet Carolina girls."

I laughed too. "Well, we Carolina girls are the best in the world." I took Graham's hand, and rubbed the gold band that I hadn't seen him without since the day we said those vows. "You do want more children, right?"

Then he said something that, not too soon later, he might have lived to regret. "Oh, Khaki. As long as you're their momma, I'd have a whole litter."

Jodi

RUNNING YOUR KNEE INTO A TRAILER HITCH

When it's getting to be rhubarb season, and you're thinking 'bout putting it up, you gotta do it quick as you can. Them first cuttings is the right time to freeze. Wait too late and all you got is a fibrous old stalk, tougher than nails.

After I said out loud that maybe I oughta give you up, I thought I'd just give it a little time, figure out if I could make it through without drinking again. But I could just hear my grandma's voice in my head, talkin' about that rhubarb. And I knew if I was gonna do it, it had to be right soon.

But deciding to give up your child is damn near like having to choose whether to cut off your hand or your foot. Don't matter what you pick, you ain't never gonna be whole again.

I don't know who said time heals all wounds, but they ain't right. 'Cause don't matter what I do, I won't never get over giving you up. That's why growin' up is so hard. You can know right clear in your heart that you did the right thing. But that don't keep it from hurtin' like running your knee into a trailer hitch, all day, every day, over and over and over again.

Buddy and me, we decided the last night of our trip we would be fancy and go out to dinner. His treat—seeing as how I had four bucks to my name. I was real sad that night, tryin' to figure out what I was gonna do, but already knowing the right thing, like you always do. I wanted so bad to be the momma you needed—without drinkin' myself into the common ground at the trailer park.

So Buddy was just drivin' along, and I said, "You know what, I don't care what my daddy said. I'm gonna get on welfare, keep my baby, and pray real hard to stay clean and sober."

I don't know if it were a coincidence or a sign from God but right in that same dag dern minute I saw a tiny girl, probably not more than eighteen months old, outta the corner a' my eye. Her house was damn near falling down, weren't nobody watching her, she weren't wearing nothing but a diaper that looked like it hadn't been changed since Bush was president, and she jumped right in a puddle of God only knows what. I was fixing to tell Buddy to do something, but he was already on the phone with the police.

I was getting outta that truck, saying, "We cain't just leave her there!"

But the sheriff pulled up, and I got to crying instead a' helping.

"It's okay," Buddy said. "The police will handle it."

And that's when I knew.

I shook my head and through my tears said, "No, Buddy. That's what I'm talking 'bout. That could be Carolina out there."

"What d'ya mean?" he asked, taking his hand off the steering wheel to rub my shoulder.

"That momma in there, she's probably all right when you get right down to it. But she ain't got no clue her kid's out here in the cold, worse'n a orphan 'cause she's passed out."

Buddy waved his hand and said, "Naw. She probably just slipped out the door in a second like kids do."

That minute you was born and I saw that pretty face, I swore to heaven that I'd protect you forever. I couldn't near imagine any momma not feeling that way. But I didn't say any of that to Buddy because he wouldn't have understood anyhow.

"Oh, Jodi, just give it time. I'm sure it gets easier."

I stared out the windshield into the black night, the stars twinkling above my head, feeling as lost down here as I would up there. "That's the thing," I said. "Being a momma ain't supposed to be about what's easy."

Khaki

THE EVIL WITCH

My design column in *House Beautiful* was the first opportunity I had to elevate my career from ordinary to A-list. I'd grown up writing stories and reading magazines, and when my boss, Anna, mentioned that she could get me a meeting, I knew I could nail the interview and land myself on a national platform that would make my career. The night before that interview, I couldn't sleep at all. I tossed and turned like a psychiatric patient wiggling free from a straitjacket knowing that this one event had the power to transform my life.

That night was exactly, to a *T,* the same as the night before we came home from New York. I ran over and over in my head what I would say to your birth momma, how I would ask her for the ultimate gift, how I would convince her that it was the right thing without insinuating that she was a bad mother or an incapable one.

I had that same thick shell my momma did, but inside, I wasn't as confident as I appeared. So, as soon as I woke up, I called the boldest, brashest woman I knew.

"Good morning, my love," Bunny said.

Bunny, who had started as a client but quickly become one of my best friends in the city, was always an early riser. Tall, broad, and lean but boxy, she was born to be an athlete just like I was born to be a mother. She satisfied her inner Flo-Jo by taking a long run every morning before her three children woke up and her husband went to work.

"May I come over?" I asked, simply.

"Are you here?" Bunny asked, enthusiasm rising in her voice. "Why didn't you call me before?"

I bit my lip, feeling guilty that I had been so wrapped up in you I hadn't even seen one of the people in my life who had always been the best to me. But Bunny was one of those great, low-maintenance friends who didn't ruminate over trivial things like a missed visit. So, without apologizing, I said, "I'm here. And I need your advice."

"Okay," Bunny said, her voice laced with a teacher's authoritativeness. "Can we meet at Le Pan Quotidien? I'm dying for a soft-boiled egg."

I laughed. It was that classic Bunny decisiveness that I needed. Thirty minutes later we were sitting across a rustic farm table, coffee in hand, eating delicious, fresh-baked organic bread with soft-boiled eggs on top. "Mmmm," I said.

"Everything is simply better when you do as the French," Bunny said, her golf ball–sized diamond sparkling in the low lighting, making her creamy, milk chocolate skin look even more luscious. She peered at me across the table, and, lowering her voice, as we were sharing the table with three newspaper-wielding men, she said, "You're pregnant, aren't you?"

I sighed. I took a sip of my coffee and said, "No. I'm not pregnant. But I'm trying to figure out a tactful way to ask Graham's cousin if we can adopt her baby."

Bunny laughed that bawdy, uninhibited laugh that was one of the things I loved best about her. "Oh, honey, why? Take it from a batshit-crazy woman, only children are amazing."

I gave her a look that wordlessly said she was being neither sensitive nor helpful.

"Okay, fine, fine. Can't you offer her money?"

I shook my head. "Isn't that against the law?"

Bunny readjusted her sleek ponytail and said, "Law, schmaw. Who's going to turn you in?"

"Bunny, come on. I need real help here. We can pay for her medical bills, baby-related expenses, and the living expenses she accrued during her pregnancy, but she isn't like that anyway. What do I do?"

Bunny took a sip of coffee. "You just ask. What's the worst that can happen?"

I looked up over my egg and said, "I'm afraid that if I ask, I'll push her away, and then she won't even let me keep Carolina while she's at work anymore." I paused, staring into my coffee cup. "I can't bear the thought of not being in Carolina's life at all—or Jodi's."

Bunny shrugged. "That won't happen."

I rolled my eyes. "So that's your sage advice? That's why I walked all the way over here? If you can't do better than that, you can pay for your own breakfast."

Bunny brightened like that $6.95 was all that was standing between her and a new jet.

"I didn't know you were paying. In that case, I would ask her to think about her little girl, to consider the advantages she could have living in a family like yours. And make sure you give her the choice of whether she wants to be involved in her life or not."

I gasped. "What if she says yes? I mean, is that okay?"

Bunny nodded like she was a child psychologist specializing in adoptions and said, "Oh, yes. I remember reading in *Vogue* that adopted children actually thrive when they are able to know and grow up with their birth parents." She took another bite, and, so I could see the yellow yolk bursting in her mouth like a paintball, said, "Open adoption is the way to go."

"Isn't that kind of confusing?" I asked, wondering why I had spent so many of those dreaded low-carb years denying myself the utter deliciousness of fresh bread.

Bunny shook her head. "It's better for you,

really. Then, when she's pissed that she's in time-out, she doesn't have fantasies about her birth mother being a princess who's coming to save her from the evil witch"—she paused, wiped her glossy mouth, and pointed across the table—"i.e., you."

Back at the apartment, where Graham, amazing husband that he was, was trying to pack while watching two children, I burst through the door. He kissed me like I'd just returned from hiking Mount Everest. "What?" I laughed.

He kissed me again. "If I ever make a comment about your job not being as hard as mine, please remind me of this day. Alex has pulled every garment that I was trying to pack out of the suitcases, and Carolina keeps crying, and I don't know why."

I ignored him and said, "Do we want to let her be involved in Carolina's life?"

Graham looked around. "Who?"

I threw a pink blanket at him and said, "Jodi, of course."

He smiled. "Sweetheart, I told you before that you have to get yourself prepared for the fact that she'll probably say no to your little proposition."

I gathered all of my toiletries, tossed them in my suitcase, and said, "I know, I know, low expectations, blah, blah, blah. Is it okay for her to be in Carolina's life? Would it be too hard or confusing?"

"You know, babydoll, I think if she does us the amazing honor of allowing us to raise her child, we should leave that decision up to her." Graham zipped his suitcase shut.

I nodded. A shiver of fear zipped through me too. What if Jodi was always possessive over you? What if she felt entitled to mother you even if she let us adopt you? I sat down, cross-legged on the floor, reached over to where you were kicking contentedly on a blanket, and put you in my lap. You blew a little spit bubble, and I smiled, my heart on fire with love for you.

"Mommy," Alex said, running in. "Carolina pooped earlier and it came all out her diaper!"

I turned to Graham. He laughed and shrugged his shoulders. "The man is correct," he said, grabbing Alex by the waist and tossing him into the air. Alex giggled, and I was reminded of how terrified I had been about how another man would be a father to him and how, when Graham had walked back into my life, that fear disappeared. Maybe the same thing would happen with Jodi. I prayed silently that God would give us both that quiet calm and peaceful knowledge of the right thing. And, without any warning whatsoever, the questions that had been zooming like cars at the Indy 500 stopped, and I had the clearest thought: You can never have too many people who love you.

Jodi
YOU CAN LIVE

I remember gettin' real tickled in school over Mark Twain saying that cauliflower is "cabbage with a college education." I think that's right near like me and Khaki. And that's all right 'cause I like cabbage real good. Cauliflower too.

I used to think Khaki were so happy and upbeat all the time 'cause she didn't care one whit about what other people was feeling. But once we got to know each other good I realized that she feels everything. She just don't want nobody to know, so she keeps it all inside. So I just got my nerve up, and I ask her one day, "Khaki, how you do it, girl? After all you been through, how do you get up every day and act so happy?"

She shrugged. "You know, Jodi, when you've looked death in the face you realize your next breath isn't guaranteed. You can either sit at home and wallow in fear and self-pity or you can live." I nodded. She said, "I've done both. The latter is a hell of a lot more interesting."

And that's when I figured that we was the same. Rich, poor, educated or not, we all got some tough mess to deal with in this life. And the only way we're gonna get through, that we can get to healing, is to know that it takes total surrender. To God, to life, to the universe. Stripping down and getting all raw and vulnerable, that's how I got off the sauce and Khaki got outta bed after her first husband died. And just like that pretty mornin' sun rising over the pond at the farm, it dawned on me that Khaki, she understood me better than I'd been knowing.

I knew right good in my heart that when I asked Khaki what I were about to ask her that she would seem all tough and together. But inside, right near that tender heart, she'd be weeping a whole river for me. And that's what a kid needs in a momma. You gotta be able to feel so deep and so hard and so sad for people but then still get on your smiley face and live your life.

When I was coming up, giving up my baby ain't something I thought about any more than I dreamed a' getting a Harvard scholarship. But you get to learning that we don't know what paths are being carved in the riverbeds of our lives any more than we know our expiration dates. (Though I can guess it on food pretty good.)

But what I did know, what my grandma been trying to teach me since I were little and sitting on her knee at church, was that people need Jesus. But I guess after I prayed that Momma would quit drinking and that didn't happen, I prayed that Daddy wouldn't die and that didn't happen, and I prayed that I would get a handle on my drinking and that didn't happen, I just lost my faith somewhere. But that Buddy, he reminded me that week in Atlantic Beach that just 'cause God don't always give us the answer we're looking for don't mean He ain't listening and He ain't answering. And, wouldn't you know, that week I prayed so hard it was like God flew down and give me the answers.

Here's what I got to telling God that week: "Lord, I ain't twenty yet, and I'm so bad off Buddy's gotta hide the mouthwash. I ain't got no job, no money, no way out. But I got this baby. I get to feeling like I want to hold her and kiss on her and love on her, but it ain't been a month yet, and I'm already near off the deep end."

I closed my eyes right tight and breathed real deep, and I tried to picture giving you up. But I dern near got sick all over the coffee table. But then Khaki, like she been talking to God too, she said, "Bringing Carolina back to you's gonna tear me apart."

And then there was that precious baby naked in the mud puddle. And it didn't take that Harvard degree to figure on what's the right thing here.

I cried more tears that week than all the other tears I've cried in my life combined. I darn near coulda give all them people in the famine water. Knowing that I wouldn't get to see my baby smile her first smile or step her first step or speak her first word—it were like finding out Daddy had cancer again times about a million. It wasn't gonna be me rocking you to sleep at night or feeding you or kissing your scraped knees or soothing your broken heart. But I wasn't what you needed. And I knew it. And I feel right blessed by that.

I was all clogged up with my tears that morning as I got up, puttin' on my nicest, prettiest dress, all peach and flowing, the one that Daddy'd saved two months to be able to buy me for the homecomin' dance. I wanted to look real nice, make Graham and Khaki see that you would grow up to be sorta pretty. I walked out on the beach, 'cause, even though it was smack-dab in the middle of winter, it weren't that cold that day. Buddy, he was still sleeping, so I just walked along, all by myself, them freezing waves crashin' over my bare feet, that dress blowing around, my long hair flowing back in the chilly wind. The crisp, fresh mornin' air, it made me feel like I could breathe, like maybe my lungs could keep working even after this horrible thing I was gonna do. And with the sun reflecting on the ocean, glittering and dancin' like diamonds, making the world seem safer and happier, not quite so scary, I thought, *Maybe I can raise her myself after all.*

But, in real life, trudging back up that sand toward the house, finally feeling them goose bumps that broke out all over my body, weren't no way on God's green earth. And that devil, he put it in my head that Khaki and Graham, they might not say yes, they might not want to keep you near as bad as I was thinkin'. But there weren't no other answer. Weren't no way I could give my baby to a stranger.

I let myself in, and Khaki and Graham, they was already sittin' right there in that wood den by the kitchen. They looked like Barbie and Ken, all perfect and shiny, and Khaki, she tried to give me them cookies you could smell baking in her momma's oven, not knowin' I was sicker than any flu I'd ever come down with.

I knew that I had to pile on out with it quick, 'fore I lost my nerve. 'Fore that little pitchfork-holding man on my shoulder got me all convinced I should keep you for myself.

But Khaki, she got to talking first. She was as cool, calm, and in control as I ever seen, but, like I said, you don't ever know what's going on inside your momma. Graham, now, he looked like he'd eaten too many of his momma's famous fried pickles. Khaki leaned in all close to me and said, "I want you to know before I say what I'm about to say that whatever decision you make is absolutely fine with us, and we will do everything in our power to help you no matter what."

Oh, Lord. They're gonna send me to rehab again.

"You know that we love you and we love Carolina, and we only want what's best." She paused, licking her lips. "I know that you are going through a difficult time with your drinking and that must be scary."

She didn't have to say no more. I could see myself all locked up in one a' them hospital rooms again, all white-walled and making you crazy.

"And I know that you are so young, and raising a baby all alone is terrifying and solitary and maddening sometimes no matter how old or experienced you are or how much help you have."

Khaki was sweet and steady and talkin' real calm and good. And then that Graham, he just blurted on out, "We want to adopt Carolina."

Khaki looked at him like he was gonna be real sorry. I got to crying so hard, I couldn't near see the room no more. It was relief and sadness and all them other things all rolled into one and pouring out my eyes. Khaki came and sat next to me right there in my little chair and put her arm around me tight.

"We're fine with any decision you make, but know that if you decided this was what you wanted you could see her as much as you wanted or not at all, depending on what you thought would be best."

That made me stop crying right quick. I ain't never thought I'd get to see you no more. Part a' the reason I was so sad is 'cause I knew I weren't just saying good-bye to you, but to Graham and Khaki and Alex too. But maybe it weren't as bad as I thought. "Wait? I can still see her and all? Is that all right for her?"

Khaki shook her head and pulled me in close. "I always say the more people who love you the better."

And then I sobbed and sobbed again 'cause weren't no living person in the world that loved me, and I wanted my baby to have nothing but love. I said, all snotty and red-faced like when I was drinking, "If we do this, it cain't be about what's best for me or best for you. It's got to be about what's best for Carolina."

Khaki, she was crying right hard too now, but probably 'cause she were sad for me but so happy for her.

She said, "Of course. We'll figure it all out together."

I leaned over, puttin' my head down on my knees 'cause I was feelin' faint. "How could I do it, Khaki? How could I give up my youngen?"

She shook her head. "I don't know, sweetheart," she said, sittin' a little straighter. "The only way you could do it is if you truly believed in your heart that growing up with Graham and Alex and me would be best for Carolina. And if you don't think that, then it won't hurt our feelings."

I stood up, stretchin' out a little, and Graham wrapped me in that big bear hug that there ain't nothing else like. And I knew you was gonna have that bear hug every single day for your whole growin'-up life. And it made me just a little happy.

I said, "I want to see her worse than anything. But I cain't get to holding her and smelling her sweet head and still let you adopt her."

"Wait—" Graham said, him getting all teared up now too. "Are you telling us that we can?"

I nodded, but them tears was so lodged in my throat I couldn't say nothing. I pulled away from that big bear hug, not wanting no comfort. I got out the door quick, running way down the beach, almost to the ocean, plopped my bony butt in that cold, wet sand, that beautiful dress I'd pined for so long and hard gettin' ruined, and sobbed and sobbed. It weren't like nothing I'd ever seen, being able to cry that hard for that long. I don't know when, but Buddy, he come and wrapped me up in this big down comforter, and whispered, "No sense in you freezin' to death out here."

But it didn't matter none. I couldn't feel nothing. Buddy, he stroked my back for pretty much the whole damn night. But I were in pain so real and so deep and so scary I couldn't move or thank him or nothing like that.

I could live a million years, and I don't think I'd never feel like that again. And there won't ever be a day I don't live that pain. But I love you so much that I knew all I could do is give you the life I didn't have, the one I wasn't fit to give. Sittin' right out there in that sand, foam gatherin' at the edge of the shore, I couldn't reckon how I could love you so fierce and still give you away. I couldn't figure whether that made me the most selfish person in the world or just a little bit selfless. I don't know the theory of relativity or the speed of light or any a' that other math. But I knew right well, watching the moon rise that night, that no matter what them smart scholars say, love is the hardest equation.

Khaki

SERIOUS TEARS

I've never been one of those designers who descends on a room with her tape measure and graph paper, charting out every perfect dimension. I go to the room, get a feel for it, and when I see the perfect pieces, I just know. I can feel that they are the right proportion and scale for the space without a yardstick.

When Alex was born, he was kind of like me with those pieces of furniture. He *knew* I was his mommy. From the moment he lay on my chest and breathed that first sigh of relief, we began the type of love affair that a woman doesn't know she'll ever have until it happens to her.

And I think that's how, even those first nights in New York, I knew that I was meant to be your mother. I might not have given birth to you, but I was the one who could calm you down, get you to sleep, make you relax. And I felt that same surge of love like a spiking fever whenever you came to me for solace.

It has never, not for one single second felt anything but right between you and me. You are my baby. You are Graham's baby. You are Alex's sister. And that's that.

Loving you like I do has made me realize that giving birth has very little to do with motherhood. And that, even in the absence of a hormone surge, new motherhood turns me into an emotional mess. When Alex was born I cried so much that your aunt Charlie was afraid I was in the throes of a severe bout of postpartum depression. But then I was devastated over the loss of Alex's daddy, so sad that here I was, so magnificently in love on my own.

With you, I think the tears were a mixture of sorrow so deep it's a hole to China and gratitude so soaring that it's the peaks of the Andes. I had pined for another baby for years, and here you were. But I knew what it was to feel that pure connection with a child, and so I knew what Jodi must have been going through. And I wept every time she crossed my mind, which was often.

It was okay, because, angel that you were, you cried some serious tears yourself. Alex never cried, and so I kept taking you to the doctor and

189

sobbing, "She's crying because she knows I'm not her real mother."

Every time, he would pat me on the shoulder and say, "You are her real mother. She has colic."

That would appease me for a day or two and then I'd be back.

I finally realized that no co-pay in the world was going to fix this, so I took you over to see Mother and Pauline, who had no idea what had transpired. When I walked through the door, Mother was in the library, and, peeking her head around, called, "Frances, honestly, are you going to babysit that child for the rest of your life?"

I smiled, nodded, and said, "I *am* going to, as a matter of fact."

Mother scrunched her nose and shot me an annoyed "What?"

"Graham and I are adopting Carolina."

Pauline came running in from the kitchen, as best as you could run at eighty-five, in support hose with a stocky build. "I been praying for years you get another baby. I tole you!"

Mother gave me a look like I had just told her I was taking a leave of absence from my life to become a groupie for an indie punk group. She rolled her eyes, sighed, and gestured for me to hand Carolina to her. She wrapped her up and said, "You better spend a lot of time with your grandmother so you'll grow up with some damn sense."

You opened your little eyes, and we all laughed. Mother looked up at me. "Khaki, I swear. You can't just take someone's baby."

I crossed my arms. "You see," I said, "that's what's wrong with you and Graham. You're too narrow-minded. I knew this little girl was meant for me, and so did Jodi. Families aren't always born, Mother. They're made."

Pauline nodded and said, "Uh-huh. Girl's smart, Miz Mason."

I smiled at Pauline. It was abundantly clear who had raised me.

Mother smiled a little. "I guess that's true. After all this time, Pauline is sort of like my sister."

Pauline looked at me skeptically.

"It's true, Pauline," I said. "Mother would've bossed her sister even worse than she bosses you."

I paused for a moment, wondering if I had overstepped my bounds. Mother and I rarely talked about her parents and sister dying, that childhood tragedy that had defined so much of her life and, looking back, must have been responsible for many of those moments that I felt she kept me at arm's length. But Mother laughed, and you looked up at her and cooed.

"All right." Mother relented. "I'm happy if you're happy." Then she said something that I hadn't even thought of, something that made me feel like the house was on fire and I couldn't get to you and Alex. "But you know she has a year to change her mind."

I shook my head frantically. "No, Mother. She only has seven days."

Mother cocked her head and put her fingers up to the pearls around her neck. "Honey, you and I both know what happened with the Taylors."

I bit my lip and looked over at you, feeling the tightening like a noose around my neck. I had convinced myself that I was safe, that the seven days had passed and you were ours. But the harsh reality that a family I knew well had been forced to give their child back in a brutal court case was a pill I couldn't swallow. And all because of a tiny, tiny mistake on some paperwork.

Pauline could read my face. "Chile, you ain't got no business worrying yourself over something like that. You just go on being a momma." Then she smiled. "See," she said, winking. "I tole you all it'd take was a little bacon grease."

I smiled, trying to push away the thought, remembering the devastation of that mistake being found eleven months into the Taylors' adoption.

"I'm just saying, is all," Momma said. "The Taylors told me the statute of limitations on those things is usually considered a year."

But I knew a lot of things would have to fall into place for that to happen. Jodi or Ricky would have to want you back, we'd have to get a judge that didn't owe Daddy for something or another . . . I swallowed my fear, walking over to adjust a stack of books on a gorgeous campaign chest I had bought for Mother's redesigned library. It was a competition between us. I'd turn them straight, and then, when I was gone, she'd turn them back at an angle.

"I've gained like five pounds, thanks to you," I said to Pauline, feeling my breath return to normal.

"Khaki," my mother said warningly. "Weight gain is a slippery slope."

You made a little gurgling sound, and Mother cooed down at you, "Not for you, darling. You're supposed to gain weight." As if she had assuaged your fears, you closed your eyes again and drifted back off to sleep.

I sat down and sighed. "So, I'm trying to decide if I'm going to keep my surgery date two weeks from now or if I'm going to reschedule."

Mother sat up straighter and peered at me. "Why on earth would you have the surgery now? You have a baby."

"Yeah . . ." I said in a long, drawn-out way. "But it's probably not the best thing in the world to have a bunch of junk clogging up your insides. I feel like I need to get it out."

"I come over and hep you take care of the chil'ren," Pauline said.

"Maybe you should wait until they're a little older," Mother said.

But I knew from experience that toddlers were much more taxing on a body than babies—especially babies that you didn't birth.

I took you back home, put you in your bassinet, and curled up on the couch to order more diapers, bottles, and another bouncy seat from Amazon. When I logged on, a message reminded me that it was time for my auto-ship tampons to be delivered. *That can't be right,* I thought. I had seen a brand-new box in my cabinet when I put my makeup away that morning.

About that time, Graham slammed the back door, and, as he was walking to my office, called, "I'm going to pick Alex up from school. There's a sale on fishing rods at the Neuse Sports Shop, and I want to take him to pick a couple out. And Momma's going to come watch the kids so we can go hear the Embers play at Pearson Park tonight." He breezed through the doorway and stopped dead in his tracks when he saw me, which was my first clue that my face was whiter than an Irish virgin.

"What's wrong?" he asked.

Kristin, Scott, and Bunny's prediction raced through my mind. "Oh my gosh," I said, under my breath. I looked up at my husband. With that particular mix of joy and terror that only one subject-adjective combination can create, I said, "I'm pregnant."

Jodi

DON'T FEED THE BEARS

I know good as my own face in the mirror that my grandma never left the United States. So how she started loving Italian caponata, I ain't got no idea. But when I'd wake up at her house, them weekends we'd have "Camp Grandma," she'd be just a-whistlin', stir-frying eggplant. I'd climb up on the stool, right beside her, and help her chop herbs and onions and celery and garlic.

After all that choppin' and that weird, Italian breakfast, Daddy'd pick me up and we'd head on to the zoo. He'd always say, real serious like, "See how it says 'Don't feed the bears,' Jodi?" I would nod my little brunette head, hair matted with sleep, a momma who didn't love me enough to brush it and a daddy who didn't notice things like hair.

"If we feed the bears we take away their instinct to hunt on their own. The zoo give 'em prey to hunt, just like they would in the wild. If they quit having to find their own food, they get fat and lazy and don't do nothin'."

You don't gotta be real smart to figure out he was tellin' my little youngen self all about his politics. But, now, don't go getting the wrong idea. My daddy, he believed just like me that we all get down our luck sometimes, and, when that happens, you gotta help out your neighbor. Says so right there in the Bible.

And I'd be the first one to tell you that, right about then, I needed a little help from my friends. I was so ashamed 'bout what I done, so embarrassed that everybody was gonna know I had a baby and I give her up.

That night before, Marlene had been over to cheer me up. "Don't nobody our age want to raise a baby their own self. Ain't nobody blaming you, girl."

More than making me feel better, Marlene was whining her pants off. "I mean, how in the hell did Karla think this was 'blond'?"

Marlene put her fingers up at her ears, making air quotes. I thought Marlene's hair looked great. It was toned down and blended. She looked something right near classy. Well, I mean, classier.

"She got done and I just told her right then, 'Girl, this hair ain't trailer park enough for me. If you're gonna be practicing for cosmetology school, you gotta give the customer what they want.'"

I rolled my eyes. "Marlene, you look better than I ever seen you, so shut up."

She smacked her gum and smiled just a little.

I said, "I gotta find a job or I'm gonna get to starving to death by next week."

Marlene put her finger up to her lips like she was thinking real hard. "Well, you should go back to school. You was always the smart one in the group."

I wouldn't a' said it out loud or nothing, but I'd always wanted to go to college right bad. I wanted to see them professors in the bow ties and sit under one of them old oak trees them college brochures always got. Maybe even play some a' that Frisbee.

Marlene got me outta my dreamin' saying, "You know, you should go to Lenoir Community. They got this program in nursing that'd be perfect for ya." Marlene was smacking her gum so loud now I wanted to smack her.

I flared my nostrils. "I ain't sure I want to be a nurse, cleaning up all them bodily fluids and whatnot."

She shook that bouffant so hard stray pieces was falling out on the floor like leaves in the fall. "Well, my friend Amber's friend Tiffany went, and she started sleeping with one of the doctors there, and he put her up in her own place, and he's leaving his wife for her."

"I ain't got no interest in stealing some poor woman's husband."

Marlene waved her hand at me, still smacking away. "You cain't think about it that way when you figure you're findin' *your* husband."

"Marlene," I said, like she were a youngen.

"You tell your friend Amber's friend Tiffany that that doctor ain't never gonna leave the pearl-wearing, benefit-attending mother of his three beautiful children for some bleached-blond tramp trying to screw him for a free apartment."

Marlene plopped down on the sofa, looking offended, and crossed her arms. "Why you gotta be so damn negative all the time?"

I sorta stacked the magazines Khaki had brought by on the coffee table, their spines in perfect, straight rows like them elementary school classes lining up to say the Pledge of Allegiance.

"I ain't negative, Marlene. I'm practical. Kinston ain't Hollywood, and this ain't *Pretty Woman*." I sat down too. "Plus, I can guarantee that your friend Amber's friend Tiffany don't look like Julia Roberts."

Buddy got to pokin' his head in the door right about then. "Hey, Jodi. Got a question for ya."

I hadn't seen Buddy since I give you up, since he got me through like he did. I sobbed so long on that beach I think them crops back home was rotated. I ain't never met a man like Buddy, one that would let you cry, not tell you to stop, one who would listen but not tell you how to fix it. I didn't know there was a man like that.

Marlene got up, straightened her skirt, and said, "What a good-lookin' visitor."

She were giving Buddy what she calls her

198

"bedroom eyes." If you ask me, looks more like she's having a stroke or something.

"Hey, Buddy. I got an answer," I said, and waved to Marlene as she brushed past Buddy. She put both her hands on his chest on her way out the door.

"How 'bout canning some of them vegetables and making some jam and pickles and coming to the farmer's market with me when it opens up?"

I looked around my teeny kitchen, and, like Buddy were right there in my head, he said, "I already asked Graham, and he said for you to come set up shop at their house." He paused. "I mean, if you're ready to be over there, that is."

I got to feeling kinda nervous and sick and excited all at the same time, like I was waiting for a boy to call or somethin'. Khaki and Graham and me, we'd agreed I would wait a month before seeing you. I couldn't near think about it 'fore then anyhow. But then, our social worker that was helping us through all this mess, she said it weren't uncommon for babies to see their birth mommas right often. Lots of 'em were even living under the same roof. I weren't real sure how it'd be, being your aunt Jodi, not your momma. But all I said to Buddy was, "So, you want me to sell my stuff?"

Buddy nodded. "Everybody's got vegetables, but I thought if we could offer something more it would make us stand out from the competition."

"You know I'll help you out any way I can. I owe everything to you and especially to Graham and Khaki."

Buddy put his finger on his mouth. "Funny because, not two minutes ago, I was up there and they was talking about how they owe everything to you."

I smiled. And, you know, I didn't get in bed with a single married man and found me a job anyhow.

Khaki and Graham, they hired me to go with Buddy to the Tuesday, Thursday, and Saturday farmer's markets right there on the spot like they'd been talking about it all along. As soon as spring hit, I'd start. And I could sell my stuff too, and I didn't even have to pay for my own stand. Things was starting to go my way. The best part of all was that Graham and Khaki, they said when you worked for them you got your own health insurance. Now I know good and well what health insurance costs, and I cain't believe they was telling me the truth. But I ain't never been so proud as when I went back to the doctor for my checkup and I had my very own health insurance that I had earned my own self.

I showed up at Khaki and Graham's that day to get a feel for their kitchen, see if I could get all my mess in there and start cannin' as soon as stuff started coming off the vine. Like she were scared to see me full on, Khaki peeked her head around the corner.

"How you feeling, sweetie?" she asked.

You didn't have to be real smart to reckon that Khaki, she was scareder I was gonna take you back than I was that Ricky was gonna get me again. But my word, it was better than any piece a' legal paper—and I signed a damn lotta them things too. I nodded. "I think I'm doing as good as I can. I think I might be all right."

She were still looking all nervous like, but there weren't nothin' else I could say.

"Can we sit down for a second?" Khaki asked, pointin' at them stools under the island.

I nodded, getting that antsy feelin' like a potty-training toddler who has to go. If you'd been standing in that room, you woulda felt it too. It were like the air got to blowing a different direction or something. And I felt that sick coming up in the back a' my throat like I been drinkin' again. You could tell it right off: She and Graham changed their minds 'bout me being in your life.

"I don't want you to think that this changes anything," Khaki said. "But I'm pregnant."

My brain got all freezed up like I been eating too much ice cream or something. And instead of panicking about not getting to see you, I panicked that they was gonna give you back.

She laughed, but I weren't sure if I was happy or not. "We're so excited!" she said.

I reckon I would be right excited if I were her too. She and Graham, they been wanting a baby

201

all their own so bad. But my heart got to hurtin' for you, like you was so little you didn't even know it yet but you was already getting tossed around like the garbage. "So then I guess you're giving Carolina back to me?"

Her eyes got all wide like a rabbit in the woods who just seen a fox. "Of course we aren't," she whispered real strange like her voice wouldn't come out regular. "She's our little girl."

Then she got to fiddlin' with her ring and you could tell that she knew that weren't the right thing to say. But it was true. It burned me through like rubbing alcohol on an open cut, but that didn't mean it weren't right.

"If you're worried about us taking care of all of them—"

I put my hand up to stop her and shook my head. You didn't even need to know Khaki that good to get to realizin' that she'd love the whole world if they'd let her.

"So I guess all them sticks and leaves you been drinkin' worked after all."

"Who woulda thought?" She smiled and dashed outta the room so fast I weren't sure she'd ever been there. A minute later, she was pushing a huge box into the kitchen with her foot, all kinda cockeyed like. She put her hand up and said, "Now before you get all sassy and protesting, I'm not giving you these. I am investing in your business. But you had to start off on the right foot."

"Investin' in my business?"

"Well, yeah. If you're gonna be canning and making jam, you gotta have jars."

I leaned over right far and pulled out a smooth, clear jar, with a round pink, green, and black label. It said: *Jodi's Cans and Jams*. It had a profile of a girl in an apron all sketched out. I guessed that were supposed to be me. I smiled and bit my fingernail. I liked the looks a' that girl, all pony-tailed and happy.

Khaki asked, like she been underwater holding her breath, "So, do you like them? Because if you don't like them you don't have to use them. I can just take them out back or to the church bazaar or something."

I was getting right choked up, so I didn't say nothing.

"I mean," she continued, "you've got to put the labels on after you've already finished the canning, obviously. I just put this one on to show you."

I hugged her real tight and said, "I love them so good I don't know what to say."

She smiled like the judge just put a tiara on her head and said, "Oh, I'm so happy."

"How'd you get all them things done?" I asked.

She waved her hand like it weren't nothing. But I could just hear her on the phone with some designer talking him into gettin' all them things done overnight and putting them on some sketchy

Greyhound somewhere so they'd get to Kinston right about in time for her to surprise me. I got to thinking that Buddy sure was gonna be impressed with me now with all my jars.

"So, um," I said, real nervous like. "Is it okay . . . I mean, can I see her?"

Khaki looked at her hands, right weak like, and I got to feeling it again. She give me them jars but she wasn't gonna let me see my baby.

"First, I need to talk to you about something that's been weighing on me." She sighed, and I could see the tears getting to her eyes right good. "That day that you came and asked me for money for the abortion . . ." She sighed again, real sad and low like, and she was trying to swallow them tears that were near to escaping from her eyes. "I would never in a million years have thought this was how it would have turned out. If I had known—"

I could feel that lump in my own throat, and that fear, it got to running in my veins like ice water. But it weren't that maybe I couldn't see you no more. It was: *What if you ain't never been born?*

It was my turn to look down at my hands. "This giving Carolina up, it's been the worst damn thing I could ever think on." I swallowed hard and looked up. "But it ain't nothin' compared to imagining living without Carolina in the world. Don't matter who's raisin' her."

She hugged me real tight and whispered, "You promise?"

I nodded and bit my lip. It was all that was keeping me from crying.

"Graham," Khaki called. "Can you bring Carolina down?"

I weren't sure how I'd feel seeing you. And it was real sad, sure. But I felt so proud, 'cause here you were, perfect and beautiful. And I had done that. I had made you.

"Hi there, little girl," I said, touching your soft head. "You're so big."

I just sat real still and watched you sleep, looking at your little face and thinking on how bad I missed you. I was so sad you weren't mine, but I was so happy that I had done this great thing for the people that I loved. It weren't mine, but I had made a family. And I knew I had to stay sober and start a good life for myself. 'Cause, no matter what, I'm your momma. Handing you to Graham, it was like ripping out my lungs and still trying to breathe.

It will get easier, I told myself. But even I thought maybe I was lying. It was near impossible to walk back into that kitchen. But working and being busy, that's the only way to get to feeling better. And when Khaki come in and helped me, practicing Grandma's favorite jam recipe with them frozen berries from last spring, I felt right grateful. We got to fillin' that first jar, and you know what? I felt proud for the second time that day.

"Khaki, I just want to thank you so much for—"

She cut me off. "No, thank *you*. You have given me everything I could never have had on my own. There's no way in the world to pay a person back for making your life complete. I am in your debt for eternity and whatever I can do to help you isn't nearly enough."

I wanted to say more. I wanted to thank her for helpin' me with my cans. I wanted to thank her for being the momma that I just weren't. I wanted to thank her for marrying Graham and turning him around like a boy on a bicycle headed the wrong way home. But she didn't want my thanks no more than I wanted her pity. So we propped right there on the counter, side by side, staring all loving like at the second creation that we would birth and raise together.

Khaki

DRIVE-BY SHOOTING

When I've found the perfect piece that will absolutely make a client's design scheme, but it has a painfully long lead time, I don't tell them about it until close to the delivery. I figure there's no point in them having to spend all that time feeling as anxious and excited as I do.

I'd like to say that's why I didn't tell my parents I was pregnant with Alex until two weeks before he arrived. Instead, I didn't tell them because I was terrified of what Mother would say. Even though I had been married, I knew she would feel all the same that my having a baby on my own was totally unacceptable. In those days, I had dreamed about how it might be to come home and tell your parents you were pregnant to the sound of schoolgirl squeals and wedding-day tears.

When Graham and I got married, I knew that when I got pregnant again, since they were so over-the-moon for Alex, Mother and Daddy would be beyond thrilled that we were adding to our little family. What I hadn't counted on for even a second was that, when I went to tell them the news, I would just have adopted a baby. By any standards, even mine, that was high school cheerleader overzealous.

That's why, when Graham whispered to me in bed one night, "Honey, I hate to ask, but are you at all nervous about what the doctor said, you know, about how you might not be able to carry a baby?" I didn't give it a second thought. Anything this nuts had to have been prearranged in heaven.

I knew how hectic this was going to be, but, instead of having to hear from Mother how ridiculous I was, I did the obvious thing. While I was snuggling you in bed, trying to slip my earrings on without waking you from your nap, I looked up at Graham, who was tying his tie for dinner, and said, "Sweetheart, I'm so glad you are volunteering to tell everyone we are pregnant tonight."

He stood stiller than a hunter behind his prey, his hand frozen on that slipknot. "Oh, hell no," he said. "*We're* not pregnant. *You're* pregnant. I'm not telling them."

I opened my mouth, trying to convey my annoyance without waking you up. "Excuse me, I believe you might have contributed half this DNA. I will not, under any circumstances, be responsible for telling them about this child alone too."

He smirked. "I guess I should just be glad you told *me* about this one."

That was a bit of a joke between us, as your daddy had found out I was pregnant with Alex by showing up in New York to a burgeoning pregnant belly.

"Fine," I whispered. "Then we'll shoot for it."

As your daddy said, "Rock, paper, scissors," I knew I was going for paper. As predictably as a summer rain shower, he went with rock, and I had won.

"Damn it!"

I smiled victoriously.

Graham crawled into bed beside me, stroked your soft, plump cheek with his finger, and kissed me. He put his hand on my belly and said, "So, should I tell them all how this one was conceived too?"

I smirked. "You don't *know* know that's when this one was conceived."

He nuzzled my neck. "Oh, I *know*."

When Graham texted me that night to tell me he had to go help his mom clean some stuff out of the house, I didn't think much about it. Alex had insisted on spending the night with Mother and Daddy because Daddy was going to let him stay up late so he could show him all the constellations with his new telescope. So I took my time cooking dinner, sipping my wine slowly, you sound asleep upstairs. I was just getting ready to light candles on the table when I heard a honk that sounded familiar yet lost somewhere in the recesses of my memory.

I walked outside and started laughing. Graham's daddy had had a whole fleet of Carolina Blue Ford trucks, those big old diesel ones that would last darn near forever. I thought they had sold them all when Graham got the new ones. I glanced at your sleeping figure on my iPhone monitor, still holding that lighter.

Graham hung his head out the window and said, "Hey there, pretty girl. You need a lift?"

I ran my hand down the side of that old truck, the paint peeling in patches. "So is this the junk you were helping your momma clear out?"

He raised his eyebrows. "Baby, this beauty ain't junk."

I laughed and pointed at the bed. "Is this *the* truck?"

"Oh yeah," he said suggestively.

"How do you know? I mean, they had like ten of these things."

He turned the truck off, that loud churning and clanging finally dying down. It made me realize how still and silent and clear it was. It was a crisp night, one of those evenings when you knew that any time, the leaves would finish falling, the frost would remember to come, and winter would set in just as quickly as fall had arrived before it. Graham hopped down, still in his work Levi's and boots, and took my hand. He opened that rusting tailgate with a squeak and held my hand as I climbed in the back. I raised my eyebrows at the stacks of blankets in the back. "What?" he said innocently. "I told you I was helping Momma clear some stuff out."

We both lay down, our heads on those old stable blankets, and he said, "See, look." He took my finger and traced over the letters *FM+GJ*.

"It really is the same truck," I whispered.

Lying there, the breeze blowing, I could almost be back in that night, all those years ago. This same truck, this same field, this same man. We had strayed far away from that perfect moment in young, first love. But, somehow, some way, we found ourselves right back here, in this same place, in this same love where we had been almost half our lifetimes ago.

I turned over on my side, my face inches from Graham's, and said, "I always knew it would end up like this. From that very first night in the back of this truck I knew it was always going to be me and you."

He put his hand to my face and kissed me, unbuttoning the top button on my shirt.

"Graham," I scolded. "Carolina is in there asleep."

"You have the monitor, don't you?"

I nodded, already knowing that there was nothing in this world, still, all these years later, that I could do to resist him. "You know," I whispered, kissing him again. "The way I remember this, it was a little more romantic. Candles flickering and roses and all that."

"Yeah." He winked at me. "But now you're kind of a sure thing." He took that lighter from my hand and sparked it, both of us doubling over in laughter. Graham kissed me again and said, "That night, I didn't think I could ever love you more. It's amazing how much that love has grown, how much better it keeps getting. You are still all I want forever."

Roses and candles are great when you're a kid, when those Hallmark holidays mean something and you need a way to prove to your girlfriends

211

how romantic your boyfriend is. But when you grow up, when those first fine lines start appearing around your eyes and that perfectly toned, flat stomach isn't quite as pristine after childbirth, knowing that you're the only person in the world a man wants for the rest of his life is the absolute best gift he can give you.

We lay in the back of that truck for hours that night, talking about how we met, how we got back together. We laughed about that night that Graham shocked the life out of me carrying me over the threshold of this very house, saying he built it for me even though I was living in New York and married to someone else.

I knew then that it didn't matter what happened. If we had more children, if we lost all our money, if we traded this life in for something new. We had each other to hold on to. We had this great love that he had never given up on and that I never would again. Candles burn and flowers dry. But that love we had, it would last forever.

You were starting to shift a little bit lying beside me in bed that night before dinner, waking up slowly, like you always did. And your daddy said, "I have had so many perfect memories with you. But that is definitely one for the record books."

We didn't discuss further what words he would say or how he would choose to tell our family about its newest member, but I assumed that he would pull them each aside separately to tell them quietly about the good news. Then there would be at least a few minutes for things to sink in before they came running to me for a lecture.

That night, my heart would intermittently race like the second hand on a watch whose battery is dying as I remembered that we were going to tell his mom and my parents. We all bowed our heads and held hands around the dinner table, Alex singing in his booster and you sitting quietly in a bouncy seat by me. Graham said, "Mr. Mason, I'll say grace."

I smiled up at him lovingly and thought how handsome my husband was and how lucky we were to have found each other again after so many years apart. I was grateful for how strong and generous he was to take the heat off me and tell our families our news.

"Dear Lord," he started, "we want to thank You for bringing our families together safely tonight to enjoy this food that You have given us. Please bless this food and the hands that prepared it and help Khaki and me to be the best parents possible to this new little baby . . ."

At that point, I was sure he was talking about you, so I was still smiling away, strolling casually down the street totally unaware that I was about to be the victim of a drive-by shooting.

Graham continued, "This new little baby that You have blessed Khaki and me with. Please keep her healthy and strong over the next months as she carries this child—"

That was as far as he got because I kicked him under the table so hard that he yelled, "Ouch," his mom gasped, Daddy laughed, and Mother said, "Have you completely lost your minds? I mean, do you really not understand how babies are made, Frances Mason, because I swear that talk we had all those years ago must not have taken."

Daddy was damn near tickled, laughing so hard he had to wipe his nose with his handkerchief when Pauline said, "No wonder you been gaining weight."

Graham's mom said, softly and sweetly, in direct contrast to Mother, "Darlings, do you know how this is going to be? It's going to be like having twins. How lovely."

"No," Mother said, pointing her finger at you. "Not lovely. It's going to be worse than that because it's going to be just as much work, but without the benefits of shared homework or the same stage of development. You're going to be up all night with one and chasing the other around all day trying to keep her fingers out of electric sockets." She paused and shook her head. "No, no, no," she said, standing up to emphasize her point. "I forbid you to do this."

That got Daddy going all over again because, I mean, really, how are you going to forbid someone to have a baby?

"Oh, Miz Mason," Pauline said. "Baby girl will get some good help, and everything's gonna be all right."

I put my hand up to stop Pauline. "No, Pauline, I think Mother's right. Actually, what I think I'm going to do when I go into labor is tell the baby to stop trying to come out until she's ready for it." I shot Mother a look. "Does that sound like a good idea?"

"Khaki," Graham said, putting his hand on my shoulder. "Don't get all worked up; it's bad for the baby."

I glared at him. "Seriously? This is how you decide to tell them?"

"I can help you," Graham's mom said. I loved her, but her "helping" was coming over and telling me all the things I was doing wrong. It was about as helpful as when Alex "helped" me clean the kitchen by pulling everything out of the cabinets.

Then Mother smiled serenely, and I knew something evil was getting ready to come out of her mouth. "I know," she said, "you can give Carolina back to Jodi."

"Oh, Miz Mason," Pauline said, shaking her head.

I had had enough, so I stood up quietly, threw my napkin onto my plate, and walked out to the front porch. I rocked for a while, examining the patch of tobacco in front of the house, wondering if you or Alex or this new baby would ever do anything so awful that I would make you crop it as punishment. I remembered Daddy telling Mother, "You can't make them crop tobacco. That's a man's job. They're just little girls."

I could almost hear her replying, huffily, "If they insist on using language like men, they can crop tobacco like men."

I am convinced that there is nothing harder in life. Maybe giving birth, but it's a close call.

I heard the front door swing shut, and I didn't turn to look around. I could smell Daddy's Old Spice and pipe tobacco before he even got to me. He sat down beside me and held my hand.

"I think it's wonderful that you're having a baby, baby girl." I didn't say anything, and we both kept rocking in the moonlight. "I can scarcely believe that my little girl is so grown up that she is going to be a momma three times over."

I turned my head and smiled weakly. "Do not tell Mother I used this word—I'm not cropping tobacco again—but having these three tiny babies scares the shit out of me."

Daddy laughed jovially and said, like I knew he would, "Lord won't give us anything we can't handle."

"I know, Daddy, but sometimes I wonder how I'm going to do it all. I want to be a great mom, and do my job well, and make time for my husband. Sometimes I'm terrified that I'm screwing it up and that I'll look back and wish I had done something differently."

Daddy was quiet for a moment, and then he said, "You know, Khaki, two men have come to ask for my little girl's hand in marriage now." He chuckled. "Graham has come twice, actually."

I didn't see how making me remember my dead husband and how I had turned down my current husband's first offer of marriage, when I was twenty, were going to make me feel better. But I let him continue anyway.

"After Alex died, when I looked back, all I did was wish that, on that day when he had come to see me, that I had said no. I wished that I hadn't let him marry you and then you wouldn't have gone through all that pain and heartache."

"Daddy," I interrupted, but he said, quietly, "Let me finish."

"The thing that I've learned," he said, "is that when life gives you an opportunity, the only thing to do is to be open. You have to keep saying yes. That's how you realize who you're supposed to be and what this life is supposed to have in store for you."

I nodded. "Hey, Daddy."

"Yeah, baby girl."

"I love you, and you mean the world to me." I bit my lip. "But I would have married Alex regardless."

He smiled and nodded. "I thought about it for

months after his funeral, and that was the conclusion I came to too."

I could feel tears in my eyes, remembering Alex telling me the story of asking for my hand in marriage, of how nervous he was, how unsure. He told me that when he asked Daddy if he could marry me, Daddy said, "Son, there are two types of men in the world: the ones who want to bridle the horse, and the ones who are content to let it run free. I know which kind I am. If you're that same kind, then I think it'd be all right."

And he had been. I had grown and blossomed into the woman I am today partly because Alex was content to let me be who I was—loud mouth and all. I felt that familiar sadness, like the red dripping right off my heart and into my stomach.

I smiled at Daddy and said, "Well, thanks for being excited for me."

"Oh, I never said I was excited," Daddy said seriously, and I swatted his arm.

"Guess it's a good thing we aren't living full time in New York anymore, huh?" I thought of Kristin back in the city, Alex's amazing, talented, fabulous nanny, and wondered if I would ever be able to find anyone as incredible right here in North Carolina. People say finding a nanny is like finding a husband, but I think it's harder. It's nearly as large a commitment with all of the compromise and none of the makeup sex.

Jodi

THROWING-AWAY RIPE

Every jam-makin' woman in the county's got her own thinking 'bout how ripe fruit's gotta be to make award-winning preserves. But, seeing as how I've won more awards for my jam than all them put together, I think I'm in a pretty respectable place to say that berries ain't ready for the pot until they are good and ripe—almost throwing-away ripe.

So maybe that's why I don't think people is made to live alone until they're good and ripe too. At nineteen, I just weren't ready—and it was lonely as all get-out in that trailer.

Ain't no arguing that I shoulda listened to that voice in my head when Ricky wanted me to move in this place. That voice, it was saying, *It's too soon to move in together, Jodi,* and *You deserve a man that treats you better, Jodi*. But I woulda swapped skin with a convict on the run to get away from my momma.

When I told Ricky that Graham was gonna let us park the trailer on his land he swung me around in the air and said, "It'll be just like having our own farm." Then he had smiled all honest like. "I promise you that one day I'm gonna give you that white house with the red tin roof that you want so much, and land of our own for our babies to run and our crops to grow."

I had ignored right hard the fact that Ricky was about as lazy and no-good as they come. He wouldn't never hold down a job long enough to get a house. But pretty words, them things is as distracting as shiny diamonds.

When Ricky come stumblin' in drunk and said, "Wish I could have taken home one of them hot chicks at the bar instead of getting in bed with an ugly bitch like you," I shoulda known better than to move in with him. But I just got to thinking on how he was drunk, and, when he'd been sober, he'd been all nice to me.

Graham and Ricky, they built a foundation underneath that trailer, and Khaki and me planted a red tulip border all the way around the outside while Alex chased butterflies. All fancied up like it was, that single-wide looked like one fine place to live. Looks don't mean nothing, though. It don't matter how many pieces of designer furniture and flowers Khaki put all over that place. If love don't live inside, it ain't never gonna feel like home.

If you ask me, a pantry all fulla homegrown food, that's kinda like love. "See," I was showing Buddy one of them first days at the market, "you can buy this beef stew, pull it out and eat it any old time."

"Do you think that's how Mrs. Fearnow got started?" Buddy was teasing me. And I liked it.

"I don't know. But I bet she did. People'd line up just to shake her hand and give her a big old hug, and she'd tell 'em how she made her stew right in her own kitchen for their family to enjoy."

Buddy laughed.

A woman in her midseventies who'd been poking all around our bins for a while come up to Buddy with a vegetable in her hand and said, "What's this?"

"This here's fennel." He pulled back one of the leaves just a hair and said, "Smell that." She smelled, and so did he. "See how it smells right like licorice?" Her nose got to scrunchin' like her humped back. She leaned over on her cane and said, "I don't think I'd like that."

"Oh, no," I chimed in. "All you gotta do is boil it in a little chicken broth, and, once the chicken broth boils out, add a little butter and sauté for a minute or so." I closed my eyes, thinking about the delicate flavor, the way it melts in your mouth like cotton candy. "It's one a' the most delicious things I ever eaten."

Buddy nodded all enthusiastic. "You'll have a new favorite vegetable. You'll be calling me on the phone in the dead of winter saying, 'Buddy, you gotta grow me some of that fennel in the hothouse. I cain't live without it.'"

The woman was laughing right along with us

221

now, putting her hand up to her white, set hair and said, "All right, then. You've talked me into it. I'll take the fennel, the rest of the things in this bag, and a jar of preserves." She turned to me and said, "Young lady, do you make this preserves?"

"Yes, ma'am."

"Well, you do a fine job," she said, pulling out her wallet. "My husband had a stroke, and he rarely communicates anymore. But when I spread that preserves on his toast in the morning he takes a bite, smiles, and says, 'This tastes just like my momma's.'" Tears got all in her eyes, which was good, 'cause I was a mess. I couldn't a' been any happier if she had told me that her husband loved that jam so much that he was gonna leave me their house and all their money when they died.

I hugged her like we was kin, handed her an extra jar, and said, "Now he can enjoy it twice as much."

She tried to pay, but I weren't lettin' her. I ain't got much, but when I could help somebody out, you better believe I was.

She headed off and Buddy winked. "Wow. A name like Smucker's cain't compare to your sweet smile."

I shrugged. "We just pushed fennel on that poor woman like a pot dealer on some middle school kids."

We both got to laughing right hard. I arranged my jars again to make up for the missing two.

And, do you know I sold every single jar I took to the market that day? Almost everybody'd bought something before. And the people who wasn't even planning on buying any cans got talked into it by the ones who already had.

"Best pickled asparagus I've ever had," one woman told a man in line behind her.

"I don't like asparagus," he said. His white hair and tanned face, lined right good from the sun, reminded me of my daddy.

"Don't matter," the woman replied, "you'll like this."

And dern if he didn't take a pickled asparagus and a jar of beef stew. "Better than a TV dinner," he said.

I weren't sure if that was a compliment, but I was feeling like the Paula Deen of Kinston. I loved makin' things damn near better than anything. And being busy, it was right like tobacco on the bee sting of losing my baby. I think bein' busy and thinking 'bout you was all that kept me from drinking like I wanted.

I helped Buddy load the truck up that night, and he said, "Looks to me like someone's got a lot of cooking to do between now and Thursday."

Thursday was our busiest day—and in Raleigh, a much, much bigger city. If I had sold out on a Tuesday that meant I would need to bring three times as much to the Thursday market. It felt good working hard, like them long days at the garage where I got in bed with that happy tired that meant I had done my best and earned my keep. The extra cash in my pocket didn't hurt much neither. I fell asleep right quick that night, like I hadn't since I give you up. I got to dreaming of buying a little white clapboard house with a red roof and makin' my jars right there in my own kitchen. Buddy, he was there too, sittin' right on the stool by the stove. I waked up quick, gasping and choking like I was damn near drowning.

I got to figurin' that night that maybe, somewhere underneath our jokes and teasing, there might be more than just jam brewing between Buddy and me.

Khaki

HELPING

More than for my keen eye and unexpected pairings, I'm known for having the most perfect vision in the middle of the night and getting up to call my clients. It might be a little unorthodox, but, honestly, sometimes you get such a good idea at three A.M. that you can't contain yourself. Well, I do, anyway. Graham says regular people get up, write down the idea, and come back to it first thing in the morning.

So, that night when I woke up with a burning

idea for a book, he said that most people wouldn't have the guts to call their editor in the middle of the night. But I'm not most people. I'd dare say that most people would be a lot more successful if they'd worry a little more about making things happen and a little less about what's appropriate. Plus, once your enthusiasm cools, the idea is half dead anyway.

After spending the entire afternoon with Jodi in my kitchen canning and boiling and learning recipes, I couldn't stop thinking about how that girl with so much talent and so much drive was going to do something that would turn her life around. She thought that just selling out her twenty jars at the market was her big break. But I had bigger ideas. So, at three A.M., when I sat up in bed with the answer, it only seemed right to call Patrick Zimmerman—who had edited both of my books—immediately.

He answered, which isn't my fault, really. If you don't want to talk to people at three A.M., then you let it go to voice mail and call them when you're ready. That's what I say. Graham says that people always answer at three A.M. because they assume that no lunatic is going to call them then unless it is a dire emergency. He means to say that I am a lunatic. But the joke's on him. It *was* an emergency.

"Patrick, I have the best idea for a new book that you are going to die to get your hands on!"

"Who is this?" Patrick asked, sleepier than a bear in hibernation.

"It's Frances Mason," I replied, breezily.

"Frances Mason," he repeated. "Of course it is."

I ignored that because I think he was also insinuating, as Graham had, that I was the only lunatic who would call him in the middle of the night.

"You know I'm always up for helping you display whatever your next amazing project is, so could this possibly wait until the morning, Frances? I have a big meeting—"

I cut him off because, no, it couldn't wait until the morning. "Well it's not exactly one of my projects, and someone else might have the idea by the morning."

I proceeded to tell him that Graham had this fabulous cousin who made the best jam in the country and could can and pickle like people didn't even know how to anymore and that she should do a cookbook. Plus, with everyone so preoccupied with gut flora lately, it would be an easy sell because she actually ferments her sauerkraut, pickles, and salsa—even sour cream.

"Why don't you have her write up a proposal and send it to me?"

I laughed. "Don't be silly, Patrick. Obviously I'm calling you before her."

"Obviously," he sighed.

"Well," I explained, "I wouldn't want to approach

her about it and then you say no. That's not good for a young girl's self-esteem."

"She's a young girl?"

"Nineteen."

"Hmmmm . . ." I could hear in his voice that Patrick was starting to wake up. "That's kind of an interesting angle. A young girl who's a culinary whiz. Where was she educated?"

I rolled my eyes. These city folk had no concept. "In Graham's grandmomma's kitchen."

"Of course she was," Patrick said under his breath. But he relented, probably because he knew he wasn't going back to sleep until he agreed with me. "I think that sounds like a pretty salable idea, Fran. Not salable enough to justify calling me at three A.M., but if you're willing to use your name to help with the marketing I think we could make something happen."

"Yay!" I squealed. "I can't wait to tell her. She'll be thrilled!"

Only, she wasn't thrilled. She looked like she had gotten a glimpse into the slaughterhouse and was newly vegan.

"No, no, no, no, no," she said, shaking her head. "I cain't do that. The recipes are all in my head anyhow."

I put my hands on my hips. It was beyond me why all these perfectly good people in my family wouldn't listen to me. Graham says it's because I'm too controlling and that people can handle their own affairs. But I'm not controlling. I'm *helping.*

"Jodi, sweetie, you'll be fine. I'll help you every step of the way. I'm telling you, this could turn your life around."

"Don't nobody want to see my pictures in a book."

She was so silly. Jodi was a perfectly beautiful girl whose features had never applied themselves. "Nonsense. This could be the start of something for you, Jodi. This could be the career that you were born for, that could fulfill you and make you a decent living and make sure that you're never in a position where people like Mr. Phillips at the cleaners can boss you around again."

I knew I was getting a little carried away. I mean, a first book wasn't going to set you for life. But I tend to get overly excited when I get an idea in my head. Jodi didn't look convinced. I smiled. "Forget about *your* pictures, Jodi. Just think about all of those gorgeous, glossy spreads of your food that will be laid out in those pages."

"We'll see," was all Jodi said in response.

Where I come from, *we'll see* almost always translates to *yes.*

Jodi

FREE WILL

I cain't near stand it when I hear people talking 'bout how home-canned food ain't safe to eat 'cause it carries bacteria.

"It just ain't true," I told Buddy.

We was sitting outside on one of them early spring days, all breeze and warm air and bare feet. We was surrounded by the freshest, greenest asparagus you ever seen. I just heard some cranky old woman saying to another that she wouldn't never eat somethin' canned that wasn't from the grocery store. I had to bite my lip near in two to keep from saying, *Oh yeah, my food that came off the vine two days ago is so damn dangerous. You go on and get to eating that mess that's been sitting on the grocery shelf for five years.*

Buddy nodded and looked at me over the *Psychology Today* he was reading. That big, burly, dirty-nailed cowboy is always studying up on something or another. "You know what else ain't true?" Buddy said.

I shook my head.

"Free will."

The earth damn near shifted as my grandma banged on the roof a' that coffin to come smack

229

some sense into his head. "So, what you're saying," I said, "is that the whole God, free will, we-make-our-own-choices-and-decisions thing is totally made up."

"I ain't saying it," he said. "This article's saying it. Them researchers, they say we ain't got any control." He threw the magazine onto the hunter green card table that's got all our scales and cash register and mess. It landed with a big ole smack. "Our neurons do all sorts a' random stuff, we do what they say, and then we think we made the choice."

I rolled my eyes and said, "You get me all involved in your church and get me dern near believin' again and then you go and say something like that?" I was acting iller than a whole nest a' hornets, but, oh my Lord, I cain't tell you how relieved I got to feeling. What if I weren't in control a' my drinkin'? What if I didn't have no choice but to give you up? What if it were just my brain the whole time doing its own thing and then actin' like it were me that made it up my own self?

But I weren't saying nothing of the sort to Buddy. That farmer's market, it was buzzing like an oven timer. "So what if all these people cain't decide for themself whether to buy some of my jam? What the hell we doing here?"

Buddy patted my knee, and, I ain't lying, it gave me the shivers like that warm air'd turned snowy.

Buddy, I knew he found me right amusing. I'll admit it: I tried entertainin' him just to see him grinning like a dad whose Boy Scout won the pinewood derby.

"So, look," he said, like I ain't said nothing, "speaking of free will, I hear you've got a choice to make."

I cocked my head. "Choice?"

"The cookbook," he said, counting out five dollars change.

I winked at the man he handed it to. "I'm telling you, you toss that kohlrabi in a little olive oil and bake it in the oven and it will change your life."

That Khaki, she knew how to get right what she wanted, that was for damn sure. Buddy turned his attention back to me and said, "I'm sorry, I mean, I know being from around here, people like me and you, we get these kinds of opportunities all the time. But I'm not sure I'd let this one slide by."

"Ha ha," I said. "I know people like me don't get these kinds of opportunities. But it's real scary, you know?"

Buddy shook his head. "The dark is scary. Bugs is scary. Drunk mommas and daddies wasting away and ex-boyfriends trying to kill you is scary." He piled five turnips into a green paper basket and said, "Writing a cookbook ain't scary, darlin'."

I know he called everyone *darlin'*. But, oh my

Lord, it was like my name getting called at the church raffle. My cheeks was getting right red, so I fanned myself and said, "Sure is hot out here today."

"If you want to be cool, be a writer." Buddy winked at me and turned and got to talking about sprayin' with a regular, who was smelling a bunch of dill. "Graham, he'd never let his kids play around in a field all full a' chemicals. So you don't never have to worry about that with us."

Outta the corner of my eye, I saw a little boy, 'round Alex's age, lookin' on a big old pile of Coke crates. I knew that Alex would be crawling up them things faster than you could whistle Dixie, so, without even looking around for a momma, I started running right at him. Sure enough, he got up that first crate, and the second one he was holdin' got to falling right as I grabbed him. He laughed, not knowing that he was damn near to being a bloodstain on the concrete. His momma, she came running up in her long dress and three-inch wedges. Who wears that to the farmer's market I ain't sure, but them Raleigh women came to get vegetables looking like they were ready for a night on the town. Not like in Kinston where everybody wore their sneakers and looked like they had some dang sense.

"Oh my gosh, Jack!" That momma was 'bout as blond as Marlene. She got to running best she could in them shoes. I put Jack back on the ground, and his momma said, all them bracelets she were wearing tinkling, "Thank you so much. I turned my back for one second."

"Oh, it ain't no big deal," I said. "I've gotta lot of nieces and nephews, so I'm always looking out for kids."

It were damn near like an ingrown toenail calling you my niece. It took my breath away hard. You weren't gonna be calling me "momma" in a few months. I wanted to cry, but, instead, I got right mad.

"You're gonna be a really great momma one day," Buddy said when I got back to the table.

I looked at him like I'd sooner sell my organs on the black market.

"What?" He was looking all confused.

"I ain't never gonna have any more youngens," I said firmly.

"Why the hell not?"

That was the stupidest damn thing he'd ever asked me. "It wouldn't be fair to Carolina."

Buddy shook his head and turned to ring up a customer. "Have you tried any of Jodi's famous jam?" Buddy asked a woman so thin it were real clear she ain't never had sugar.

Just like I was thinking, she shook her head and said, "I don't eat jam."

Buddy weren't the kind to give up easy. "What about sauerkraut? It's the best in North Carolina, and there's one jar left that's got your name on it."

She got all excited and her tennis dress was just a-quivering. "I love sauerkraut! I'll take it."

Didn't nobody at this market ever ask how much nothing cost. I smiled at her, said, "Thank you," and she shocked the livin' daylights out of me by saying, "I've heard from my friends that you are an amazing canner."

I shifted my eyes from her pretty face, all shiny and groomed, and said, "I don't know there's much to be good at or not." My accent was getting more backwoods and country talking to her with her city, fancy Southern.

"Oh, yes there is," she said, her ponytail just a-bobbin'. I couldn't figure she knew much 'bout nothing besides getting her nails done. "My friends and I are starting to grow our own gardens, and some things are so plentiful that we don't know what to do with it all. Do you think you could come by sometime and give us some advice?" She got all nervous. "I mean, um, we'd pay you of course," she stuttered.

I was more flattered than a girl on a tenth date with a confirmed bachelor. "Well, actually, if you check back with me, I'm gonna have a cookbook coming out real soon that's got all my best secrets in it."

Buddy was shellin' some peanuts for a little girl with a big bow in her hair, but our eyes met all the same. Later, he said, "For someone who was so unsure about changing her life, that sentence sure did slide right out."

I shrugged. "I didn't have no choice. My neurons made me do it."

Khaki
EMERGING VOICES

I know how I feel about most things without much thought. Velvet, no. Linen, yes. Burgundy, no. Gray, yes. Plaid, no. Animal print, yes. Even those things that I haven't formed an immediate, snap opinion about, I'm able to wrap my brain around pretty well.

The one gap in that imagination is that, as much as I try to put myself in one's shoes, I can't imagine how a father must feel about his children. I know it's not the same as a mother, but I can't pinpoint what the feeling might be precisely.

Sitting across the table from Graham at Chef and the Farmer that night, our favorite, farm-to-table restaurant in Kinston, Graham gave me some insight, reminding me that this house full of little feet and emerging voices was what he had always dreamed of too. Amid the hustle and bustle of the Thursday night crowd, many of whom had come from out of town to enjoy Chef Vivian's award-winning creations, I said, "I'm so glad that you get to have a child of your own."

His face contorted like I had just told him I had been screwing his best farmhand for our entire marriage. He snorted and said, "It must be true that pregnancy makes you nutty."

I stopped my fork, full of the most magnificently flavored, bone-in pork chop you'll ever eat—from Daddy's farm, thank you very much—right before it got to my mouth. "What does that mean?"

"Khaki," he protested. "I don't know if you've forgotten because it's our date night, but I already have two children of my own."

It was the single greatest thing that man has ever said to me. And he has said a lot of things that sit prettier than the top tier of a wedding cake.

He squeezed my hand across the table, taking a sip of the Weeping Willow Wit from right across the street at Mother Earth Brewing and said, "But I have to admit that feeling little kicks in your belly and having a baby know my voice before she's even born is awesome."

"She?"

He nodded. "It's a girl for sure."

I didn't bother to argue. I had known Alex was a boy, so why couldn't Graham know that this baby was a girl? I smiled, thinking of how much Graham adored you. He was amazing with Alex, of course. They threw balls and rode around on the tractor and wrestled on the floor and ate hot dogs and got dirty. If you hadn't known the whole story, you would never have been able to tell that Graham hadn't always been Alex's dad.

But the way he looked at you was something different entirely. It damn near broke that big teddy bear heart when you cried, and you felt the same way about him. You had this special baby smile that only crossed your lips when your daddy came in the room.

Lying in bed that night after a divine dinner, I had to force myself to stop daydreaming about my beautiful girls in their giant hair bows and focus on the recipes Jodi wanted me to edit because we were going to have a big weekend. Charlie, my best friend from childhood, and her husband, Greg, were coming from California to meet you. I had told Charlie a million times not to bring anything for you, but, secretly, I was hoping for a wrapped-to-perfection treat from Jacadi.

I was holding my breath and that envelope full of large index cards Jodi had written each recipe on. I was too nervous to even open them.

I set it beside me again, its weight sinking into the plush down like a horse in quicksand, and sighed.

"What's the problem, babydoll?"

"I'm just wondering what the hell I was thinking. I mean, I can't even imagine the amount of editing I'm going to have to do to even get Jodi's stuff ready for Patrick to look at it."

Graham laid his open *Sportfishing Magazine* on the fluffy comforter and said, "No way. Jodi is super smart. She was always at the top of her class."

I shook my head. "Yeah, but the way she talks . . . I can't even imagine how she writes."

Graham shrugged and said, "Well, no time like the present to find out."

Now, I know I'm from the South. But I'd consider myself at least a quarter New Yorker, which means I'm maybe not fully jaded, but pretty jaded nonetheless. It takes a lot to shock me. And my mouth was just hanging there wide open like I was having my teeth cleaned. That girl, who couldn't seem to get *was* and *were* straight in a single thing she said, had managed to write: *This isn't a book about Michelin stars or master sommeliers or four diamonds. It isn't a book for swanky nights out with high heels and cashmere. This is a book about real living. It's about the best things—fresh-picked food, laughter around a table of love, and learning everything you need to know at your grandmother's knee in her kitchen. The faster the world seems to spin and the more hectic things become, the more we long for a return to those simple values. There's always time to slow down for a good, home-cooked meal—especially if your cupboard and freezer are full of the finest ingredients the earth has to offer. This is the stuff of life. The way memories are made. And it can be all yours—as easy as pie.*

I set the paper on the bed, removed my glasses, rubbed my eyes, put my glasses back on, and read again. Then I looked over at Graham. "She nailed it. I mean, she absolutely writes like she was born to do it."

Graham winked at me and turned back to his fishing article. "Yup. Just 'cause we talk wrong don't mean we don't know what's right."

I pored over her recipes that night, laughing and wiping a tear over the little anecdotes that accompanied each one. And it made me realize how strong Jodi was, how she took a life ripe with strife and struggle and chose to remember the good moments. She had made those lemons into lemonade. And I knew that my instinct had been right. I didn't blame Patrick for not wanting to present this based on a proposal alone. But I was pretty sure this work was going to blow him away.

I must have fallen asleep somewhere in the jam section because the next morning I awoke to the sound of voices flooding the kitchen. I looked over at the clock, confused, and realized it was almost noon. I could have killed Graham for not waking me. I brushed my teeth and tiptoed carefully down the stairs. Those first few months I'm pregnant I'm like a momma bird with her egg.

I'm so afraid that if I sit wrong or stand wrong or move wrong, the baby is going to fall right out of the nest.

I squealed when I saw Charlie holding you and Greg sitting on the floor with Alex, playing with a dump truck that he must have brought from California. Charlie, looking quite unlike the law firm partner she was, was clad in a pair of Umbro shorts that she must have had since high school, her light brown hair in a messy ponytail, looking like she hadn't seen the sun in a decade. Greg, on the other hand, was deeply tanned, his ear-length hair held back with sunglasses, in jeans and a slim-cut dress shirt that made you know he spent quite a bit of time in the gym. I was always stunned, when I saw them in real life, by what an odd-looking pair they made.

Charlie looked at the clock. Then, without saying a word to me, she looked at Greg and said, "Oh, good Lord in heaven above."

"What?" Greg asked, confused.

"Khaki is pregnant *again*."

"How do you know?" I protested.

"Well, it *is* noon, Khak," Graham said.

I smiled demurely. "A fifth Jacobs will be joining the family very shortly."

Charlie rolled her eyes and Greg winked at her and said, "Well then, I guess it is a good thing that we're moving back here. Someone is going to have to help you take care of all these children."

I stopped dead in my tracks and peered at Charlie. "Wait. What?"

Charlie smiled. "My firm wants to open a Raleigh office, and Greg thought open fields and riverbanks could be new painting inspiration—for a few years at least. We're moving back to Kinston, and I'm going to commute to Raleigh a couple of times a week."

Forgetting completely about my pregnancy and my fear that the baby would roll right out, I leapt to throw my arms around Charlie's neck.

"It gets better," Graham said.

I gasped. "You're having a baby!"

Charlie cringed. "He said better, Khaki, not apocalyptic."

I put my hands on my hips. "Why would it be so bad for you to be pregnant? I think you'd be a great mother."

Charlie crossed her arms. "I know you think it would be so great for me. You've made your point. But not everyone has to be exactly like you to be happy."

I shifted my body language to say that that was true, and she understood. "I didn't say I *wanted* you to be pregnant," I amended. "In fact, I'm kind of glad you're not, because then you wouldn't get to be my kids' cool, fun aunt Charlie because you'd be too busy."

"Speaking of." Charlie smiled and reached behind the island to produce a Jacadi box.

"Yay!" I squealed, and Graham said, "Are you ever going to let them tell you the best part?"

"The Jacadi isn't the best part?"

I turned to Greg, and he shook his head.

"You know how Momma has been wanting to downsize ever since Daddy died," Graham said, "and since I built this place for us and we won't take it off her hands she has been pouting?"

"No!" I exclaimed.

"Yes!" Charlie shouted back. "We're buying Mrs. Jacobs's house!"

I turned to Greg. "Are you okay with all this? I mean, do you feel like you've been kidnapped by aliens who are forcing you to inhabit Venus?"

The South was a bit of a different planet, when you got right down to it. Greg just shrugged in his cool, California surfer way, pushing his long hair out of his eyes and said, "I'm all about life experiences."

I turned back to Charlie and could feel myself salivating like Pauline's fresh-baked cheese biscuits were about to come out of the oven. "Anything you want to ask me?"

"Of course, Khaki. Would you be so kind as to assist us in getting the new place looking straight?"

I clapped and jumped up and down and gave Graham a big kiss. "I know, babydoll," he said. "You've been wanting to clear that place out for two decades."

Graham's mom could have borderline been on one of those shows about hoarders. She lived in this grand, gorgeous home with the widest hand-carved moldings you've ever seen, door casings that would make you cry, and a free-hanging staircase that would take your breath away. And she had every square inch so crammed with hideous knickknacks and furniture that you could barely breathe, much less take in the incredible display of architecture around you.

"Actually," Charlie amended. "Could you do it however you want and send me the bill?"

I nodded and patted her on the shoulder. "You know you don't even have to ask."

Charlie trying to decorate a home like Graham's momma's was like Shaq trying to comfortably drive a Prius. Furthermore, she couldn't have cared less if the place had folding chairs and empty cardboard boxes for a coffee table. As long as she had her comfortable mattress and a sofa to curl up on and watch *Downton Abbey*, life was good.

I put on my happiest face, smiled down at you and Alex, and said, "Hey, Char, can I talk to you for a minute in the living room?"

"Khaki . . ." Graham started. "I told you everything is fine. You worry too much."

I pinned on an enthusiastic grin. "You don't even know what I'm talking to her about, Graham." But he did know. And he'd known me about two decades too long not to know my lying face.

Charlie studied my face and said, "Is everything okay?"

I sat down on the couch and she followed suit, tucking her feet up underneath her.

"It's fine," I said, still sort of lying, having been unable to sleep well ever since my conversation with Mother about Jodi getting you back. "I know you're the best at what you do, but I just want to make sure . . . I mean, I know you wouldn't make a mistake, but I guess I just worry . . ."

Charlie reached over and took my hand. She set her eyes on mine and said, "Khaki, I swear. There isn't one margin space out of place on those adoption papers. They can look high and low from here to hell and back and they're not going to find anything. And Ricky had already signed his rights away. I mean, I didn't do that paperwork, but it doesn't seem like he's clamoring to be a dad or anything."

I nodded. "I didn't want you to think I didn't trust you, but Momma was just reminding me about—"

Charlie nodded. "I know. The Taylors. That's the most god-awful thing I've ever heard, and I think they should put that judge in prison." She said, very slowly, "There's no way she can get her back now."

Then she smiled. "And, besides, you know there isn't anybody in this county that would make a move against your daddy."

I smiled too now, feeling at least ninety-five percent better. "Okay," I said. "You're right." I stood up, and, walking back toward the kitchen, said, "You know how nutty pregnancy makes me anyway."

"Your words, not mine," Graham called. He put his arm around me and squeezed my shoulder. "See," he said. "Feel better?"

I nodded, smiled, and was pleased to find that this time, I wasn't lying at all.

"Okay, crew," Graham said. "Momma is going to be here in a few minutes to watch the kids. We've got a Triple Overhead release to celebrate down at the Tap Room . . ." He looked at his watch. "And there are only a few drinking hours left until it gets dark."

Mother Earth Brewing was one of the staples of Kinston's downtown redevelopment, a LEED-certified and award-winning brewery that not only used local farmers but also drew tourists from all over the country.

Charlie saluted dutifully. "Support your local brewery."

Greg looked up from his perch beside you on the floor and said, "Promising me that we'd go to Mother Earth every night for happy hour is one of the only ways that Charlie got me to move here." He smiled and in a truly horrible Southern accent said, "Best beer this side of the Mason-Dixon line."

Graham patted him on the back and said, "We know. We've done the legwork."

"Thank God we have a driver for a few more months is all I can say," Charlie said, elbowing me in the side.

It was so normal and so natural that I could feel tears gathering in my eyes like so many leaves on the sidewalk. My best friend was back where she belonged and my family was growing by the minute. It didn't matter the weather. I knew that, in my life so far, this was my favorite season.

Jodi
TWO OF THEM

Cooking and canning, them things is right like second nature to me. I can make somethin' in my kitchen easy as pie—even though Grandma's hand-rolled, homemade pies ain't easy. But writing down all them steps, remembering all the ingredients, trying to explain something that's near like breathing to me—it were right harder than I thought. But me and Khaki, we was gonna visit Patrick Zimmerman that day. So I had a taped-up manila envelope all full a' recipes crammed in my bag with my driver's license and my first boarding pass.

It's right funny that I was near grown and you was still such a little thing when you got your first boarding pass scanned. When I told that stranger at the farmer's market about my cookbook, it felt so damn good I couldn't stop. It was soft and sweet on my lips like a long kiss or a cool bite of an ice cream cone. It was still like I told Buddy, though. I was scareder than a weed in a field a' Roundup. I was so used to scraping by, not doing nothing too good or right, that I was afraid I'd do this one thing and it'd be too hard to go back to being so ordinary.

But that Khaki, she said, "Oh, honey, I'll teach you everything I know. Getting what you want isn't about anything more than being totally certain. If you're absolutely sure that what you're fighting for is the right thing, then there isn't anyone in the world who can stop you."

I weren't sure if that was true or not. I was one of them girls so full a' doubt I weren't sure I'd ever do nothing good. But that day, looking out the airplane window in the outfit that Khaki give me, I thought she just might be right: Maybe I could have my jam and eat it too.

Me and Khaki and Graham, we'd gone 'round and 'round about us all spending the weekend together, if that was all right for you. We'd talked to our social worker and some therapy lady and read all over the Internet. Graham finally put his foot down right hard—which he don't do often when it comes to Khaki. "This is absurd. We agreed to do what was right for Carolina, and all this anxiety is what isn't right for her."

He was right. Babies, they know when the people around them is wound up.

Graham and Khaki, they acted like being on a plane with two babies and another on the way weren't nothing. Graham fed you a bottle so I didn't have to see somebody else being your momma. Khaki and me, we played tic-tac-toe with Alex. But he was so excited over the gum he got to chew to keep his ears from poppin' he didn't care about nothin' else. I woulda been right nervous somebody'd get to crying or something. But Graham and Khaki didn't act like they was one bit concerned.

I weren't real sure how I'd take to flying. But being up in the air felt like freedom. Couldn't nobody get to me or hurt me.

Khaki looked up from the tic-tac-toe board and said, "Now you don't worry one bit about this meeting. I'll be there the whole time, and Patrick is about the sweetest thing in the world. What people in the South say about Yankees doesn't pertain to him."

I nodded, but I'm sure I was right green.

Khaki smiled real reassuring. "And this is only a preliminary meeting. So we shouldn't get our hopes up that they are going to buy the book." She squeezed my hand. "And that's a good thing because if you change your mind you don't have to do it." She paused, and whispered, "But I probably don't have to tell you that I think you should!"

That stewardess in her uniform, she said we landed in New York. But it might as well've been Mars for how different everything looked. I ain't never seen nothin' besides trailer parks and fields and them regular buildings downtown, so skyscrapers and all kinds a' people all crowded on the street, it were right different looking. I was fixing to get scared, but Khaki, she held my hand the whole time. I said, "You do know you're not my momma, right?"

"For Lord's sake, Jodi, I'm scarcely old enough to be your big sister." She winked.

Graham, he told me one time that it didn't make no difference that Khaki had moved to New York and married somebody else. He knew sure as rain makes the grass grow that they'd be together.

"Khaki has been mothering since she could talk," he said. "I knew we'd need at least five bedrooms because Khaki having a bunch of babies is just like one of those hogs down at her daddy's having them. It's only natural."

Khaki had to go to a meeting, so Graham and me, we took you and Alex to get some "barbecue." Now, listen here, New York may know fashion designers and art, but they don't know pork. I whispered over to Graham, "Is it just me or do our *gas stations* serve better barbecue than this?"

He laughed. "Maybe we should face facts that when we're in Manhattan, it's wiser to eat as the Manhattanites do."

I didn't have a dern clue what Manhattanites ate, but I knew damn well it weren't this.

We were quiet for a second, and he said, "So, Jodi, do you really want to do this cookbook or is my wife pushing you into it?"

I shrugged. "Thinkin' 'bout my name being on a bookshelf gives me butterflies. But I'm gonna walk in that big-city office, and they'll see right quick I'm some trailer-park hick from nowhere, North Carolina, and tell me to leave."

Graham wiped his mouth and laughed.

"What?"

"Just the idea of someone trying to tell Khaki to leave anywhere. I can envision two guards, one holding her arms, and one holding her feet, her kicking those fancy shoes she wears, you following behind trying to calm her down."

I laughed too.

He said, "I want you to realize that you're smart and you're young and you can do anything you want to do, whether this is it or not."

"I think I might actually like to do the cookbook." I smiled. "Seems like a real nice way to remember Grandma, don't it?"

A real fine mist gathered in Graham's eyes. "It really does. But just so you know, cookbook or no, she would be so proud of you she wouldn't know what to do."

It made me feel so good I weren't even real nervous walking into Patrick Zimmerman's office.

Patrick, he smiled at me real cute, all dimples and teeth under his gray hair. It made him look right young. Then he said, "So, I hear you're the canning queen of the South."

I couldn't believe how brave and normal it sounded when I answered him right back like it weren't nothing. "Don't forget picklin' and jammin' too."

He laughed, looked at Khaki and said, "Look out, world; there're two of them."

I ain't never thought of myself like Khaki before, all strong and brave. But hearing him say that, it was near like when Daddy used to tell me I was his best girl. And, for the first time since giving you up, it made me feel like I was worth something again.

Khaki

ANY ATTENTION

Every now and then, I'll just be hanging around at home, and it will hit me that I completely despise the room I'm sitting in. Of course, I've designed every room in my life. But it goes without saying that tastes change. Sometimes, no matter how perfect something once seemed, it's time to reassess.

Being pregnant with my third child was the stimulus for completely reevaluating not only my house but also my entire life. I stopped by my antiques store the first day we were in the city to chat with Daniel, who had turned into the full-time coordinator of everything furniture. He kissed me, examined my burgeoning bump, and said, "Oh, darling, you look fab-u-lous."

He was lying. All those women I grew up with who said, "Girls steal your beauty and boys let you keep it," were right on. Grace was a criminal caught red-handed before her little eyelids were even formed.

We walked around the store, where I casually wiped a spot of dust here, switched an accessory there, but, all in all, it was somewhat devastating how well Daniel did without me. We communicated via FaceTime daily so that I could see what was going on, but, when you got right down to it, it was his store now, not mine.

"We are in desperate need of several chests-on-chests, headboards, and secretaries," Daniel said, clicking through a list on his iPhone. "I think we're okay on dining tables and chairs, but if you see anything amazing when you're buying, we do have a tad bit of extra space in the warehouse."

That was when I realized it: If I was going to have another baby, I was going to have to let some things go. "When *you're* buying," I said.

Daniel stopped, ran his hand through his thick hair, crossed his arms, and said, "Come again?"

I smiled. "When you're buying."

"But I live here," he said, wiping his hands down the front of his signature, pressed-to-military-standards khakis. "You buy in North Carolina."

I nodded, and when a smile spread across his face, I could tell that he was starting to get it. "There are no less than fifty direct flights from LaGuardia and JFK to Raleigh every single day. And if you get super brave you can head on to New Bern or Greenville."

"Oh my gosh," Daniel said. "This is so major. You would trust me to do the buying?"

Handing over control has never been one of my strong suits. "Well, let's not get carried away," I said. "I might check in on you from time to time."

There were two bright sides: One, Daniel had fabulous taste. Two, the places I was sending him to had very few opportunities for critical mistakes.

"Obviously, you'll get a raise," I said, "and use your company card for travel expenses."

"Can I—"

I cut him off and said, "You can start flying first class when I do."

"Damn," he said under his breath. "That will be a quarter after never."

I shrugged. "It's absurd to pay five times the price for an hour and a half flight." I kissed him on both cheeks and said, "Okay, love. I'm off to see Anna."

Every year when I had this contract renewal meeting with my boss, Anna, she looked increasingly nervous when I walked through the door. I held the majority of the firm's biggest accounts and attracted the biggest jobs. We always skirted around the issue of me opening my own firm, and, hands down, it made the most sense. My clients would follow me because they didn't need a big-name design firm as long as they had a big-name designer.

This year, I noticed that Anna's chestnut hair was a couple of inches shorter and the black patent French chairs across from her lacquered French desk had been changed to Lucite. And, this year, she wasn't mincing words. "So that I don't have to sit here for an hour making small talk and feeling like I need a ginger mint, please tell me if you're leaving me or not."

I had fully planned on leaving her. It made no sense to stay. I could hire my own accountant and assistants, and I could keep a much larger percentage of my profits. Staying at her firm was the worst business decision I could make. Graham and I had gone over and over the situation and decided time and time again that staying with Anna made about as much financial sense as growing your money by planting it in the yard.

But here's the thing: What the job cost me in money, it made up for in convenience. I wasn't living in the city, and finding great staff was so difficult. At Anna's, there was always someone to run and take measurements or pick up fabric samples or send me pictures from Waterworks. Plus, I loved coming into the city and rushing straight to see Anna so that we could collaborate on our latest ideas.

So I smiled and said, "I know it makes me crazy, but I'm sticking with you."

She walked around the desk and hugged me. "Do you think you should at least become a partner or something?"

I shook my head. "I'm about to have three kids, Anna. I barely have time to brush my teeth."

I kissed her, and, as I walked out the door, the phone rang.

"I'm so glad it's you!" I practically squealed. Before Scott could even say anything I said, "Do you want to meet for coffee at Zibetto?"

On my walk to the restaurant, I thought about getting back to the apartment and how I needed to soak some oats to make the homemade oat yogurt that you loved so much. And Alex would want a new batch of those strawberry muffins he had no idea were so good for him. I needed to get Jodi to make some applesauce, because she scolded me last time I bought it. You were in desperate need of new socks, Alex had completely outgrown every bathing suit he owned, and I needed some gorgeous sandals. Combine that with a phone interview for the book, a cocktail party with signing, paying the bills for both houses, and picking out tile, and this momma was starting to feel tired, tired, tired.

When I walked through the door, Scott was already sitting, looking rather dismayed. I took a moment to savor the white tiles, white marble counter, and glass shelves. One of my favorite things about Zibetto was how meticulously clean it was. If you could keep glass shelves and white grout sparkling, you could certainly keep a cappuccino machine to my standards.

Scott stood up to kiss me, pout still firmly in place. I rubbed my expanding belly and said, "What is the matter, my little love?"

Scott fiddled with the spoon on his cappuccino

plate and said, "Don't you think two daddies would be better than none at all?"

I thought of my father, the slow smile that was warmer than the inside of Scott's coffee mug, the soothing smell of pipe tobacco that floated wherever he was. "Honey," I said, "if I'd had two dads and no mom I can't even figure how much I would have saved in therapy bills. It would boggle the mind."

"Then why hasn't anyone picked Clive and me to be parents?"

I gasped, wiping the foam off my mouth. And it shocked me to realize that, while it was good, I would take the soy latte down at Queen Street Deli in Kinston any day of the week. The first time I met my sweet daddy there for coffee, I ordered my one-pump white mocha. He said, "You know, I'll take that same thing."

I whispered to the man behind the counter, "Just put it on my tab." My daddy is the kind of man who brews his own Folgers in the morning because eighty-nine cents at the Rightway is too expensive.

But Daddy said, "Now, you know my girl isn't paying."

I grimaced as he pulled out that ten-dollar bill and couldn't believe it when he didn't say a thing about the price. He held his tongue the entire half hour we were down there catching up. But the minute we got back on the sidewalk, he hiked up his pants and said, "Lord, Khaki. I thought I was meeting you for coffee, not putting a down payment on the building."

We both laughed, but those coffee dates have become a regular thing for us now. And Daddy always says, "Now, darlin', just you don't tell your momma I'm spending money on coffee. It'd ruin my reputation."

I smiled again, thinking that daddies really were the best. Then I said, "You and Clive are going to have a baby?"

He shrugged, his shirt so starched that when his shoulder went back down, the fabric above it stayed in place. Of everyone I'd ever known, Scott couldn't tolerate a wrinkle. I didn't know how he was going to take aging. With a vial of Botox and a jar of Crème de la Mer, I assumed.

"We got on some adoption lists, but nothing has happened yet." He sighed. "So I need to ask you something."

I could feel the panic rise through my body. He was going to ask me to carry his child. I loved Scott, and he had been one of my best friends for years. But I couldn't bear the thoughts of forming a nine-month bond with a child and then being separated. Praise God, my sister and Charlie—for whom I would have carried a child—already had children and didn't want them, respectively.

Scott smiled. "Does hubby have any other

teenaged, knocked-up, alcoholic cousins we could help out?"

I laughed, the tension melting away like the fluffy top of my drink. I took another sip and said, "Unfortunately, the rest of the childbearing-aged family is free from addiction." I thought back to my conversation with Daniel a few months earlier and added, "Daniel told me surrogacy is really in right now."

Scott ran his finger through his hair, and said, "Yeah. That's Plan B. But we both feel very strongly that one of our callings as a couple is to love and nurture a child that needs a home and a better life."

I could feel the tears rise to my eyes, when, fortunately, Scott pointed to my belly and added, "Maybe we could take one of yours off your hands. Poor kids won't get any attention."

We both laughed, but, through my laughter, I thought of you, my bright-eyed, beautiful little angel. I leaned over and patted Scott's hand. "All I know, honey," I said, "is that when you least expect it, God will bring you the rest of your family." I winked at him. "And then you'll understand why I'm so crazy."

Jodi

ALWAYS

If I had my pick a' things, you can bet your bottom dollar I'd pick somethin' fresh over somethin' canned any day of the week. Most of my regulars at the farmer's market, they'd get to agreeing with me—'cept when it comes to green beans. Green beans, they sell canned two to one over fresh.

That got me to thinking that maybe I'd be able to keep going to that market dern near all year long. Mostly, once October hit and it started getting right colder, we had to pack it up. But thinkin' about all that time to myself, not having much a' nothing to do, it got me to worrying. I was feeling pretty good again, not wantin' to drink so much all the time. I didn't want nothing to get in the way a' that—'specially not me having too much free time.

I couldn't sleep one night, just staring up at the water ring on the ceiling, worryin' about fall crops and Graham not planting none and me not having nothing to do all that long, cold winter 'cept hole up in the trailer with a bottle. So I just got on up real early, pulled on my rain boots over my pajama pants, and got to walking. I didn't have to wonder where Graham was. That tractor was whirring in the distance, loud and clear like a train announcing its return to the station. It weren't Graham I got to first, though; it was Buddy. I wanted to run away and hide looking a mess like I was, not a stitch a' makeup on, not so much as a brush through my hair.

He waved, turned off the engine, pulled his glasses off, and ran his hands through that fine, thick head a' hair. He coulda been in a Pert Plus commercial. Or John Deere. It were a deadly combination for a country girl. And it got me to thinkin' that wanting to do the farmer's market all year round had as much to do with Buddy as with my drinking.

"You miss me while you were in New York?" he asked, winking.

That red was running right up my cheeks, giving me away. Weren't a damn thing I could do 'bout it. *Pull it together, Jodi.* I wanted to be real clever and quick on my feet, fire something back kinda flirtatious and tough all rolled into one. But the best I could come up with was, "You miss me?"

He grinned. "Always."

I put my hand up to my forehead like I were shading the early-morning sun. But I was really hiding my ruby slipper face.

"Puh-lease," I said. I was like a grade-school girl again, my first crush leaning against my locker making my heart get to flutterin'. "I just need to see Graham."

"Well, climb on up, darlin'," he said.

My mouth kinda dropped.

"What? I didn't figure you as too prissy to ride a tractor."

I fluffed my hair. It didn't do no good. *Never, ever walk out of the house again looking like a hag*.

I got to climbing on the tractor, near about fallin' out when Buddy held my hand to help me. Oh my Lord, I prayed so hard he couldn't smell my dirty hair. I got to figuring the fresh grass clippings and diesel fuel was smelling stronger than me.

He cranked the engine right hard, wrapped his arm real tight around my waist, and whispered, "Don't worry. I won't let you fall."

Too late. That tan arm all tight 'round my waist, it were too much for any girl not to fall, really. I was so far into my fantasies of Buddy and me splashing in the ocean, lying in the sand, reciting vows . . . When I could make out Graham in the distance all my worries 'bout them fall crops had floated on by like a bubble in the wind.

"Thanks for the ride," I said. I climbed down real slow.

Buddy, he didn't let go a' my hand when my feet hit the ground. He grinned. "I took the long way."

"You damn well better stay away from my cousin," Graham called over the roar a' his tractor.

He killed the engine, his earplugs dangling 'round his neck.

"Whatever you say, boss," Buddy called back, winking at me.

As he drove away, Graham said, "So, something going on there I need to know about?"

My brain, it couldn't stop my mouth. "Oh my Lord, I hope so."

We both got to laughin' like our hearts ain't never been broken. "He's always giving me a hard time, that's all."

I waited a long minute, crossing my fingers that Graham would say Buddy must really like me. But he just nodded.

"Anyway, I'm here 'bout the fall crops."

Graham looked skeptical because we both know fall crops ain't really his specialty. He smiled. "Well, then looks like this'll be a pretty short conversation."

"Just hear me out, all right?"

He nodded.

"I was just thinkin' that the way I been selling so many a' them cans, maybe it'd make sense to keep going through the fall. If we could just plant some onions and cabbage and cucumbers and maybe do some lettuces and collards and kohlrabi, we could still have some fresh stuff to sell at the market. And maybe the Piggly Wiggly'd be interested since they buy our stuff in summer. But then I could make pickles and sauerkraut and fermented vegetables and all that good stuff."

Graham's face got all twisted up like he ate some bad oysters or somethin', and I started to realize how hot it was getting. "Jodi, you know I'd do anything for you, but . . ." He jumped off his tractor, dust flying out from under his boots. "I'm just not sure we can justify that. It's a lot of work taking care of all this land."

I nodded. "I know, I know. But we could just plant a little bit, and I can help you. I'm right good at plantin' and such." I cleared my throat. I didn't want him to feel guilty, but I said it anyhow. "Look, Graham, girls like me, we gotta stay busy."

He smiled and patted my shoulder, finally catching on. "Well, you and Buddy get that all worked out and I'll help how I can." He winked at me, and I could feel that red rising again just talking about Buddy.

"Hey, look," Graham said. "You doin' okay, Jodi? I mean, with all of it. The drinking, giving up Carolina. All that?"

I swallowed right hard. "Yeah. I mean, it's made it right easier for me to get to be around her. It's hard and it hurts, but Khaki, she always treats me like . . ." I paused, 'cause I could feel them tears getting into my eyes. I swallowed, and I tried not to get choked up but I couldn't help it. "She treats me like I'm Carolina's momma still too."

In his deepest voice, Graham said, puffing up his chest, "Honey, Carolina might need two mommas, but I'm cowboy enough for two daddies." He tipped his hat to me.

We got to laughing again. Graham, he always knew the right thing to say to make you feel better right off. Couldn't nobody dream up a better daddy for their baby.

"All right, well, I guess I'll just have to talk Buddy into my new fall plantin' scheme if I want to keep working."

Graham squeezed my arm all supportive like. He hopped back into his tractor seat. "Yup. But I have a feeling you could talk Buddy into dern near anything." He cranked the tractor, getting back to the long day a' work ahead. "You want a ride back?"

I shook my head. It weren't that far. Plus, I felt like skipping and dancing and twirling around all the way back home, just thinkin' that Buddy might like me too. And I tried to lie to myself about it, but me and God and all them saints, we knew the truth: I was hoping to run into a different cowboy.

Khaki

AMAZING GRACE

The thing that no one ever tells you about being a mother is how unfathomably guilty you feel all the time. I felt like I had committed a crime and ruined your youth by being locked up in prison every time I left to pick faucets or approve a blueprint. I reasoned that if I were a doctor or a humanitarian, I would feel like my work was necessary, like I wasn't leaving you and Alex for some fabric swatches.

But now I know it doesn't matter what you do. You feel guilty for leaving your children and going to work. You feel guilty for spending too much time with them and making them spoiled. You feel guilty for letting them learn to cry it out in their crib. You feel guilty for letting them sleep with you and never training them to sleep on their own.

It's a constant, vicious cycle, and no one can tell you what's the right thing. I had spent years squelching the anxious, analyzing woman in my head; I was trying to keep her quiet, to love you instead of constantly worrying that I was doing the wrong thing.

Alex, fortunately, was out of our bed for the most part, having taken to his new role of "big brother" and wanting to differentiate himself from the babies. Unlike our son, you didn't care one bit about sleeping in between Graham and me. In fact, I learned quickly that you slept best in your crib in your own room. When you were nine weeks old, I woke up one morning in a panicked sweat and sprinted down the hall to your bedroom, certain that I would soon be screaming "Call 911" to Graham. My infant CPR class was running through my head like a filmstrip on a projector. The only explanation for why you hadn't woken up all night was that you were dead, obviously. But there you were, sleeping peacefully, swaddled and glowing like a little angel. Alex hadn't slept that long until he was two. But, like I said before, every child is different.

I was grateful that you were a sleeper because being pregnant with baby three, taking care of babies one and two, working on two design projects in another state, and doing marketing and appearances for the sale of my latest book were keeping me busier than an ant hill intent on carrying an entire sandwich back to their queen. Why I had also agreed to coordinate the church bazaar, I can't tell you. Needless to say, I was tired.

Three weeks before my due date, I resigned myself to the fact that I was finished traveling and that working was out of the question. With Alex, I had been thin and fit with a little basketball on my front and, obviously, you were my easiest pregnancy and birth. I don't know if it was something about being pregnant with a girl or being back in the South, the land of salt and pork fat, but I was swollen, exhausted, and pregnant from the top of my head to the tips of my toes.

I was thinking that I wished someone would come over and help keep an eye on you. You had recently discovered how you could pull up on the toilet, crack the lid open with one hand, and splash in it with the other. People asked me why I didn't get those child-safety toilet protectors.

Those people have never been thirty-seven weeks pregnant.

When I answered the phone and it was Jodi's voice on the other line, I was relieved. "My water is off for some reason," she said.

"Come stay with us!" I said, probably a little too enthusiastically. "I need a little company."

I think it was the first time since the adoption that neither of us hemmed and hawed over whether it was the right thing. You loved her; she loved you. We were a crazy, mixed-up, blended family. We were embracing it.

I scooped you up under my arm, carrying you like a pile of lumber, to which you squealed with laughter, and headed off to make up the guest room. While I was changing the sheets, trying to negotiate my pregnant belly and the corners of the fitted sheet, the phone rang again. It was Charlie.

"My power is out," she lamented.

That had been a common occurrence that summer, especially in the neighborhood where Charlie and Greg's rental house was. It was so excruciatingly hot that the power system couldn't keep up with demand.

"Well, then you and Greg come on over and spend the night," I said, thinking that Alex would be thrilled to be back in bed with Mommy and

Daddy. I was less thrilled, as sleeping with Alex was like sleeping with Mia Hamm when she was dreaming about winning a championship.

"I don't want to be any trouble," she sighed.

"Good," I replied. "Then I'll let you change your own sheets."

I padded back downstairs and placed you in your Jumperoo, where you sang and babbled and carried on. I peered into the fridge to see what I was possibly going to feed a family of seven for dinner. Slamming the fridge door closed, I said, "Pizza it is!" to no one in particular.

"Pizza what is?" Mother said from behind me, her voice laced with judgment.

"Mommy!" Alex squealed as he turned around and ran to me. I leaned down to kiss him, intensifying the shooting pain from my back down my legs.

"Charlie and Greg and Jodi all need to stay here tonight, and I can't cook for that many people since I can't fit behind the stove."

Mother rolled her eyes. "Then you'll all come to my house, obviously." She waved her hand and her charm bracelet tinkled like bells in a windstorm. "Pizza." She shivered, and I realized that I could already taste those jalapeños.

Then she said, "Do you think it's okay if Jodi stays here?"

"Mother, please. I'm doing the absolute best I can, and I need not to be judged every second."

"Fine, far be it from me, your mother, to interfere with your life," she said under her breath. Then turning to Alex, "I'll see you tonight, darling."

He replied, "Bye-bye, GG."

"It's *grandmother,* darling. *Grandmother,*" she enunciated, her lips like a blowfish trying to wiggle its way off a hook.

Alex looked up at me, and I ruffled his hair. Tuesday afternoons were his special time with Mother. They went out for lunch and orangeades and then he and Daddy rode around on the tractor. He had such an amazing time every week, and I savored those special hours with you.

Jodi arrived as Mother was leaving and said, "I swear I paid the water bill."

"I wouldn't have even considered that you hadn't," I replied.

"Can I help you get ready or anything?"

I shook my head. "Your bed is made, and I told Charlie that she can put her own sheets on."

"I could have put my own sheets on too," Jodi protested.

"Yeah, but you gave me your child," I said, patting her on the back and winking. "I owed you."

Jodi laughed, and it occurred to me that that was the first time I had been able to make a joke about the adoption.

Two hours later, Mother, Daddy, Pauline, Benny,

Jodi, Charlie, Greg, Graham, Alex, you, and I were all sitting down to a lovely supper, graciously prepared by Pauline, when Mother said, "Khaki, you'd better not eat any of those collard greens."

"They're the most nutrient-dense food on the planet, Mother. Why on earth would I not eat them?"

Pauline poured herself a cup of sweet tea and said, "Oh, Miz Mason, that's just an ole wives' tale."

Her husband Benny motioned for the bowl of greens and said, "Nuh-uh. My momma went into labor with all six of us the night after eatin' collards." I smiled, thinking of the Benny I had met all those years ago in New York and how, as soon as he had gotten back home, that neutral accent had faded right back to Southern.

Jodi looked at the ceiling. "Come to think of it, I think I ate collards the night I went into labor."

I could feel myself cringe. Even though I had made a joke about it only hours earlier, I was unsettled. That warning from Mother still rang in my ears: "She can take her back for a year, you know." It was almost like I wanted Jodi to be with you but also forget that she had ever had you, take an eraser to the chalkboard. You were *my* daughter, the voice inside my head screamed, in direct contrast to the outer me that said we were both your mothers.

"Okay, okay," Charlie said. "Collards, schmollards.

This baby is coming sometime, so I think we all better get prepared." She reached into the purse hanging over her chair and produced a spreadsheet. "I've worked up a tentative baby care schedule that I thought might be fair for everyone—"

"Wait," I interjected, my fork halfway to my mouth. "You have made a spreadsheet for the baby?"

"They all been talking 'bout it on Facebook," Jodi said.

I looked at Mother skeptically. "*You* are on Facebook?"

She wiped her mouth and set her napkin beside her plate haughtily. "I'm a poet, darling. Must I remind you that I have *fans?*"

I smiled, thinking of how many years Mother had tried to get her poetry published, and she said, "Speaking of, my book is being released in November and, obviously, it's too cold to do the release party in Manhattan."

"Obviously," I said, thinking that November was my favorite time in Manhattan. In all likelihood, with a two-month-old baby, I would miss it this year.

"My friend Laura wants to host the launch party in Palm Beach so that everyone doesn't have to be so dreadfully cold."

Jodi covered her mouth with her napkin, and I could tell she was trying to muffle her laughter.

I raised my fork in the air. "No, no, that's fine. You all run off to Palm Beach and leave me with my three children. I don't need any of y'all to help."

Uproarious laughter from the table ensued. Even you laughed.

Mother was the only one with a serious face. "Of course you'll all have to come, darling."

Graham shot me a look that wordlessly said my mother was a crazy alien who clearly had no idea what it was to have a child.

"Mother, I'm not sure that—"

"You're coming," she snapped. "This is the biggest thing that has happened to me in decades, and my whole family needs to be there."

I was used to a life filled with travel and hauling children all around kingdom come. But taking three kiddos on a plane wasn't something I was anxious to do. When it was Graham, you, Alex, and me, we were at least playing man-to-man defense.

"And you," Mother said to me accusingly. "I have been to every launch party you've had all over the country, so I don't care if your baby is three days old, I expect you to arrive smiling, happy, and *thin*."

I caught Jodi laughing again out of the corner of my eye. "Oh, right," I shot at her, a laugh in my voice too. "Since you're twelve and lost your baby weight in a week you would think that was funny." I mentally kicked myself. Why did I keep *reminding* her? I turned back across from me. "Mother," I said, "I won't even be able to exercise again."

She squinted at me and said, "You are coming, Frances Mason."

I sighed. "Fine. I'm coming. But I can't promise thin."

"Where are we staying?" Graham asked.

Mother started to open her mouth, but Charlie interjected, "Please, Mrs. Mason. Allow me." In her best Mother-impersonation voice, Charlie said, "The Breakers, darling. Is there anywhere else?"

As I crawled into bed that night, Graham groaned.

"What?" I asked, irritated, thinking that if anyone was groaning, the one with an extra twenty-five pounds of pressure on her hips should be the one.

"I hate Palm Beach," he said.

I yawned, sliding into the cool covers, closing my eyes, so ready for sleep. "No one hates Palm Beach, sweetie." I patted his hand.

"I think it is the most egregious display of ridiculous wealth that I have ever seen. In this economy, it's almost inappropriate."

I opened one eye. "I've known you for two decades, and I've never, ever heard you say 'egregious.' "

He nodded. "That's how serious this is."

I was too tired to argue. "Okay, honey. Then we'll tell Mother we can't go."

"No, I mean, she's right. She always comes to your stuff, so we have to go."

"Well, then let's face the fact that we're going to have to suffer through a long weekend of mai tais on a sparkling beach with our personal butler spreading our towels out in our cabana."

I rolled over onto my left side heavily and said, "Not to mention the caviar and top-shelf liquor that will be forced on us at Laura's five-star launch party."

Graham kissed me and said, "You're right, honey. I'm being silly. As long as my family's there, I'll be okay."

"Great," I said, unable to keep my eyes open.

A shot of panic ran through me that another baby was about to be here, and I was going to be even more tired. Knowing that my friends and family would help share baby duty felt like the time I borrowed Mother's favorite Chanel bag without permission, lost it, and then found it in Charlie's trunk. I was bathing in relief. In truth, I didn't know how we were going to handle all of these babies running around and work at the same time. That reminded me that tomorrow, without excuse, I had to start looking for a nanny. About that time, you started crying, and I pulled the covers back and rushed to your side. You were standing up in your crib, fat tears rolling down your chubby cheeks. I picked you up and put you on my hip as best I could with a tremendous roadblock between us. I kissed your little forehead and said, "Do you want to sleep with Mommy and Daddy tonight?"

You laid your head on my shoulder, and I knew for certain that no achievement in life—no book deal, no million-dollar sale, no Nobel Prize—could top the feeling of a tiny child resting her head on your body and dozing off. I was practiced at having children in my bed, so even having you on one side and Alex on the other didn't hinder my sleep.

The ringing phone beside my ear, however, did. Graham could have slept through a tractor-trailer ramming right through our room, but I was a much lighter sleeper. By some miraculous transpiration, the phone woke neither you nor your brother, but my heart was racing. Graham had been right all those months ago, after all. People do answer the phone in the middle of the night because they automatically assume it's an emergency. In those seconds before I said, "Hello," my mind leapt to so many worst-case scenarios. Daddy had had a heart attack, the house had been broken into, Pauline had passed away peacefully in her sleep. When I heard my sister Virginia's voice on the other line, I started crying right then and there. We didn't talk that often, so for her to call me in the middle of the night, something must have been wrong with Mother or Daddy.

It sounds terribly selfish, I know, but I was a little relieved when she sobbed into the phone, "Allen left me."

I picked up the cordless and tiptoed into my bathroom, where I shut the door, sat down on the closed toilet lid, and said, "Oh, honey, what happened?"

"He's found someone else," she wailed.

How could that creep Allen have gotten one woman, much less two? I thought.

I told Virginia that she was welcome to come over, though where she would have slept is beyond me as we were Bethlehem on a cold, December night. There was literally no room at the inn.

"I'll come over tomorrow to talk," she sniffed. I yawned and padded back to my bed, and when I got back between the sheets, I realized that they were wet. I figured that your diaper had leaked, but when I touched your pajamas, you were bone dry. That's when I noticed that I was soaking wet too, from more than your average pregnant night sweats. I guess the shock of being woken in the middle of the night and the focus I had on what Virginia was saying had prevented me from realizing it before.

"Graham," I hissed, finally awake enough to

realize that the disgusting squish I kept feeling was my broken water. "Graham," I whispered again, this time a little louder.

"It's okay, sweetheart," he mumbled. "We'll get it in the morning."

I threw a baby shoe at him, and he finally opened his eyes. "Why would you do such a thing?"

"Because I'm in labor."

Graham rubbed his eyes, bolted up in bed straight as a ship's mast, and ran to his closet. He began tossing things in a bag. I looked over his shoulder.

"Honey," I said, "why would you need a ruler?"

He shrugged. "Don't I have to tell you how many centimeters you are or something?"

I shook my head. I realized why my poor husband had begged me to go to a birthing class. He truly was clueless. "Should we wake the kids to tell them bye?"

Graham shook his head. "Nah. Just tell Charlie what's going on. May as well let them sleep while they can." He winked at me.

Perhaps I shouldn't have even woken Charlie because, by the time the nurse had admitted me to my hospital room, Charlie, Greg, Mother, Daddy, Pauline, and Jodi were all there. You were soundly asleep in your car seat, and Alex was snoring again, arms flailed, face mushed into Greg's shoulder.

Charlie said, "I called Stacey too, and she said she'll be here before things get really rough. Just in case, she e-mailed me a list of poses for you to do."

Stacey was my best friend in New York slash yoga instructor slash birth coach with Alex. I would never have made it through without her.

I was thankful that everyone was so interested in my birth, this crazy, patchwork quilt of a family that we were. But now that we were at the hospital, I had one overarching thought. I looked at Graham and said, "It's too early."

At that moment, Dr. Painter breezed into my room and said, "You're thirty-seven weeks, Frances. That's full-term." He elbowed Daddy in the ribs. "At least it was back when I was in medical school." They had a good laugh—Daddy and Dr. Painter had gone to high school together—and Charlie and I rolled our eyes in unison.

I shouldn't have worried about having to defend myself. Mother said, "My child and my grandchild are at stake here. Maybe we could all be a little more composed."

"I'm going to check you now," Dr. Painter said.

I looked around the room at the massive number of people and said, "Oh, no, don't worry. Please, everyone stay."

They must have taken me literally because Daddy and Greg actually sat down. "Fantastic," I said under my breath.

Dr. Painter reached underneath the sheet, and announced, "Five centimeters! Is this girl a pro, or what?" Then his forehead crinkled, and I panicked. He rolled back on the stool, popped his glove off, and said, "Looks like this little one decided to do a last-minute flip."

Charlie gasped. "Do not try to turn the baby!"

As horrified as I was, I actually laughed. "Why on earth not?"

"Because I read that babies born breech have magical healing powers," Greg interrupted.

Charlie shot him a look. "Noooo, Greg. Because I read that it can hurt the baby."

Greg looked at me seriously. "The healing powers thing is true too, though. I swear."

"I think you should do a C-section," Mother interjected.

Daddy said, "Perhaps you should let the doctor make the decision," and Mother said under her breath, "Just trying to help her have a baby with a pretty head, is all."

Dr. Painter, who was a generally jovial man, put on his sternest face and said, "If you weren't there when this child was conceived, if you could please leave."

Everyone left but Charlie. I looked at her and said, "I don't recall you being there when this child was conceived, love."

She crossed her arms. "I know. But I got to be in the room when Alex was born, so, you know, I just kind of assumed . . ."

I squinted at her. "Charlie, you threw up all over

the floor, and one of the nurses holding my leg had to come clean up after you."

She shrugged. "Practice makes perfect?"

Graham waved to her and, looking dejected, our last stray family member made her way to the waiting room.

When it was finally quiet, Graham lay down beside me and put his arm around me, rubbing my belly.

"We can try to turn the baby," Dr. Painter said. "But there are risks."

"I don't want risks," I said. "Let's do the C-section and call it a night."

Graham looked at Dr. Painter. "But that's more dangerous for Khaki, right?"

Dr. Painter got up and started washing his hands. "Every procedure has its risks, but Frances is in excellent health and should come through a routine cesarean beautifully."

"Okay," I said, looking at Graham. "When they pull the baby out, you go with the baby."

"What do you mean?"

"I mean, don't stay with me. Follow the baby around, don't let it out of your sight, and bring it right back here to me as soon as you can."

Dr. Painter laughed. "The baby will be tagged at birth. There's no way to get them mixed up."

"Dr. Painter," I said. "With all due respect, I've seen enough of those Lifetime movies that I'm not taking any chances."

He laughed and said, "I'm going to go get ready, and the nurse will come in to get you and Dad prepped for surgery."

"Send my family in, please," I called.

Charlie burst in the door first and said, "Stacey and Joe aren't here yet."

"Well, by all means, let me stay in labor another five or six hours until they arrive."

She sat on the edge of the bed and kissed my head. "I'm just teasing you. It's going to be fine, you know."

I looked at Jodi. "Could you bring me my babies, please?"

Pauline came in carrying Alex, and I could tell by the way her lips were moving that she was praying harder than a sinner on his deathbed. And I was awfully glad of it. Alex climbed into bed beside me and examined my IV line. "Why do you have all these tubes, Mommy?"

I could feel the tears pouring down my face as I said, "Because you have to have tubes to have a baby."

It was the simplest explanation I could think of. Charlie handed you to me, and I smelled that sweet baby smell at the top of your head and held you close. You were still for a moment and then looked up and smiled at me with the two tiny bottom teeth you were so proud of.

"I hope I don't take your childhood away from you," I whispered.

It was like you knew what I was saying. You leaned up and gave me the openmouthed, slobbery "kiss" that you had been perfecting.

"I promise that we'll still spend tons of time together."

Graham rubbed my neck. "Honey," he said. "You heard what Dr. Painter said. It's a routine procedure, and they do it all the time."

Then I started crying again. "I know that," I said. "I just realized that their lives are going to change so much, and they don't even know it."

Alex peered into my face and said, "Mommy, is my new baby coming out today?"

"Yes, love. Your new baby is coming out."

He nodded in approval. "That's good, because Carolina needs another person to play with."

"Why is that, sweetie?"

He shrugged. "Oh, you know. I like to play with her but sometimes she gets ignoring."

We all laughed. I kissed you both again, and my heart was breaking into fragments because you sobbed as Mother took you away from me.

I waved good-bye to everyone, and Graham reclined beside me again, one leg on the floor. "You know what, babydoll?"

"What?"

"Their lives are going to change but in such a good way. They are going to have a blast growing up together."

Less than an hour later, when Dr. Painter handed

your sister to me, I realized that Graham, as usual, had been right. In that instant, I quit worrying. I knew that this beautiful baby had been given to our family out of one thing and one thing alone: God's amazing grace.

Jodi
A TICKING TIME BOMB

Every damn body thinks they can grow a garden. I always hear people sayin', "Oh, yeah. I think I'm going to grow my own vegetables in my yard this year." They don't have a dag dern clue. They don't get how much time it takes, how you gotta commit your whole self. Them crops, they'd just as soon break your heart as grow for you to eat 'em. It's the same thing with babies. You get to spending some time around a baby, and you start thinking you know what being a momma's like. You don't. I mean, I only been a momma for two weeks, but there ain't no comparison between taking care a' somebody else's baby and having your own. And it ain't just being so sore and tired your body gets to feeling like it's superglued to the couch. You're all weepy and you don't never know what's gonna make them waterworks start flowing like a hydrant being tested.

Khaki, she was having to go through all that

mess, but she were so happy because her best friend Stacey from New York got there an hour after Grace was born. So Stacey, Charlie, Mrs. Mason, and me was all helpin' her out.

I damn near got to crying, that girl was hurtin' so bad. The social worker mighta turned up her nose, but I couldn't help myself. I said, "I'm staying a night here and there to help you out. I can at least bring Grace to you when she gets hungry." I waited, but she didn't say nothin'. "I mean, I'll come after Carolina's sleepin'."

"But, Jodi, you have to work. I don't want you to get worn out helping me."

I shook my head. "I can nap for a couple a' hours most days."

I mean, yeah, I wanted to help Khaki real bad. But I was also real scared. Every time that trailer got to groaning or creaking I was convinced it was Ricky coming for me. In the light a' day, I weren't that nervous. I mean, I knew Ricky would take Khaki's daddy real serious. But it was like every time I walked through that door I could just remember me being pinned up against that counter, them crazy eyes a' his flashing. And my palms would get to sweatin', my heart racing and my throat getting all dry.

Khaki nodded. She tried right hard to smile but it didn't take. "I hate to say yes. But I really want to. You know?"

I knew damn well better than she could ever

imagine. I knew when I let them keep you. I knew when I took a job and health insurance. I knew that sometimes a girl don't have many good choices but to say yes. It don't matter what my daddy said.

Khaki patted the comforter beside her, like she was inviting me in. I snuggled in all close, fighting real hard not to close my eyes. "Jodi," she said, "why on earth would you think that you shouldn't have any more children?"

Buddy and Khaki, they was about the two worst secret keepers in the world. I shrugged. "I cain't imagine having another youngen. Then I'd know how good they was and know that I'd give one up."

"Honey," Khaki said. She tried to lean forward, winced, and then lay back down. "You can't punish yourself forever."

But I think she got where I was coming from. Having a baby and thinkin' on what you give up—that were punishment.

She sighed. "So how's the stuff Patrick wanted you to prepare coming? Is there anything I can help with?"

"It sure is nice a' him to spend so much time helping me get the book ready and all before they even decide if they're gonna buy it."

Khaki smiled. "Patrick's a good one. He just thought a manuscript would be stronger than a proposal in this case, and, looking at it all coming together, I have to say it's amazing."

"Yeah," I agreed. "And even if they cain't publish it, I'm real happy that all them family recipes is in one place so I can pass 'em down. I almost got it all done for you to take a look at 'fore I send it back."

I could hear you fussing just a little, ready to get outta the crib.

I turned to walk down the hall to get you. But then I turned back around right quick. "Thanks for makin' it so I could do this. You never know. It might be my ticket outta here."

Khaki gasped. "Out of here! You want to leave Kinston?"

"I'll still see Carolina every week. Won't nothing come 'fore that."

The doorbell rung before we could finish talkin'. I grabbed you and ran downstairs.

"I thought I might find you here," Buddy said, when I opened the door.

I smiled, my legs feelin' right like Jell-O.

"I was just thinking," Buddy said, "you been here workin' so much I thought you might want a little rest. I can make it through the market alone this week if you wanna catch up on your sleep."

I guessed Buddy didn't know that goin' to the market with him's the best part a' my week. I shook my head. "Nah. I like bein' there right good. Kinda feels like home, you know?"

He smiled. "All right. I didn't want you to quit

coming or nothin'. I's just trying to be gentle-manly."

I could feel that blush rising up my cheeks. He was getting ready to walk away, and I realized I didn't want him to. "So, Buddy," I said, real quick before he could get turned around good, "speaking a' the market, I got something I've been meaning to talk to you about."

"Yes."

"Yes, what?"

"Yes. I'll plant fall crops and help you keep going to the market all year round."

"Are you sure, I mean—"

He put his hand up to his cowboy hat and shook his head. "Jodi, I know you're still right young so maybe you don't get this without me being real clear: I'd do pretty much anything in this world for you."

I couldn't believe he said that. My heart was poundin' so hard I couldn't even say nothing.

So Buddy just kept on. "You and me both know them parsnips'll make it all year and the garlic too. We can plant us some peas and onions, rutabaga, arugula, cauliflower. I thought we'd do some herbs too. Cilantro and dill do real good in the cold."

I cleared my throat, trying to regain my consciousness from Buddy saying he'd do near anything for me. My voice came out kinda shaky when I said, "That sounds great. Peas is one of my favorite things to can. They were my grandma's favorite. And dill is so good on them pickles I want to make."

"Great," Buddy said. "It's a plan. I love working, so I'm right excited about the whole thing."

Right then, that sister a' Khaki's, she didn't even say hello, just ran on past me and Buddy like we weren't even there.

Buddy raised his eyebrows and said, "Well, I guess I oughta let you get back to it."

"Hey, thanks," I said. "It's real good for me to be working."

Buddy winked at me. "It's right good for us all."

I closed the door and followed Khaki's sister, practically floatin' on a cloud from gettin' to see Buddy when I weren't even expecting it. I turned my face right up toward yours, thinkin' how it really did feel like you was my niece now. When they said something 'bout you being their girl, I didn't even think, *Yeah, because you carried and gave birth to her.* There hadn't been one time lately I'd tried to stuff you in my shirt and get you on back to the trailer with me.

Virginia, she barely peered in at Grace and said, "Oh, she's beautiful."

She lay right up there beside Khaki and them tears started flowing and a-flowing.

Seeing as how she just give birth, that Khaki got to cryin' real hard too. She said, "Please stop crying. It hurts my incision."

I handed Khaki a tissue, and Virginia grabbed it outta my hand real quick. I rolled my eyes big enough that she could see. I weren't nobody's sister, but I knew it weren't okay to dump your problems on a new momma no matter who she is.

But Khaki, she got to comforting Virginia. "It's okay, sis. You're going to be fine. You're going to find someone new and better, and you're not even going to miss Allen."

"But I've been with him since high school," she sobbed. "I haven't been on a date in twenty years."

Khaki nodded real supportive and sobbed back, "When Alex died, and I had to start dating again, it was so awful. I wished he would be alive and I didn't have to find another man to love me."

I weren't sure it's exactly the same when your husband dies as when he leaves you for his daughter's preschool teacher. I rolled my eyes again. I ain't never been too tough. I mean, I let men walk all over me and my momma tell me I ruined her life and was too afraid to go for some things I really wanted. But I was gettin' just good-feeling enough from my new job and whatnot that I started to stand up for myself—and the people I loved—a little bit more. Plus, I'd been up dern near all night trying to perfect my recipe for dilled green bean pickles, figuring if the flavor was better when they was hot packed or cold packed. My fingers were sorer than all get-out from that bean snapping, and I'd had just about enough.

"Virginia," I said real firm like. "I gotta get Alex, and Khaki, she needs to get to napping."

It were like she weren't even crying all a' sudden. "It's okay. I'll stay here with Khaki and get her anything if she needs it."

I made my lips real tight and thin. "Visiting hours is over."

Virginia looked at Khaki real sad like she's some puppy needs saving, but Khaki shrugged. "Whatever the nurse says."

"I don't know who you think you are," Virginia hissed like a wet cat as I walked her to the door.

For the first time in my entire life I didn't *think* I was anyone. I damn well knew.

Khaki

PARANORMAL ACTIVITY

I absolutely love decorating with the color pink. While I don't think it has to be only for little girls' rooms, Graham wasn't too keen on the idea of having his house resemble a princess palace. So, we never found out the sex of baby Grace, but when your daddy decided she was a girl, I went with his instinct and had that room painted pink before he could even tell me to wait. I had picked a rug, curtains, a crib, a changing table, an armoire, a diaper pail, a toy chest, a bookshelf, a mirror, a pair of paintings, and a store's worth of clothes, shoes, and baby blankets. What I had failed to choose was the most important and by far the most difficult thing: a nanny.

The last thing you want to do when you get home from the hospital and are juggling three under five is look for a new nanny. I had intended to have this all worked out before Grace was born, but, obviously, I thought I had three more weeks.

Looking for a nanny is, to me, essentially the same as dating. If I know there's no chance I'm going to marry you, I don't waste a bunch of time. When my first interview of the day walked through the door, though, I thought that maybe we'd go ahead and say our vows so I could get back in bed. She had long blond hair, crystal-blue eyes, a clear complexion, and a voice like a midnight train rolling down the tracks. I loved her immediately.

"I thought you might want some references," she practically whispered, handing me a list of names and phone numbers. "I used to be a full-time nanny for four children, and it was the best experience of my life."

I tried to shift positions but found it too painful, so I stayed slouched down on the couch instead of sitting up straight. "Do you have any experience with babies?" I asked.

"Oh, yes," she said. "Two of the four children were twins, and I helped their parents bring them home from the hospital."

Charlie walked in about that time, throwing a handful of peanuts into her mouth and handing me a plate of the orzo with vegetables that had been the only thing I could stomach since I got home. Charlie smiled weakly, glowered at me, and said, "Sorry to interrupt." She walked around behind that field of glowing blond and mimed, *Are you crazy?*

I smiled like nothing had happened. My husband and I had spent decades trying to be together. It was doubtful that one dead husband and one dumped-at-the-altar fiancée later he was going to have an affair with the nanny. Nevertheless, I could hear Mother's voice in my head. "When you hire a nanny you make sure she's old, heavy, and unattractive. In a weak moment, a man might be with a woman who's old or heavy or unattractive. But things would never be so bad that he would succumb to all three."

The tiny me in my head pushed away Mother like you push away Alex when he's trying to get a toy you're playing with. (It's so cute!) My nanny candidate continued telling me that she had formerly been a vegan chef and liked to cook and clean when the children's schedule permitted it. "I don't believe in sitting around," she said, and I almost cried, picturing her folding the five loads of laundry per day that our family now produced. I'd read that cloth diapers prevent diaper rash, and I couldn't bear the thought of those raw little tushies.

I was about to say, "You're hired," cancel the rest of my afternoon appointments, and go on about my day when I asked, "Is there anything else I should know about you?"

"Well," she demurred, teeth whiter than freshly fallen snow gleaming at me. "I'm having a baby five months from now, and I'm planning to stay home for six months." Then she had the nerve to add, "Do you pay for maternity leave?"

I gritted my teeth, forced a smile like Alex into church clothes, and said, "We'll be in touch."

As I slammed the door, Stacey sauntered in like a ballerina, her curly brown hair pulled up in a ribbon, and said, "Surely you aren't crazy enough to hire her."

"She's pregnant," was all I said in reply.

Greg came in and said, "Pregnant or no, she can be my nanny."

Charlie slapped his arm.

I said, "She had the nerve to ask if I would pay her for maternity leave."

"Maybe you should have asked if you could help with her baby," Stacey said, and we all laughed. I writhed in pain and shot her a look. "No one is allowed to say anything funny for four more weeks."

Stacey and Charlie agreed to take over the next four interviews so that I could get some much-needed rest. Three hours that felt more like five minutes later they were up in my room, plopping résumés on my desk with a pleasing "thunk." Charlie dropped the first one and said, "Scientologist."

Stacey cringed and said, "If we've learned anything from Katie Holmes, it's that you don't mess with that no matter how sexy it is."

Another slam of paper and Charlie pointed between her legs and said, "Inappropriate piercing."

Stacey shuddered.

I put my hand up. "Wait a second. Do we care about that?"

"We don't care so much about the piercing as that we've known this person for twenty minutes, and she told us all about it," Stacey said.

"In an interview to be your nanny," Charlie added.

She had a point. "Okay. Please have good news for me on this next one."

Another thump and Charlie said, "Hate to tell you, sweetheart. Criminal record."

I peered at Charlie. "How on earth do you know that?"

"Please, I'm a lawyer," she said like she was saying, *Please, I'm in the FBI.*

I put my hands over my eyes and said, "Well, that

settles it. Stacey, you're never going back to New York, and, Charlie, you and Greg are going to have to sell Mrs. Jacobs's house and move in here."

"Don't give up yet," Stacey said in her best motivational speaker tone. "You have one more interview at four thirty."

When Diane (pronounced *Dee-ahn*) breezed through my front door, I have to admit that I judged her on her outer appearance. She looked a little like the Wicked Witch of the West, with long, unruly gray-and-white hair, glasses, a pointy nose, and an all-black outfit.

"At least you don't have to worry about your husband screwing her," Charlie said out of the corner of her mouth.

I had to clear my throat to keep from laughing. She met only two of Mother's three criteria, but I thought that maybe being skinnier than the stray cats wandering around downtown might be as big a turnoff as being overweight.

You crawled up to her, put your hand on her leg, and didn't even cry when she picked you up. You were fascinated with her glasses all through our interview, and I thought that maybe, just maybe, I had found the one. When she said, "I've been so lonely since my husband passed away," I felt myself tear up. When she added, "So I'm available for nights, weekends, and I could even go away with you if you wanted," the tears dried faster than a bathing suit in the sun.

I held my breath when I asked, "Is there anything else I should know about you?"

She shook her head and said, "Just that I absolutely love children, and they tend to love me too."

That was clear from the fact that, for a child who was into everything and never stayed still, you had sat with Diane for forty-five minutes, examining her strange jewelry. I looked at Charlie and Stacey, and their knowing glances confirmed my thoughts: Diane was going to work out great.

She had four children, eleven grandchildren, and decades of baby-raising experience; I couldn't think of anyone better. So I sent you and Diane to join Alex in the playroom while I went upstairs to feed Grace. We had agreed that for a week Diane would come over for an hour or so at a time so you could all get acclimated to each other.

When I walked back downstairs, gripping the rail for dear life, realizing how much we actually use those poor, incision-ridden stomach muscles to do *everything,* I heard Alex laughing. I was thinking that I sure had made the right decision with Diane, and said, "What's so funny, honey?" I noticed Diane in the corner, holding you on her lap, looking like Stacey when she's deep in meditation.

Alex started laughing all over again and said, "Mommy, we're talking to ghosts."

I could feel the confusion written all over my

face. "You're pretending there's a ghost in here?"

Diane piped up in an eerily monotone voice like a Clear Eyes commercial gone wrong, "I am a medium, and I'm helping a soul cross over."

"Now?" I asked, my voice getting high and squeaky like a bike wheel in need of WD-40.

She cracked one eye and said, "It's a gift, not a time clock. I can't turn it on and off."

With that, I snatched you off her lap, doubling over in pain, and said, "Thank you very much, Diane, but I don't think we'll be needing your services."

She got up, looking befuddled (I mean, honestly, why would a person care if her nanny was helping souls cross over instead of watching her three children?), and handed me her card on the way out. "This is a very old house," she said. "I sense a high frequency of paranormal activity here."

I nodded. "Of course you do."

The house was actually only ten years old, so the logical part of me knew that Diane was mistaken. But it didn't keep me from feeling totally creeped out.

"If your lights start flickering or you feel breath on the back of your neck at night, call me."

Every hair on my body stood on end. I looked nonplussed, but I immediately went in the house to call Graham and tell him that he had to come home right away, as we had a high level of paranormal activity. I could tell he was trying not to laugh when he said, "Okay, honey. I'll leave the crew of twenty-five I've got in the fields and rush right over to save you from the monsters in the closet."

"Not monsters," I hissed like an aggravated cat. *"Ghosts."*

"So I take it the nanny search isn't going well."

"Well, let's see," I said sarcastically. "We've had the pregnant chick, the pierced weirdo, the Scientologist, the convict, and now the medium. You could say this isn't what I had pictured."

"I'll see if I can ask around for someone too, sweetheart." He paused and then said, "Hey, you know . . ."

"Hey, you know what?"

"Jodi is working for us anyway and—"

"No," I interjected, feeling my momma bear instincts rise to the surface like oil on water. I couldn't decide if I was worried that Jodi would see how wonderful you were and want you back or if I couldn't imagine asking someone to take care of a child she had birthed without getting to be her momma. Either way, it was a firm no.

"Maybe one of the guys has a wife or sister or somebody."

I sighed. I thought of the laundry and cleaning that even the four-days-a-week cleaning lady couldn't keep up with, the interminable amount of cooking that had to be done for children at different stages of eating, the hours on end of breast-feeding, the sleepless nights, the cupcakes for school, the field trips, the birthday parties. I didn't know how I was going to do any of that much less fly back and forth to New York, promote a book, design homes, run a store, pay payroll taxes . . . "Maybe I should quit work."

Graham laughed like the time Alex pulled his pants down and peed in front of church.

"What?" I asked.

"Oh, honey," he said. "You're not the kind of woman who can quit work and be okay."

I wanted to argue, but I was sore and tired. Plus, I knew he was right. My children were my life, sure. But my work was my identity.

One of the most important things to consider when taking on a new design project is the emotion of the space, the feeling that the family wants a room to convey. Most of the time, I like to bathe a room in neutrals and textures so that it can adapt to whatever mood a person is actually feeling. It is okay, after all, to not feel new-puppy pleased all the time.

While decorating Jodi and Ricky's trailer, I most definitely veered from that course. I filled it with pieces I hadn't been able to move from the store and focused on yellow as the main component of the color palette. Ricky was such a loose cannon that I always thought if he could walk in the door and immediately feel happy it would be best. Too bad it didn't work. The truth of the matter is that, sometimes, no matter how many times you kiss that damn frog, he's never going to turn into Prince Charming.

We had done everything we could to protect Jodi from Ricky: scared the daylights out of him, had him sign his rights away to you, and gotten a restraining order. The private investigator who tracked him down promised that he was skeezing around Mexico, but I still got the feeling that every time Jodi had to go back to that trailer, she felt a bit like a dog with an abusive master, fearing his return.

Somewhere in the first month after Grace was born, when Jodi was staying the nights with us, I stopped worrying about the dynamic between you two. It seemed normal and easy, like she was a fun and well-meaning aunt. I could sense her relief that she hadn't been a mother so young. I wished that we could have helped her more, but she didn't need me mothering her, I reminded myself about ten thousand times a day.

Recovering from a C-section on no sleep had been particularly difficult for me, and I wasn't ready to leave the house for a couple of weeks after Grace was born. One morning, though, I had had enough. Graham was at work, I was alone with three kids, and I thought I would rip my fingernails off one by one if I had to look at those same four walls any longer—even if they were papered in a handprinted Scalamandre.

It was just the grocery store, but anywhere I could walk outside, get in my car, and drive away was okay by me. Jodi asked sweetly, "Khaki, you sure the doctor said it'd be all right to drive?" I shot her a look, and Charlie chimed in, "I'm not sure it's such a good idea." Stacey didn't say anything because she was the least assertive of the group. But I could tell she didn't approve.

"Ladies," I said. "I am a thirty-two-year-old woman. I feel perfectly fine. If I can take care of three children, I can certainly drive a car."

That was sort of an overstatement since I had had Jodi, Charlie, and Stacey there to help the entire time, not to mention daily visits from Momma, Daddy, and Pauline. But still, even when there's help everywhere you look, kids want their momma.

I was through the produce aisle, perusing the rows of Oreos and chocolate chip cookies that weren't proper fare for girls on a postbaby weight loss plan, when I noticed a woman who looked familiar out of the corner of my eye.

When I got close enough to see her jaw smacking open and shut like a screen door in the breeze, I recognized that it was Jodi's friend Marlene.

"Hey there, Khaki," she called.

I waved back, hoping to avoid a conversation.

When she stopped her cart beside mine I knew I was out of luck.

"Sure is nice of y'all to take Jodi in like that," Marlene said, and I marveled at her ability to smack her gum and talk at the same time.

I laughed. "We didn't take her in. She has been helping me with the babies. I couldn't have survived without her."

Marlene crinkled her forehead. "Oh. But you know she's scared outta her mind to go back to that Ricky-infested trailer."

I was reading the ingredients on the back of a box of crackers when I began to feel sad. The thing about feeling sad when you're a hormonal train wreck is that you absolutely can't hold it together. So, there I was, a leaky watering can in the cracker aisle, and Marlene, whom I had met one time, was holding and comforting me as I sobbed.

"Oh, honey, it's okay," she said. "I wish somebody'd took care of me like you're taking care of Jodi. You done everything for that girl."

Then I started crying all over again for all the children in the world who were mistreated and uncared for. "It's just not fair," I said.

I spotted Pauline out of the corner of my eye and tried to get myself back together. "That my baby over there?" she called, pushing her cart toward me, a woman on a mission.

I nodded. "I'm fine, I'm fine."

Pauline pushed Marlene out of the way and held me to her ample chest like she had when I was little and someone had hurt my feelings at school. "You tell me what's wrong right now, baby."

I realized I was still holding a box of crackers, and, wiping my eyes with my free hand, I said, venturing a smile, "So many of these crackers have hydrogenated vegetable oils and genetically modified ingredients, and without even knowing, people feed them to their *children*."

Pauline howled with laughter, and Marlene and I joined her.

In the car on the way home, I allowed myself to think the things that I pushed away hardest. I faced my biggest fear, that Jodi would want to take you back. And I finally let that little voice in my head say, *Carolina is going to love Jodi more than you.*

I realized how selfish it was to deny a girl I loved the safety she craved because I was insecure.

Then I called Graham. "What do you think about Jodi being our nanny?"

"I think I thought of the idea a long time ago."

I winced as I turned my body to check my blind spot before switching lanes. "I mean, how do you feel about it in terms of Carolina and the adoption and all of that?"

Graham sighed. "I know that the therapist and the social worker and the books and our friends make like this is supposed to be this ridiculously complex blending of families. But we were already family before, you know?"

I nodded, even though he couldn't see me. "The kids love her so much."

"Right," Graham agreed. "And Carolina is at that stage where she cries for everyone. I'd rather her be happy with Jodi than miserable with a stranger." Graham sighed. "And, beyond all that, Khaki, we forget that the girl is twenty. I mean, what were you doing when you were twenty?"

He knew what I was doing at twenty because it pretty much revolved around him. I was staying out too late, going to parties, talking all night with my sorority sisters, sneaking into his fraternity house every now and then. I was going to classes to pass the time, having no idea what I was going to do with my life. And Daddy sent those checks every month like clockwork. I didn't know anything different than having people taking care of me everywhere I looked. I thought I was being this independent woman, but in reality, I had no real responsibility for anything besides my grades, something that had always come easily to me. Above all, I was in my little bubble, safe from harm, and felt totally invincible.

And then there was Jodi, working her tail off every day, trying to pay for her own house, her own car, her own insurance, already having been through one of the most horrible things I could imagine. And she didn't have anyone that she could count on. Anyone besides us, that is. I could feel the tears gathering in my eyes again, so torn between my fear and that deeply ingrained knowledge that you take care of your family first and always. Even when you're scared or hurt or angry, family always comes first.

I swallowed the lump in my throat and said, "Okay. So maybe we could try it short term?"

"Sure," Graham said. "I mean, think of all the people in family adoptions where the mother and the baby are under the same roof the whole time. If it doesn't work out or any of us feels uncomfortable, then we'll go back to the weekly visits."

"Graham." I paused.

"Yeah."

"Do you think . . ."

"She's not going to take her back, Khak. She's not."

When I walked through the front door, you were napping, and Jodi was rocking Grace while Alex colored on the floor. I sighed deeply like I hadn't exhaled in a month and said, "Jodi, I hate to ask you for anything as much as you've done for us, but I've thought and thought, and I can't come to any other logical conclusion."

Concern passed her face, and she said, "You can ask me dern near anything."

I shook my head and sat down on the couch across from the rocker. "I know you need your independence, and I want that for you more than anything." I looked hyperbolically nervous. "But I was wondering if you could possibly stay at our house for a while—I mean, all the time, not just a night here and there."

Jodi looked like she had just gotten a full scholarship and her book was being bid on at auction. She bit her lip. "You done so much for me, Khaki. I'd help you with near about anything."

"I've talked to Graham about it too. Let's all stay open and talk about the situation with Carolina. If anyone feels uncomfortable, we can always take a step back."

Jodi nodded. "I'd feel right good 'bout all of them being taken care of by family. Better than some stranger off the street."

I nodded. "Obviously, we'll pay you a salary, and you'll stay here and eat with us whenever you want."

So that settled it. Just like that, with two minutes of discussion, Graham and I had yet another child to feed, clothe, and house. I told him that since we had always wanted four kids, I was trying to get a jump on that as quickly as possible. He said at least this one was potty trained.

Jodi

HAVING IT ALL

When you got crops growin' you cain't very well leave 'em. So I ain't the kinda person that goes on vacation. I can count all the vacations I ever took on one hand. Grandma and Pop, they rented a house at the beach and took all the cousins one summer when I was nine. We was all of us crammed under one roof, slurpin' down orange sodas and getting sunburned. It was so much fun they promised to take us every year. But wouldn't you know Pop died that very next year, and, without him, Grandma didn't have no money for extras like vacation.

But Daddy, he took me to the beach when I was thirteen 'cause he was doin' some car work for the folks that owned the Oceanana. That playground equipment had been all I could think about. But I were too big to try them swings, too ashamed to let myself feel that freedom. Me and Daddy, we was like royalty staying in a hotel room that had its own sittin' room and kitchenette.

Daddy, he cooked fish that his friend caught. I didn't like it none, but I ate dern near every bite so he'd know how grateful I was. We got to walkin' on the beach, feeling free 'cause we was away from Momma, an orange-sherbet sunset sinking into cotton-candy clouds.

My friend Marlene's parents musta felt real sorry for me when Daddy was dying 'cause they rented a place in the mountains and took me along when I was sixteen. When me and Buddy went to the beach and I got to go to New York, those were the last two.

I knew pretty damn near nothing about the world. But I was feeling right cocky 'bout knowing my way around a airplane. When we went to New York, we drove to Raleigh, went right through them security guards, got some snacks, and waited in some chairs while I got to looking around for that "gate" that now I know don't exist. We got on the plane, flew with a whole buncha people, got off, and a man with a sign met us to get in the car.

I was goin' through all that in my head again so I wasn't embarrassed goin' off to Palm Beach for Mrs. Mason's book party. But I got all throwed right off the bat when we drove to the little airport not ten minutes from the house and waited around outside a tiny little plane.

"Why didn't we go through security?" I whispered to Graham.

"Khaki's parents chartered a jet for this trip."

I got to searching my brain for the word *chartered*. Only thing I knew about chartering was somethin' with making a new state. "What's 'chartered' mean?"

Graham smiled. "Rented."

I mean, I don't know near nothing 'bout traveling, like I said, but any fool could see this was a darn sight better than waitin' around in that musty airport. And it was real nice to just be with people you liked. The inside reminded me of Khaki's Mercedes, all leather and wood trim everywhere.

'Course I thanked Mr. and Mrs. Mason about a million times for inviting me and said hey to Khaki's sister Virginia, Charlie, and Greg. I weren't trying to, but I overheard Mrs. Mason say to Virginia, "I don't know why on earth she can't be sensible and leave those children at home like you did."

Khaki don't never leave her children.

I heard a man on the news saying that winning the Mega Millions lottery was the best feelin' in the whole world, but that ain't right. Having somebody love you so much they cain't even leave you for vacation is the best feelin'. And I got all warm inside just knowin' that you was gonna get to feel like that.

A whole flock a' fancy black cars was waiting when that plane landed with a real smooth little bump. At first, I thought we was in trouble or something, all them black car noses pointing at us. I heard Khaki whisper, "Seriously, Momma, Bentleys? Don't you think that's a hair excessive?"

Khaki's momma, she got kinda snippy about it.

"This might be the only book launch I ever have, and I will celebrate as I see fit."

Mr. Mason, he was all happy and calm and smilin'. He just said, "Girls, please don't argue. This is a special time for the whole family to be together."

Virginia took Khaki's hand, and they got to laughing right hard 'bout something must've been a sister joke as they slid in the backseat.

Like I said, the only hotel I'd ever stayed at was the Oceanana. So "hotel" to me meant a small, concrete building with doors on the outside. I had already got to picturing hunter green floral bedspreads and cups with plastic wrap over them. Not a damn thing in this world, not even them *Town & Country* magazines, coulda prepared me for drivin' up that brick driveway, eyes jumping 'round between rows and rows a' perfect palm trees, the ivy-covered walls and shiny building taking my breath away. This looked like somewhere kings and presidents and princesses stay, not country girls like me. And everybody else, they was just a-chattering away like it weren't nothing.

With my bag slung over one arm and you on my hip, I like to have tiptoed into the lobby of that giant hotel. Every place I'd ever lived combined weren't near as big as the front hall. Two men in uniforms said, "I'll get that, ma'am." They took my bag, and I wasn't even worried they were stealing it. Ain't nobody ever called me ma'am before.

"Some place, isn't it?" Khaki said.

That's when I realized my mouth was hanging open. The ceilings was painted with pictures and all them arches everywhere and glass chandeliers bigger than me. "It looks like the pictures of the Sistine Chapel in my old history textbook."

Khaki nodded. "It's beautiful, for sure."

I couldn't near imagine how much it must've cost for all a' us to stay in a place like this. But I woulda bet that first sweet corn a' the season I didn't make it in a year. People, they was always talking 'bout Mrs. Mason getting all that insurance money when her family got killed in that car wreck. But I hadn't had a damn clue what that money could buy.

"Let's get cleaned up and meet out by the pool for lunch in thirty minutes," Mrs. Mason said.

I followed Khaki outta the elevator, near bumping into her. She led me into a bedroom all blue and white and clean and crisp and the ocean and sun just shining in everywhere you could look.

"I hope you don't mind sharing a room with Alex," she said. "Carolina and Grace are going to sleep with us." She pointed to a door and said, "Our rooms are adjoining, so we'll prop them open, and we can all go in and out."

I peeked my head into a marble bath like my

heart couldn't take nothing else so amazing. I knew I hadn't said one dern word since we got there.

Mrs. Mason swished on through and said, "Is everything to everyone's liking?"

I just hugged her real hard.

"I'll take that as a yes."

Mrs. Mason, she was 'bout as warm and fuzzy as a porcupine, but I didn't blame her none. Losing all them people she loved when she weren't more than a grade-school girl, that's bound to make you hard inside. She said, "Hurry up, now. Get your suits on. I'm sure everyone is hungry."

"Jodi, Jodi," Alex called, all excited. "Which bathing suit should I wear?"

Khaki, she answered him all sugarplum sweet, "Do you want to see which one Daddy is wearing and you can match?"

"Yeah!" he yelled, jumping onto the bed.

Khaki shook her head and whispered to me, "I want so badly to turn that bed down so he's not on a germy comforter, but I don't want my children to inherit my phobias."

Germs don't know how to even get in places this beautiful. Khaki squeezed Alex's hand and took him through to the other room, saying, "Let's let Jodi get ready, please."

I sat down on the edge of my bed real soft. I was so scared I was gonna wake up and this weren't gonna be real, not any of it. Girls like me, we didn't get to come to places like this. Girls like me didn't go on millionaire vacations and ride in private jets and Bentleys. I was gonna make it last long and sweet like one a' Grandma's butterscotch. The Walmart bathing suit and dirty flip-flops in my ten-year-old duffel bag looked a darn sight more like the trailer park's Fourth of July barbecue than Palm Beach. But that weren't none a' my concern. You could tell straight off, all them people down by the pool, they was all worried 'bout how they looked, not me.

Buddy crossed my mind. He woulda been telling me how you got to be who you are and it don't matter where you are. I would be lying if I didn't say I kinda wished he was here with me. We'd get to be all shocked about the chandeliers together. We did work together. I could call him and just see how my jars did at the market.

"So," I said, when he answered. "Did you make it through the day all right without me?"

"It was real tough," he replied. "The good news is, your stuff sells itself."

I gasped. "Did it all go again today?"

"Every last jar."

I closed my eyes, feelin' the cold Kinston air on my face. I was having a real good time here in the sunshine. But there weren't no two ways around it: I'd kinda like to be wherever Buddy was.

"I'm real glad we decided to keep on growing

314

all year. The winter used to be right depressing, but now you've changed all that." He paused. "So how's Palm Beach?"

I bit my lip. I didn't want him to hear my smile, 'specially 'cause it were more about him than Palm Beach. "Oh, Buddy. This place ain't like nothing I ever seen. Talk about country come to town."

"Hold your head up and walk tall like you belong." It was just what I knew he'd say. "Maybe you'll take me back there with you one day?" I blushed right hard. "You know, now that you're gonna be a famous published author."

"Oh, Buddy, stop," I said. "We don't know if they're gonna even buy it." But I didn't want him to stop no more than I wanted to can crickets and eat 'em.

Khaki Tinkerbelled through the door saying, "I thought you might want—"

She stopped right quick when she saw me on the phone and whispered, "Oh, sorry."

"No, no," I said, putting my hand up for her to stay. "I gotta run," I said to Buddy. "But I'll see ya real soon."

"Take me some pictures," he called. "And make sure you're in 'em."

That blush had ahold a' me good now. I couldn't even say nothin' so I just hung up.

Khaki said, "I hope you didn't hang up on my account."

Grace was propped up real snug over her shoulder, wearing the tiniest pink seersucker bathing suit with little ruffles on the bottom. There weren't nobody on earth who could get herself lookin' good and get three youngens all ready better than Khaki.

"I brought way too many cover-ups, and I thought you might want to wear this one." She handed me a blue-and-white tunic with beading all 'round the collar. It were 'bout as gorgeous as the crown jewels. "I thought it would look pretty with your eyes." She pointed to the floor. "And I wasn't sure if you brought any sandals, but it's not exactly a short walk to the pool."

We did wear the same size shoe. Not a damn thing I could do about that. I thought of Daddy telling me to never take a handout—and then I thought on my old flip-flops in my bag. "You know, I didn't bring a single dern pair."

I learned quick what a "cabana" was. And it was real nice to have a little kitchen and bathroom and couches and playpens for you and Grace to nap. We didn't even have to walk back to the hotel. Alex was on a bike ride with your daddy, and I got to thinking in all that silence what a great, big world there was out there. I ain't seen near a postage stamp of it. Seeing the world, doin' something outside a' Kinston—I ain't never thought about them things any more than I woulda thought about getting my recipes all published

316

up or having my own pretty jars for cannin'.

I got to thinking on how addin' the rest of the sugar to my almost-cooked jam made it bubble up to the top of the pot. That was me now, bubbling all over, thinkin' for the first time in my life that I could do something. Like my momma had said about her own self all those years ago, I could be somebody.

I was gettin' all nervous and such when Khaki looked over and handed me a small stack of worksheets with boxes on 'em.

"What's this? Homework?"

She laughed. "Sort of. Graham and I do these goal-setting worksheets once a quarter where you imagine yourself in ten years and then set goals accordingly."

I was right confused. "So do you want me to do his worksheet for him?"

She took a sip of her virgin daiquiri and laughed again. "No, silly. I want you to do it for you." She took another sip and said, "All you have to do is let yourself be completely free, open, and uninhibited about what your ideal life could look like in ten years if you had absolutely no restrictions."

"No restrictions," I repeated.

"Right," she said. "No 'I don't have that kind of money,' or 'I could never travel that far.' Just uninhibited dreaming."

"I cain't do that," I said. "It don't seem real realistic."

She shook her head. "Nope. We live in the U.S.A., sweetie pie. It might be hard as hell and you might never achieve it, but you're allowed to dream whatever dream you want."

I pulled my sunglasses down, feeling kinda nervous and shaky knowin' that she weren't wrong. "Will Graham be mad that I did his sheet?" I asked.

"Well," Khaki said, "the whole point is to dream of yourself in ten years and start reaching those goals today. Graham said his goal was to ride bikes with Alex more in ten years, so he was going to go do that instead."

We both laughed. As I put the pen to the paper, I got all tense and nerve-racked. Girls like me, we don't think on what we *want*. We think on how we're gonna *survive*. It kinda made me smile, thinking 'bout Marlene. God bless her sweet soul, she'd been tryin' to teach me my whole life how to dream. Lord knows, she always was.

"What if I change my mind?" I asked Khaki. "I mean, what if I write all this mess up, and then I get to realizin' I wanna do something different?"

She reached over and patted my leg real soft and sure. "Then you rip the worksheet up and start over. This is your life, sweetheart."

I closed my eyes and breathed real deep. I thought I didn't know what I wanted one whit. But when I wasn't pushing it all away, them thoughts just got to popping up. I looked right good in another cap and gown, my jars looked real cute on the grocery store shelf, and I probably don't have to tell you that that hand I was holdin' looked a hair like Buddy's. But I got to openin' my eyes real quick when I seen me holding a baby.

I spent near an hour scribbling on them pages, gettin' to figuring on how I could make my little dreams work out real good. When I was finished, I looked over at Khaki in her printed bikini. She was always complaining how she ain't got her body back yet. But, if I were her I'd be moving to California right quick so I could wear my bikini every damn day. She looked like she were dozing. But I whispered all the same, "I think I'm gonna try to go to college."

She nodded, looked on over at me, and said, "I think I'm going to sell my store."

We both turned back to stare out over the pool connected to the ocean, all glittery like a Christmas card. Sometimes, there ain't nothing more to say.

Khaki

CHEATING ON CHANEL

Living as close to the coast as we do, every now and then I get the opportunity to redesign a family's beach house. Right around Mother and Daddy's house, many of the homes have been in the family for generations. They are characterized by that amazing tongue-and-groove paneling and an uncluttered, unpretentious air of relaxation. Those homes always remind me of summers at the beach when I was a little girl. The day school let out, we packed up and headed to the coast.

One month was carved out for Camp Seafarer in the small, seaside town of Arapahoe, North Carolina. I made some of the best, most lasting friends of my life during those weeks, learned to sail, tried to shoot, and got one heck of a tan. I felt free during those summers at sea, like my life was just beginning and the best was yet to come.

I decided long ago that The Breakers is Camp Seafarer for grown-ups. The oldest of the attendants, those who come to Palm Beach during the winter for the "season"—the social season, that is—are children at camp once again.

That night, my children dressed and lined up like little Von Trapps, in matching creamy baby Dior purchased from Spring Flowers on Worth Avenue, was the first time I realized that my parents were getting old. It crept up on me slowly that night, like a tiger stalking its prey. It was the nearly imperceptible shake in Mother's bejeweled hand when she shook the governor's. It was the slightest sag under Daddy's eyes that lent him the never-rested look of a man whose best years are behind him. It was the fierceness of Mother's temper that seemed to have subsided a bit when the bartender told her the champagne wouldn't be served until nine—and she didn't so much as threaten to have him killed.

I felt Graham's strong arm wrap around my waist, his soft lips with a hint of liquor on them graze my cheek like a white-gloved hand over an antique chest. "I'm not going to lie," he whispered. "Gratuitous money flashing and all, Palm Beach is kind of awesome tonight."

He leaned back to study me in the cream, floor-length Robert Rodriguez gown that, as much as I had dreaded this event, I was more than a little excited to be wearing. Its textured bust, flowing skirt, and dainty bow around the waist were so lovely that I almost wasn't mad that Mother had clearly picked something with an empire waist in case I wasn't thin again. I did still have the tiniest baby pooch under that flowing silk. But I would have shredded the dress with Kindercut scissors before admitting that to Mother.

Mother was shining like the LOVE bracelets in the Cartier counter in my Gucci kimono gown that I had insisted she wear even though it was a clear deviation from her norm.

"It's your big night," I told her. "Branch out. Do something different."

She had run her fingers across the iridescent peach fabric and said, "I just don't know if I could. I've had the same look for so long."

I had finally convinced her, saying, "It's Gucci,

Mother. It's not like you're cheating on Chanel with Contempo Casuals."

Graham's lips met mine softly, and you, perched on my hip, laughed like we had gotten you a new light-up toy. Perhaps children sense when their parents are happy, but nothing made you laugh with more gusto than when your daddy and I kissed. I studied him in his gorgeous, tailored-to-perfection Ralph Lauren tux and said, "Sweetheart, we've got to go to more black-tie events." With his slightly grown-out winter hair, strong jawline, and eyes like the giant aquamarine cocktail ring Mother was wearing, I was certain there couldn't have been a finer-looking man on the East Coast that evening.

"You liking my tux enough to make baby number four when we get home?" he said into my ear, a smile playing on his lips.

I gasped, hit him on the arm, and said, "Have you completely lost your mind?"

He shrugged. "Have *you* completely lost your mind?"

Virginia waltzed over about that time on the arm of a very attractive, silver-gray-haired man and said, "Oh, good. So you told him about the store after all."

I smirked at her, at which she bit her lip inconspicuously and said, "Have you met my friend Fletcher?"

Graham acted nonplussed, reached out his hand,

and practically bent down to Fletcher's five foot eight from his six foot four to shake his hand. "I'm so pleased to meet you," he said, and Virginia mouthed *Sorry,* and mimed with her hand up to her mouth that she'd had too much to drink.

They chatted for a few minutes about ethanol and the shortage of soybeans and farming futures before Fletcher swept Virginia away. She looked as gorgeous as I'd ever seen her, her impending divorce the impetus for finally losing her baby weight, highlighting her hair, and regaining that effervescent attitude that everyone had always found so attractive.

"Divorce is a good color on her," I said as she floated away saying, "Fletcher, I simply must introduce you to my aunt Charlotte."

Graham nodded. "I hate it for their kids, but Allen was dragging her down big-time."

I nodded, feeling my ab muscles clench like I was in a particularly sweat-inducing body pump class, realizing that maybe I'd gotten away with it. Jodi came over, took you from me, and said, "I think I'm going to get the kiddos back to the hotel and into bed if it's okay with you." I nodded and smiled. "That'd be great. Thanks so much, sweetie."

As Jodi turned to walk away, Graham sighed and said, "Finally. We can drink out in the open now."

There was more alcohol in that room than water

in a fishbowl, but I didn't think it was appropriate for us to drink around Jodi no matter what the circumstances. It seemed like stuffing yourself full of crepes in front of a starving child.

Graham put his hand on the small of my back and led me to the bar. He said, "Oh, and just so you know, we'll be discussing whatever you're not telling me about the store later tonight."

I could feel myself grimace as I put my arms around Daddy's neck, the smell of mingling perfumes and smudges of makeup on his tux jacket from dozens of hugs. "I think your momma might have carpal tunnel from all of this."

I shook my head and looked around the ballroom, which led out onto a tremendous slate patio overlooking the pool and then the ocean. It was as packed as Ken's Grill outside Kinston on a Friday afternoon. "I know Laura was hoping to help Mother get well on her way to selling that first thousand copies, but I'll bet she got her all the way there."

Daddy nodded, looking around at the lifted faces and plumped lips filling every nook and cranny. "Do you think any of these people read the kind of poetry your momma writes?"

I raised my eyebrows, because—well, frankly— I was one of the only women in the room who actually *could* raise her eyebrows. "Do you think any of these people *read?*"

Virginia appeared at Daddy's side, breathless

and rosy as a woman who has basked in the glow of the affections of a very eligible man all night. "So sorry, sis," she said. "I only assumed that you had told him about the store."

I shook my head. "It's okay. I have to tell him sometime."

She looked over my head, clearly scanning the room for Fletcher, and said, "What were you talking about?"

I rolled my eyes. "Having another baby."

"No," Daddy said, clapping his hands together. "No, no, no, no. Three is enough with everything else you two have going on. I can't watch my daughter have another C-section and hold my breath that hard the entire time. There's only so much praying and so much whiskey in Kinston."

I laughed. "It's okay, Daddy. Graham was just teasing me about it. Our hands are pretty full right now."

Daddy said, "Good Lord in heaven help us," under his breath, turned his back, and walked away with his hand up calling, "Bartender!"

"So," I said, bumping my sister's thin, sequined hip with mine. "What's up with Fletcher?"

She patted her sleek chignon and said, "I know you're thinking he's too old for me, but, quite frankly, I think he's fascinating, and I don't care how many Anna Nicole jokes y'all make." She exhaled deeply, leaned her head on my shoulder, and said, "Okay, for real, is he too old?"

"Age is a state of mind."

She stood up straight again and said, "He's only fifty-six. That's not terrible, right?"

I couldn't imagine being with someone who could easily and legitimately have been my father. But I also knew that Cupid didn't check birth certificates. "I think it's chic, sweetie. As long as he worships the ground you walk on, I don't see the problem."

She grabbed the olive out of her martini with her teeth, chewed, and said, "I married someone my own age, and he left me for someone younger. I need a *man*. I need someone to take care of me, not someone who lies around on the couch burping and asking for more beer."

I caught Fletcher's eye across the room and noticed that debonair sparkle that only the most sophisticated, worldliest men have. I thought of Allen and his beer belly rolling over the band of his jeans and the way he used to smack me on the back. It made me shiver, and I finally realized that Diane the nanny had been right. There had been a bad spirit in our family. I winked at Fletcher, took Virginia's hand, and said, "Well, honey, what can I say? At least there's no risk of *him* leaving you for someone younger."

We both burst out laughing like we were six and eight again in the midst of a pillow fight. I wouldn't wish losing a spouse on anyone, but having my sister back was nice.

I love nothing better than crawling into bed with my husband, him rubbing my sore feet, champagne bubbling inside me, the gossip of the night fizzing over like an overfull glass. "Did you see Laura's husband following Charlie around all night?"

Graham laughed. "It's a good thing Greg is so laid-back, because that dude would have gotten a black eye if he pulled that shit with my wife."

I laughed at Graham's faux machismo, lay back on the stack of pillows that I had propped on the edge of the bed, and said, "I know I told Jodi to leave the babies in here with us, but it's kind of nice to be able to talk and not have to be so quiet."

Graham nodded and said, "Okay. We can talk about the night in a minute. Time to tell me whatever Virginia was saying about the store."

I shrugged. "I've been thinking about how soon Alex is going to be in school all day and Carolina is practically walking and Grace will be before we turn around, and I don't want to look back and think I missed out on anything."

"So . . ."

"So, I know I don't want to quit doing at least a few design projects, and I love being able to travel back and forth to New York, so the only thing I thought I could drop was the store."

Graham nodded, his hand stopping over the ball of my foot momentarily and then picking up its kneading again. "But isn't Daniel doing most of the store stuff anyway?"

I could feel myself getting irritated. "Yeah. But I'm still thinking about it all the time. I'm still the one doing the books. I'm still the one writing the checks. I'm still the one staying up nights worrying about pieces getting damaged in shipping and if the water bill was paid on time and if the storefront needs to be redesigned and whether he's marking things up too high while I'm away and—"

Graham put his hand up to stop me. "Got it," he said. "It's a lot of worry." He paused. "You know I don't care, and I'm happy for you to do whatever you want." He paused again and licked his lips. "I will support you in whatever you do, and we are fine. But farming isn't what it once was and it might be a stretch for me to maintain a very pricey New York apartment, our house in Kinston, the farm, and three children's private school educations and college savings accounts on my own."

Strangely enough, for people who talked about everything from their daily schedules to their ingrown hairs, Graham and I hadn't actually ever discussed my financial situation. Obviously, he knew Mother and Daddy were wealthy, but wealthy parents didn't always translate to wealthy children.

"You know I'd love for you not to work," he

continued. "But we might have to scale down our lifestyle a little."

I sat up, and he laid his head in my lap. I hadn't ever wanted to tell Graham how much money Alex had left for Alex and me. For one, I didn't think it was relevant since I had decided that that money was for our son's future. Plus, talking about how much money your last husband made is sort of like talking about how well he made love: intimidating and unnecessary.

"I don't know why I haven't told you this before, but Alex is set for life and beyond," I said, grimacing slightly. "Mother and Daddy have asked to pay for Carolina and Grace's educations, so we're good there. And I certainly make enough off the few design jobs I'm still doing to pay for the apartment and to keep us all clothed." I rubbed his arm the way he liked and said, "So, basically, if you can keep our house up and running, which, obviously, you did for years without me, I think we're good to go."

Graham closed his eyes and lay very, very still for a solid minute, while I braced myself like a shutter in a hurricane for his reaction. I was thinking that he knew when he married me that I made more money than he did, and that if he was intimidated by how much more, then that wasn't my problem. But then I looked into his serene face and saw the same heart of that kid I'd fallen in love with first, hardest, and last. And I softened.

"Honey," I said gently. "What are you thinking?"

He still didn't open his eyes, but a smile spread across his face. "I'm thinking how, for the rest of my life, now that I know my children are educated, I don't have one single worry in the world." He pulled me on top of him, and I squealed. He opened his eyes, kissed me, and said, "I'd be dirt-floor poor as long as I got to sleep beside you every night, Khaki Mason."

I couldn't have agreed any more.

Jodi

FATAL FLAW

I always make my own beef stock. Lotsa folks, they cain't tell a homemade broth from one you buy off a grocery store shelf. But me, I like the hours a' boilin' and strainin' and dicin' and choppin'. 'Cause it's *perfect* when I get done with it.

That broth, if it taught me something, it's that I'd be okay in college. When I do something, I do it right. And that's what school's all about.

I was scheming on how I'd get to making my dreams come true while I was in The Shops at The Breakers not believin' my eyes was telling me some people'd pay what I make in a whole month for a sweater. I saw a book that caught my eye right quick. *Tiffany's Palm Beach.* It was all full a' gorgeous pictures a' gorgeous people lying by the pool and crystal-blue waters and houses that even Graham and Khaki's house woulda fit right inside. I got to thinkin' on them other parts of Palm Beach that we had driven through, them places where poverty lives and buildings fall and desperation pushes grocery carts right down the street. It were all a part of Palm Beach. But it certainly weren't a part of *Tiffany's* Palm Beach.

Khaki, she was Tiffany. She couldn't near believe I'd want to leave Kinston. 'Cause my Kinston, it was trailer parks and drunk Momma and fightin' and Ricky trying to kill me and scraping by to have enough to eat. Khaki's Kinston, it was farmland and plantation homes and Pauline cooking dinner and the love of her life.

She and Tiffany, they don't see what me and those grocery-cart folks see.

My cell phone—the one that Graham called my "bonus"—it got to ringing. I weren't paying no attention, thinkin' it were just Khaki wanting to see if I could go to the Ocean Bar and get a bite. Alex, he'd be pointing at the clown fish swimming around right there inside the clear bar, saying "Nemo! Nemo!" And all them people'd be feeding their youngens thirty-dollar cheeseburgers like it weren't nothin'.

But that voice, it weren't Khaki's.

"Don't hang up."

I couldn't have even if I'd tried. It was like my hand got superglued to the phone, one a' them senior pranks we woulda played.

"Before you say nothing, you gotta know I'm clean again. I'm real sorry for treating you bad when you brought your baby by."

It was my momma, raspy voice and all. I got so sick I had to sit down right there in the hall. And then I got to figuring why: We had escaped by a hangnail. I cain't predict the future any more than I can change the past. But it were laid out right clear like one a' them picture books I read to you. If I hadn't give you up, if I had stayed workin' too hard for too little, being with men and working for bosses that treated me worse than an old shoe they tossed in the bin, this would be me and you in twenty years. Me calling you up, saying I were clean again, apologizing. You being sicker of my excuses than political ads in the fall.

My momma, she just kept on talkin'. "I reckon I oughta come by and we can have us a sit-down."

I knew sure as pectin makes jam set real easy my momma wanted something. I cleared my throat. "I'm outta town. I cain't."

She'd be wonderin' good where I was. But she didn't let on none. "That's all right. You just call your momma when you get home."

"Momma, how'd you get this number anyhow?"

"How do you think it makes a momma feel when her own youngen don't even give her her phone number?"

"Momma, how'd you get my number?" I repeated.

"Well, I had to get me a new phone and all our numbers is on the same account so they give it to me up there at the phone place. So, come on, baby girl, you just call your momma when you get home from wherever you are."

I could feel the anger risin' up in me, making my insides feel near on fire that my momma had got Graham feeling sorry for her and now he was paying for her phone. Some people'd say she didn't have no choice, but me, I knew better. Everybody on this green earth has a choice about taking advantage of the good people that never done nothing but love them.

But every good storybook character, they all got a fatal flaw, that thing that keeps 'em making the same mistakes over and over again. Mine is that I cain't stand to hurt nobody's feelings. Don't matter if you've broken my spirit like a wild horse, I'll keep lettin' you on back in. I cain't stand treating people bad because I know how it feels.

"Okay, Momma. I'll call ya."

I hung up feeling near like my face was under water and I couldn't get no oxygen. Momma, she was like that x-ray scanner at the airport. She could always see right through when I was gettin' something like happy. And then, like one a' them pickaxes on the ice sculptures down the hall, she'd damn near tear me apart.

Khaki

PLAYDATES AND PROSECCO

Sometimes something that has been a staple in your design repertoire suddenly changes without a moment's notice. It happens to me all the time. For years, every throw pillow I designed had the perfect, luscious, chunky fringe. Then, one day, I decided that the fringed look was over. Ditto stainless steel appliances.

So I guess it shouldn't have surprised me when, on that trip to New York, all of a sudden, forcing three tiny, tired children through the airport felt less like a luxury and more like child abuse. After a week in Palm Beach being off schedule, overstimulated, and schlepped from dinner to dinner, event to event, none of the three of you was in the frame of mind to battle a crowded airport or sit quietly through a plane ride.

You were intermittently crying in the stroller, Alex was whining as I practically dragged him to the terminal, and I was in a particularly snarky mood. "Who was it again who told Mother we would be fine flying commercial? Wishing we'd taken her up on her offer of the jet now?" I snapped at Graham.

He rolled his eyes. I needed someone to blame for this state of affairs besides the person whose fault it was: mine. Despite my bad attitude, it was an incredible relief to have your daddy with me, hauling the rolling suitcase full of "plane emergency gear" I had packed. And, no, I don't mean parachutes. Blankets, toys, diapers, wipes, extra changes of clothes, antibacterial spray, pressure-reducing earplugs, snacks, sippy cups . . . You get the idea. Traveling with three children was a Herculean packing effort. If it had been an Olympic sport, I would have won the gold medal.

Since we were going straight from balmy Palm Beach to freezing New York, we had all of our luggage shipped. It cost roughly the same amount and saved what tiny portion of my sanity was still intact. The iPad was a close second in the sanity-saving department. Your daddy set it up on Alex's tray table, and y'all watched *Tom and Jerry* the entire time, fixated on the screen like children from *The Poltergeist*.

When we landed at LaGuardia, you were strapped to me in the Ergobaby, sleeping more soundly than Daddy after a couple of beers. Grace was cooing in the Baby Bjorn and Alex was cruising through the airport, red Spider-Man sunglasses on, shirttail half out, as cool as a

Popsicle from the ice cream truck. Despite the fact that I held my breath the entire flight waiting for the bottom to fall out, everyone had done remarkably well. Well, everyone except me.

I breathed a huge sigh of relief as the freezing air outside the terminal hit my face. I had gotten us a decidedly unstylish minivan with driver, but when we stepped outside, a familiar voice called, "Hey, baby cakes."

I looked over and squealed as Bunny lifted her oversized sunglasses with a red, lacquered nail. "What are you doing here?" I asked, noticing as I ran to her that my C-section pain had gone from broken bone to paper cut very quickly. Plus, much to my elation, the scar was low enough that it would be well hidden by even my teeniest bikinis.

"Oh my Lord, that man just gets more delicious, doesn't he?"

Graham leaned down to kiss Bunny on both cheeks. Bunny loved Graham almost as much as she loved Veuve Clicquot. Being from the city, I think she had this fantasy that Graham was like every sexy, strong Southern man she'd ever seen in a movie. As I looked at him, with Grace strapped to his chest, I realized that maybe he *was* like every sexy, strong Southern man she'd ever seen in a movie.

She stepped out of the limo, gave Alex a kiss on his hair, and peered at you and Grace. You were still breath-gaspingly asleep. Bunny tapped her manicured finger on her mouth and said, "Does it offend you if I say that Carolina is the only one who looks like you?"

I laughed. "Wait 'til she opens her eyes."

Grace had your daddy's light blond hair and crystal blue eyes, while Alex was a little clone of his late father. You, on the other hand, were me made over. Aqua eyes, brown hair. It was eerie how much you looked like me even though I didn't give birth to you. Of course, my recent bottle brunette job did help the cause. Bunny kissed me again and said, "Well, they're gorgeous. All three of them." Then she linked her arm through Graham's and said, "Your family is a little *Yours, Mine and Ours* rerun, isn't it?"

Graham looked over Bunny's head at me, which was quite a feat because she was one tall drink of water. He said, "Babydoll, where's our car?"

You started to gurgle, and Bunny said, "Don't be ridiculous. I paid your driver. You're riding with me, of course." Bunny shot a withering look at Graham and said, "So glad that you're *home,* Frances." Bunny may have loved Graham, but she would always blame him for taking me away from her.

I was sure he ignored the remark.

I texted Kristin, who was already at our apartment waiting like a sequined girl for her prom date.

Bunny handed Alex a Spider-Man cupcake, and he started bouncing up and down on the squishy seat in excitement. Grace began to cry, signifying that the two-hour-and-forty-five-minute food window was rapidly closing. Bunny grabbed you from me, and, much to my delighted surprise, you didn't even peep. You snatched one of her extensions in between your thumb and forefinger and said, "Dada. Dada."

We all laughed because Dada certainly didn't have hair like that. Over Grace's suckling noises, Bunny said, "So, in truth, I have a bit of a favor to ask."

I readjusted Grace and said, "If you want me to keep your three children too, the answer is no."

Bunny screwed up her glossy lips into a pout and said, "Oh, honey. I have people to do that. This is something serious."

Graham looked at me incredulously, but I winked at him. Bunny, in regard to her children, was a grade-school boy with a crush. She couldn't act like she was sensitive and sweet even though they were the loves of her life.

She said, "I know you're so jam-packed with activities—"

"But your three-year-old son is sleeping on a mattress on the floor in a room with billowy white, silk curtains and Peter Rabbit painted on the walls."

Bunny opened her mouth, but before she could speak, I said, "Check your e-mail, please."

On the plane, I had sent Bunny a list, complete with photos, for Zeke's bedroom redesign. It included an entire wall of tortoise-framed hunting dogs that were both childlike and mature, a pair of cane twin beds I'd found at auction, and Leontine duvets in a masculine monogram. Add the industrial-steel-and-leather toy chests for the end of the beds, the bleached-mahogany, eighteenth-century dresser, and a hanging rope chair, and it was a little boy's paradise.

"I didn't have a photo of the curtain fabric," I said, "but, trust me, it's perfection."

Bunny looked at Graham and said, "This woman raises your children and runs the world. She should be wearing more jewelry."

Graham nodded. "Believe you me, I know how awesome she is. That's why I spent thirty-two years trying to pin her down."

"You've only known me eighteen," I said, readjusting my shirt and lifting Grace up to kiss her drooping eyelids. She was no match for the motion of the car.

Graham winked at me. "But I spent the first fourteen dreaming about you."

Bunny nodded. "He's good, honey. He's good."

Bunny dropped us off at our apartment, and we parted with kisses and promises of playdates and Prosecco. I threw open the door to our apartment and, as usual, the best part of coming home was the light that flooded through the floor-to-ceiling windows. It might have been a superhuman effort to get there, but it really can't be said enough: I absolutely adore Manhattan.

Jodi

THE SAME PERSON

When you get to thinking 'bout it good, the only real tough part in canning is getting all the mess ready. Shuckin' the corn, stringin' the beans, snappin' them little peas right outta the pod. But me, I was born to work with my hands just like my daddy.

I knew it good as I know it now the day I got them college applications. It weren't that I wanted to go to school so that I could do something different. I knew right good that I wanted to spend my days in my kitchen filling up jars with love all the time I was writing them essays and calling Mrs. Petty, the high school guidance counselor, for transcripts. Graham, he said that maybe if I was thinking 'bout going to college I should go to culinary school, seeing as how I knew that cooking was what I wanted. But I already knew how to cook good as I knew how to breathe. It was a different kind of knowledge I was getting after.

Mrs. Petty, she'd tried getting me to go to that early college while I were still in high school. And I guess you could say I got to wishing I had done it. But my daddy, he was dyin'. And Marlene, she and me, we was gonna go to cosmetology school after we graduated. Turns out, we stunk worse than sauerkraut at cosmetology. We couldn't near do our own fingernails. So Marlene, she got to waitressing down at Andy's, and me, I was working at the garage.

Oh my Lord, Marlene was gonna be right hot I was going off to college and leavin' her. But I didn't tell no one save Buddy that I was thinking of applying. But even then, I weren't near believin' something like that could happen to a girl like me. My family, we was mechanics, farmers, cooks. Not learners.

"Until now," Mrs. Petty said. "You were always so bright, Jodi, and I had such high hopes for you." She slid a schedule with dates for the SAT listed on it real perky like across the shiny, fake wood desk with chips all on the corners and asked, "What do you think you might like to do?"

I shrugged. "Well, I was thinkin' I might like to major in business long as I still get to take other classes like English and science too."

Mrs. Petty nodded and said, "Are you going to want to live on campus?"

I hadn't thought about it, but it weren't a hard decision. I was gonna be home for you. Plus, I couldn't stomach the thoughts of sharing some pink polka-dot room with a sorority girl who covered the sink with curling irons and makeup.

"I've got a job I like, and my schedule's right flexible. I'd really like to do both."

Mrs. Petty, she was rustling around in the laminate credenza behind her desk when she turned and handed me a bright purple pamphlet like it were some sorta medal. I knew what that meant.

"ECU is probably your best bet because you can take most of your classes online, and the commute is only a half hour when you need to go in person."

She turned again, pushin' them half glasses down her nose, her blond curls getting all up in her eyes. I looked around the room. It was dingier than ever. The dark green chair fabric was all threadbare, and the college course catalogs, they looked even dustier. Mrs. Petty's head popped back up.

"Shew." She got to wiping her forehead, slid a pamphlet across the desk, and said, "Plus, with your grades, assuming you do okay on the SAT, we can probably get you some scholarships."

"Scholarships," I repeated.

Now it don't make one lick a' sense. But me, a girl who spent her whole damn life figuring how she's gonna have enough left over to eat, I hadn't given one thought to how I was gonna pay for college. That would be right near like Khaki designing somebody's house and forgetting to pick the furniture. I was getting up, realizin' college weren't something poor girls got to do. Just rich folks.

But Mrs. Petty, she was just jabbering on, "Yeah, between the scholarships and financial aid, if you have some place to live we could probably get you through ECU on a shoestring."

Even I got a shoestring. "All right, then. Go, Pirates!"

I thanked Mrs. Petty even though them flickering fluorescent lights had give me some sorta bad headache.

She called, "Don't forget to fill out those financial aid forms and bring them back to me!"

I weren't forgetting.

"I thought you had dreams a' going off to college and walking the campus and professors with bow ties," Buddy said, when we was just sitting there on a real slow, drizzly day at the Raleigh market. "You shouldn't just give all that up if it's what you really want."

I shrugged. I didn't do it often, but, just this once, I let myself look deep in his eyes, my stomach all flipping around and a wreck.

"I ain't gonna do it for real," I said. "I ain't the kind of girl that goes to college." I looked up at him again, and it was like my mouth just couldn't help itself. I had to say it. "Sometimes dreams change."

A momma with a baby perched right up on her hip was asking me if my pickles were fermented. Khaki, she told me people was all worried about their bacteria levels. Turns out, she was right.

After the lady paid, like he'd been thinking on it the whole time, Buddy said, "I'm real glad you told me." He paused. "Sometimes you cain't make a dream come true all by yourself."

Some people, they see picking vegetables from the garden as a chore. They get to complaining 'bout bending over and sore backs and dirty fingernails. They don't like the squattin' or kneelin' or diggin'. But me, I ain't like that one bit. Seeing something I planted months earlier grow is a miracle—don't matter how many times I done it. I get down there in the dirt, planting them seeds, and even I cain't believe something delicious is gonna come from 'em. But them little seeds, they sprout every dern time. And me, that's when I know God's up there working it all out for me.

My little garden, that's where I got to feeling right normal again after my trip to Palm Beach. And it's where I got to thinking hard 'bout my college dreams. I was real glad to get back to cooking and canning—and, you caught me, to Buddy. But the thought a' having to see my momma, it was like a rain cloud over the outdoor wedding I could just see me and Buddy having.

Khaki and Graham, they asked me to housesit, which were right funny seeing as how I hadn't left their house for weeks. I pulled down that long, tree-lined driveway, and I could just make out a truck at the end. My fingers and toes got all tingly and numb like. *Please be Buddy, please be Buddy.*

When I got closer I could make out that the truck was much older than Buddy's—and a whole hell of a lot dirtier. Buddy, he was right particular 'bout keeping his things clean and orderly. He were real appreciative of everything he had, and he kept it real nice.

But then I figured it. And my heart screeched to a stop like a front tire trying to miss a baby bunny. All that stringy gray hair that was way too long for her age—it were my momma's. It took damn near all I had in me not to turn around, back out of the driveway, and keep on drivin'. But my momma, she was waving at me like a kid picking up his daddy at the airport. That was the thing about my momma. When she got clean, she just expected all us to love her like nothing happened.

She got to running, hollering, "Oh, it's my baby girl! Oh, you're so gorgeous!"

"Hey, Momma," I said real quiet. If her hug was neon pink, mine weren't nothing more than taupe.

"I's looking for Graham," she said. "But this here's an even better surprise."

"I'm just grabbin' the mail." I said it real casual, not wanting her to know I was living here.

345

Me and my momma, we wouldn't never have dreamed of even walking in a place like this. "Graham, he won't be back for a few weeks. You can come on back then."

You didn't have to be real smart to figure it. I was as sure Momma was gonna ask Graham for money as I was that putting up lettuce don't work no way you do it. And she was just standing there, looking like it weren't nothing. This weren't her first visit.

She was waiting, them huge, nothing-stylish-about-'em glasses over the makeup all piled on her face. She was still wearing them faded-out old blue jeans with the up-high waist that made her look like she got a big poochy tummy, even though she weren't ninety pounds. I knew right well they was from a Goodwill rack. And I felt sad for her. Me, I may've been wandering around in Khaki's fancy hand-me-down coat and living in this big ole house and making me a living. But me and my momma, we was the same person way deep down inside. I got to choking on the fear that I would go back to that life, that being like my momma was something I couldn't escape. I had to get her outta here.

"So, I been dying to see you ever since we talked." She swallowed real loud. "Let me see your place."

"Momma, this ain't the best time." My voice was real rushed. And I was madder than hell. This is what she does. She ain't nowhere to be found for months and then she just shows up expecting me to forget whatever I got going on. She stole my childhood, ain't never helped me none, and she was just standin' there like we was best friends.

But then she got to lookin' sad, and, wouldn't you know it? I was the one that felt sorry. And I reckoned that she cain't help who she is when she's drinking. She's fighting real hard against that drink just like me.

Them tears got all pooled up in her eyes.

She'd got me again. "Well, maybe we can visit for a minute. But then I got to get back to work." I pointed down the gravel path toward the trailer, feeling that sick on my stomach that Ricky might be waiting for me.

"So what you been up to?" I asked Momma.

She shrugged. "Well, you know, I'm just trying to get back on my feet, trying to make ends meet off of disability, keep my car payment made, keep the trailer payment made, you know."

She was fishing, but I weren't bitin'. I had just got a few emergency dollars in the bank, and I weren't giving them up for nobody.

"Gosh, Momma. Maybe you should get a job."

I didn't look at her, but you just know she was real shocked by me mentioning something so crazy.

"You still down at the garage?" she said.

"No. I'm runnin' markets for Graham and Khaki,

and I've started me my own canning business on the side."

She got all smiley and happy. "Maybe I could help you with that! I don't need much, just a little to help me get through the month. And, I mean, it's gotta be cash so I don't lose my check. You understand what I'm sayin'."

Lord knows, even sober, I could never, ever trust my momma. So I was trying to change the subject when we got to the door. But I didn't need to, 'cause Momma did.

"This sure is fancy."

Momma was looking around, real impressed by all the designer stuff Khaki'd done in my trailer. If I had showed her where I was really living she probably woulda dropped her dentures. I always told her you couldn't drink on a empty stomach, especially when you was smoking all the time. But you cain't tell her nothin'. It pure ate them teeth up.

"The baby sleeping or somethin'?"

The baby. You. I shouldn't a' worried about what my momma would think. But I were real shaky all the same. Worse, Momma thought it was all right to leave a baby at home by herself.

"Then where is she?"

I bit my lip real hard, trying not to cry. "She's with her parents."

Momma crossed her arms. "What do you mean, her parents?"

"Carolina got adopted." I didn't want to cry in front a' Momma, but I couldn't help it. It was true. I had give you away. "I just couldn't do it all by myself. It was the right thing."

I thought Momma would scream and cuss and get all crazy. But she shocked the pickled okra out of me, her chin quivering and her eyes puddling. Under that gin-soaked skin, a heart was beatin' after all. She put her head in her hands and said, "If I'd a' been there, if I coulda helped, we might coulda been a family."

I felt that sadness creeping in again, the one that makes your body weigh a million pounds, the one that keeps you from getting outta bed. It coulda been different. Momma, if she'd been sober, and she'd a' helped me out and wrapped you up tight, maybe we coulda got through. Maybe I wouldn't have felt like drinking again so hard. Maybe I coulda done it.

But then Momma, she said, "All of us."

I squinted real hard. "All a' who?"

"You, me, Carolina, and Ricky."

"Momma," I said, "Ricky's always been a no-good son of a bitch. You cain't be family no more once somebody's tried to kill you."

All she said was, "Ricky wants you back."

It were like one of them digital billboards had switched. All my being grown and a woman and smart went out and a silly girl come back. That silly girl I'd been when I agreed to movin' in with him, when I didn't ignore how sorry he was, when I didn't worry 'bout having a baby with him.

But then I thought a' Buddy, my stomach flipping right over. And it weren't just because he was so handsome. He was sweet and good and kind and strong. He was the kind of man that don't just walk away when things get tough. I shook my head at Momma. She might've tried her whole life to keep it from happening, but looking into them dark circles under her eyes, I got to realizin' it: I deserved better.

Khaki

ENOUGH PROBLEMS

When you spend your days surrounded by wallpaper books and fabric swatches like I do, creativity-boosting music flooding the room, it's easy to get lost in a daydream. Sometimes in those spurts I feel like giving everything away, quitting my job, and finding a moment of peace with my husband and my children. I can picture myself in the midst of an open field, sitting and reflecting, or hiking by a beautiful mountain stream. I dream of something simpler, free from the burdens and restrictions, the travel and stress, the frivolity of so many of the things that make this life what it is.

I think it's normal to daydream about a different

life, but it seemed like those fantasies of spending my days surrounded by my children, not missing a single moment, were happening more and more often, making me wonder if that really was what I wanted.

Of course, I'd be lying if I didn't say that I felt more confident walking into an important meeting in a killer Manolo pump. And, while sometimes I hate Scott for that, I mostly love him for teaching me that while things don't define me, sometimes they can make me feel taller, wiser, and more confident.

I could only imagine what he and Clive must have been feeling standing underneath an arch of flowers pledging their lives to each other in matching, custom Armani tuxes. I've always cried at weddings, but I think now that I've been through two myself the tears flow harder. For one, they are a reminder of the first man I pledged to love forever who went on before me. For two, they make me realize how incredibly blessed I am to have finally ended up with the boy who made me feel like I could do and be anyone, even my crazy, dichotomous, mind-changing-every-two-seconds self. I realized as I laid my head on my husband's wide shoulder, wiping my eyes, that, while it wasn't realistic to give away all my worldly possessions and spend my life sitting in a field of hay, it was realistic to pare down as much as possible.

I'd already decided to sell the store, and, while I firmly believe that volunteering is a nice thing to do, it's not necessary to be in charge of every organization in town. I promised myself I would write several resignation letters when I got home. Every hour I was away was another hour of my children's lives that I was missing out on.

For me, happiness has always been about a mix of things, not just one, and this was perhaps the hardest time I had ever had finding a balance, listening to my heart and blocking out the outside forces. But I think being able to carve your own path is a part of growing up. It's being able to say to the world, "My family comes first," without needing to apologize for it.

In the midst of Clive's handwritten vows, Graham leaned over and whispered, "I was embarrassed to tell you before, but this is my first . . ." He paused. "This is my first wedding where it isn't a man and a woman."

I smiled. "Why'd you say it like that?"

He shrugged. "I hate the term *gay wedding*. With the over-the-top flowers, gourmet food, and party music, aren't they all a little gay?"

I put my hand over my mouth to keep from laughing out loud. Scott turned his head at that exact moment, which set me off all over again, and I got tickled. Once that happens, there's no turning back. I removed a hanky from the clutch Scott had picked for me for the occasion and tried to pass off my shoulders, heaving with laughter, as sobs of happiness for the gorgeous moment where my two friends were pronounced married.

Scott winked at me on his way down the aisle, and I stood to clap with the thirty or so other family members who were there to witness one of the most important days of my friend's life. "They are so fantastic," I said to Graham. "You should see how hard a time they're having getting a baby."

"They'd be killer parents."

I raised my eyebrow. "Maybe don't put that line in your letter of recommendation to the adoption agency."

We both laughed and then, with my straightest face, I said, "So, I hope it's okay with you, but I think I'm going to be their surrogate."

I felt a little mean when I saw how ashen Graham's face got.

I laughed, and the color returned to his face. He bumped my hip with his. "That was not funny."

After champagne and dancing and cake and flowers galore, we were tucked in tight, underneath the covers. "Isn't it strange," I said, "how I can feel so perfectly myself in a field in Kinston wearing an old pair of Levi's and a T-shirt and then turn around and feel just right in the Waldorf in a Robert Rodriguez gown?"

Graham kissed me. I struggled so much with those opposing sides of my personality, wondering which one of those people I should be, how I was going to pick whether I wanted to be the farm girl or the city woman. Graham must have known what I was thinking because he said, "It's okay for you to be both, you know. It's actually one of my favorite things about you.

Sometimes in the rush of life and hectic schedules of children, I forget to really look at my husband, to see the kind lines of his face and the tight, broad shoulders. It felt far away sometimes, that moment when he told me he loved me again, that instant that I knew he had called off his wedding and the lead vest that I had been wearing sank to the bottom of the river. I would be lying if I said there weren't times when I wished that I could feel that splash-of-soda, first-days-of-love feeling all the time. The good thing, though, was that in the quiet moments like this, when I really saw the man I had married, I got that stomach-flip feeling all over again. And it was magic.

People always talk about having a creative outlet, and for years I was jealous that I didn't have one. Bunny would always say, "Don't have a creative outlet? You're a *designer*. What's more creative than that?" But I didn't feel like I was *creating* anything. A writer creates a story, a painter creates a painting, a musician creates a song. But I guess designing was so second nature to me that I always felt like I was taking other people's creations and buying them for people too busy to do it themselves.

It took me years to realize that not everyone is blessed with the ability to layer nine patterns in a room and have it come off looking relaxing and cohesive. But now, thanks to Charlie, I know. She always insisted that I was a visionary, and I always told her how ridiculous that was. If she had time to get fabric swatches and pick out furniture, she could decorate as well as I could.

So she put my theory to the test. I did every room in her house in California except one, a particularly easy one, I thought. She was in charge of furnishing one guest bedroom. That was all.

Roughly the third week of our challenge, she called me and said, "You know, Khak, you might be right. I think I'm pretty good at this decorating stuff after all."

I was a little disappointed that my theory was going to be proven true: Anyone could do my job.

Charlie had kept her guest room sealed off from prying eyes, so Greg and I had the pleasure of seeing it for the first time together. Greg isn't one to get overly involved in the material, so I didn't think he would care one way or the other what the room looked like. But when the door swung open and he exclaimed, "What happened?" my horror melted into a fit of giggles.

Charlie's face fell, and she said, "What? You don't like it?"

A black laminate bedroom set that looked like it belonged in a Vegas nightclub was the least of our worries. An overstuffed, black leather recliner was overwhelming the corner like a big-and-tall man in a coach seat, and the bed was dressed in a burgundy-and-purple flowered bedspread. A desk lamp that must have come from Staples was the only thing on the massive dresser, which was so oversized the closet door wouldn't open, and on one of the nightstands was a faux flower arrangement that perfectly matched that bedspread.

I was trying to compose myself, but the flowers set me off again. "Where, sweetheart, did you possibly get those flowers?"

Charlie leaned into Greg, who rubbed her back supportively. She finally decided to laugh herself. "I went to a class."

I whipped out my cell phone like a head stylist with his scissors and began dialing. "Who are you calling?" Charlie asked, panic filling her voice.

"The Salvation Army, who else?"

Greg grabbed the phone and hung up.

"What the hell did you do that for?" I asked. "You couldn't possibly want to live with this stuff."

Greg looked at me incredulously, and I thought a lecture about hurting his wife's feelings was coming on. Instead he said, "Fran, don't you think those people have enough problems?"

We all doubled over in laughter like a bachelorette party recapping the night after too many Pink Panty Pull-Downs. Charlie shut the door and brushed her hands together. She looked at me helplessly and said, "Well, on the bright side, we've learned that you are even more talented than we formerly believed."

I put my hands up over my eyes, trying to block out the horror of what I had just seen as if it were a dead body, not a display of truly terrible taste.

All I knew was that it was a good thing I was coming home to design Charlie and Greg's new home for them so as not to have to replicate that scene. I had been sad to leave New York, but with the store in capable hands, my design work was all I needed to focus on. And my A-number-one priority was in Kinston. It only made sense for us to come home for the holidays.

I was sharing that story about Charlie's design disaster with Jodi when we got back from New York. We were planning our Thanksgiving menu, and she was teaching me one of her new winter canning recipes. She looked terrible, like she hadn't slept since we had been gone, and I thought the story might cheer her up. When the laughter stopped, Jodi said, "Khaki, I gotta talk to you for a minute."

My heart stopped beating, and I could feel the blood drain from my face, my spoon practically stuck to the pot where I'd been stirring. My mind started racing, and I wondered how I could have been so stupid. I had known better than to let her get too close to you.

But then I looked into Jodi's eyes. I studied her sweet, honest face, and my heart rate returned to normal. And I think I finally realized that Graham had been right about your birth mother all the time. She had known what she was doing when she gave you to us. It wasn't a rash decision. And she wasn't going to change her mind.

This could be a talk about anything. Boyfriends. Ricky. Restraining orders. Maybe I was wearing the wrong bra size, and she was nervous about hurting my feelings. But whatever she wanted to talk about, she wasn't trying to take you back.

Jodi said, "I know I said you and Graham was the ones doing Carolina's raisin', and I was gonna stay out of it." She paused. "I mean, I'm real glad she's got to spend this time with y'all, and I ain't trying to make you upset or nothing. I want Carolina to have a real good life. But I don't want her all spoiled rotten and having Gucci bags and mess." Jodi leaned on the island, a little closer to me, and said, "I mean, how you do her raisin' is up to you, but I just had to say something."

How I raise her is up to me. Me. And Graham, of course. I was so relieved I kissed Jodi, this girl who had helped create my family. And, in that moment, I quit being so afraid. "Honey," I said, "I promise I won't spoil her rotten. I bought her that bag way back when she was born, to celebrate my new book. It was insane and I won't do it again." And then I added, "And, no matter what, you will always be her birth mother. Your opinion will always count."

Then I turned, walked upstairs, bolted into your room, and did the unthinkable: I woke a sleeping baby. But, just like your birth momma, instead of crying and carrying on, you greeted me with a smile and a "Ma-ma."

I sat down in the upholstered glider in the corner of your room and said, "That's right. I am your momma. Me. And I'm always going to get to be. Because you're my little girl." Then I whispered, "And no one is ever going to take you away from me."

You smiled again and rested your head on my chest, twirling my hair around your finger. I should have been upstairs working, pulling together the last elements of Charlie and Greg's design scheme. I should have been ordering bolts of fabric and finalizing rug measurements. But instead, I sat there and rocked you until you fell back asleep. And, as you breathed in and out, I realized that it was the first time I had watched you sleep that the pure joy and love of seeing your child at her most peaceful hadn't been laced with fear. And, for that fleeting moment, the world made perfect sense.

Jodi

FAMILY

There ain't many things so exciting as seeing your fancy own sign, all hanging proud and permanent over the awning at the farmer's market. It weren't just *Jacobs Family Farms* no more. Right underneath, in professionally painted plywood, it was *Jodi's Cans and Jams* too. I don't think Graham'll ever get how choked up I was over him getting me that sign, how, in that moment, it felt like my life was changing for the good. I had *done* something. And couldn't nobody take that back.

When I was a kid, weren't nothing so exciting as the first day a' school. I got to see where my seat was, if there were any new kids. That fresh-paper smell was everywhere, and I got to get new glue, no dried-up globs or old glitter all stuck on the top.

Me and Daddy, the minute the school people sent out the list, we'd be at the Walmart, picking out new pencils and folders and crayons. It was my favorite thing in the whole world. Well, except that year I was going into second grade and Daddy was working all the time and Momma had to take me shopping. Daddy, he thought Momma was cleaned up. But I knew better. She was

360

sneaking sips here and there, hiding airplane bottles in her socks and wine boxes in the roastin' pan in the oven. Lord knows she weren't cooking with it.

I was excited all the same. I climbed in the back of her Oldsmobile, that cracking leather burning the back a' my legs, them swinging 'cause they didn't near touch the floor. I got all buckled in like Daddy told me I oughta even though that silver buckle was damn near hot as a pizza oven. Momma pulled up to the ABC store, and I was getting so excited them legs was going. Daddy and me, we didn't go to the ABC store, but it made all kinds of sense that's where you'd buy school supplies.

Momma said, "You stay here and don't talk to strangers."

"But, Momma, I want to come in. Daddy lets me pick the colors of my notebooks and get the fancy pencils."

She laughed real mean, and the sting of them hurt feelings, that won't never leave me. She slammed the door right hard and walked in, leaving me to sweat in the humidity with the window rolled down.

Until the day I die, I won't never live down the shame of walking into that classroom. All them kids organizing their shiny schoolboxes and sharp pencils in their desks. Me, I didn't have nothin'. Daddy, he found out quick what Momma done.

"I promise I'll take you to get school supplies soon as work lets out tonight, baby girl," he said.

But it was too late. That first day I didn't have so much as an old eraser. My face was so hot you'd have needed an oven mitt to touch it. I walked real quiet to the desk with my cheerful name tag on it, not wanting nobody to see me, to make fun a' me for coming to school with nothing. Them fat tears was coming down my cheeks.

"It's okay," the teacher said, rubbin' my back. "Your momma will be back for you before you know it."

That's why I'm crying. I didn't care if I ever saw my momma again. She'd disgraced me in the worst way for a seven-year-old.

I got real busy remindin' myself about that seven-year-old girl that day when I knew my momma was coming to visit. I knew it weren't smart for me to be around her. It was just too tempting to take you and your birth daddy back. But she was itching red hot to see me, and I was plum outta excuses why I couldn't. At the end a' the day, that woman, she's my momma. And just 'cause she birthed me and probably did the best she could, she should get to see me. Though, Lord knows, her best was damn near a natural disaster.

But this time, I was smart. This time, she wasn't gonna fool me. Weren't no way I was gonna start loving and trusting her again just for her to damn near kill me by lettin' me down again.

I was just sitting there in my chair out front of the trailer, scraping a spot of dirt outta the plastic ridge with my fingernail, trying to keep from getting all worked up. It weren't long 'til I heard a old car bumping down the gravel path, dust jumping all out from everywhere making me hold my breath. You could see right off it weren't just Momma in the car. *Probably some new, useless boyfriend she got.*

But when he started getting outta the car, I reckoned that man was useless. But he weren't a boyfriend. It was Ricky.

It was that day in second grade all over. Momma'd tricked me again. I don't know where on God's earth I thought I was running to, but I was near to the woods 'fore I heard Momma yelling, "Don't run away, Jodi. Ricky's changed."

Changed. There was that word again. I'd been around twenty years. Only thing I knew of that could really be changed was a dollar bill.

I weren't trying to listen. But ain't nobody in the county that didn't hear Ricky scream, "I've found Jesus." He was running behind me, and weren't no way I could get away. That Ricky, he was too fast.

"Please, Jodi. We can get Carolina back. We can all be the family we've dreamed about."

It stopped me cold in my tracks, that sentence. The VCR in my brain rewound the tape of my life with Ricky. All them fantasies I had, that white house with the red tin roof, my own field, room for my babies to play, they weren't never gonna happen. But a girl with a heart all full a' dreams, she can pin them on darn near any man, no matter how sorry. And Ricky, he was always gonna say the right thing and do the wrong one.

When we was together, I hadn't seen no good examples of family or love. But now I knew what it was all about. Leaving your girlfriend when she's good and pregnant and needs you most, not even trying to clean yourself up and change for your youngen, coming back and wanting to do the right thing when it was too late . . . Them things weren't love. And they sure as hell weren't family. So I spun around on my heel real quick and glared at them.

"We done looked into it," Momma said. "We got us a lawyer. We can get Carolina back. It ain't too late."

"What do you mean, get Carolina back? Ain't no way we can get her back. We give her to Khaki and Graham, we signed all them papers."

"Yeah," Ricky said, smiling right broad. "But the lawyers said there's some kind a' mistake."

I shook my head. "You cain't tell me that Khaki Mason didn't make for damn sure that them papers I signed was all letter perfect and *i*-dotted."

Ricky smiled again, moving closer, trying to take my hand. I pulled it away. "Yours had every last *t* crossed. That's for damn sure."

"But Ricky's," Momma chimed in, "them ones

that they did back before the adoption. They ain't quite right."

I looked at Ricky and then at Momma, then back at Ricky again. It were so tempting to get you back. And Ricky *was* right with the Lord now. He was looking at me so earnest, and Momma, she was talking so sweet, they coulda roped me right on into their scheming.

Ricky smiled at me again, real reassuring like. "That lawyer, he said judges are real keen on babies being with their birth parents."

"Yeah," Momma said. "They said that little mistake'll probably do it. But if you just get up there and say that you wasn't right in the head on account a' your drinking—"

She snapped her fingers. "Then we'll get Carolina back no problem at all."

It was all a lot to take in. That pain and heartbreak that a momma feels when she gets apart from her baby. The way that voice creeps in telling you you done the wrong thing, that you shoulda stuck it out, it woulda got easier, you coulda done it and you can do it now. It made me want to smile and take Ricky's hand and skip on down to that lawyer's office and tell a little white lie up on that stand.

But then I thought about you. My sweet little Carolina. You were happy. And it was 'cause you were loved and stable. I could dream in a weak moment that I could give that to you, that me and

365

Momma and Ricky could all get saved and clean and all that. But Momma and Ricky, they lied to me one too many times.

"We could be a family," Ricky said, trying to take my hand.

And when I looked at him again, I finally saw clear. I got to remembering why we was in this mess in the first place, why I got so low, why I felt like I couldn't take no more, how all alone in the world you and me were 'til Khaki and Graham loved us back to being whole. I ripped my hand away, like a green stem from a carrot. "Let me tell you 'bout family," I hollered. "Family is there for each other. Family supports each other and loves each other and makes them hard decisions easy. Family don't take the easy way out."

Ricky and Momma, they looked all shocked and shaken. But them words reaffirmed in me like the Nicene Creed in church that I had done a good thing by letting you go. It hurt like an appendectomy with no anesthesia. But it was right.

Ricky, he was getting all mad, and I knew he might kill me. But it didn't matter none. I was gonna be free a' him if it was getting to Jesus that did it.

"You just walked right out on me, you bastard!" I said real low and mean at Ricky. "You took away my childhood and my child, so don't you come back here now saying we can be family." Then I hollered at the top of my lungs, "We won't never be family!"

Ricky lunged at me, and I could feel them hands wrapping 'round my throat. Everything, it got all still and quiet. He wasn't really squeezing or nothing. I was just faintin' like normal when things got tough.

Momma, you could hear her screaming at Ricky to stop. But I couldn't really make out nothin' but the cock of a pistol. And I knew my time here was done. And I thought a' your sweet, sweet face.

But Ricky's hands, they loosened right up and my body fell to the ground. Somebody was sayin', "What part of *restraining order* don't you understand?"

Next thing I remember, Buddy, he was stroking my hair, my head in his lap, and saying, "You're gonna be just fine. It's gonna be all right."

The old me, I woulda cried and carried on, feeling trapped right like a raccoon in an animal control pen. The new me, she had choices.

"Buddy, I gotta get out of here," I whispered. It musta been the lack a' oxygen that give me the courage, but I heard myself saying, "Buddy, I'm such a wreck. You need to stay far, far away from me." I closed my eyes for a second and said, "How could you still like me after what I done?"

Buddy shrugged and smiled down at me. "My grandmomma, she used to tell me that I would find one woman that I would always keep loving and worshipping the ground she walked on—don't matter what she did."

Surely he wasn't saying that woman were me. "Only one woman?"

He nodded. "There's plenty a' women a man could make a life with and be happy with. But only one he's gonna be so taken with that he thinks she cain't do no wrong. And she said I oughta keep looking 'til I find that girl."

I got to thinkin' on that look Buddy give me, that one that made me feel right smart and pretty.

"Only one," I repeated. "No wonder you're so afraid of being alone forever."

He put his hand on my cheek real gentle. "Oh, I ain't afraid of that anymore."

And you're not gonna believe this. I wasn't afraid anymore either.

When you plant them seeds in the ground, you got to believe that they're gonna sprout right up. If you just know real deep in your heart that they're gonna grow into somethin' amazing, that's half the battle. Khaki, she says all the rest a' life is like that too. She says I learned how to open up and believe in good things. And they came right to me.

Maybe.

All I know is, on the same day Ricky got locked up for violating his restraining order and resisting arrest, that letter, it come from ECU. Mrs. Petty, she got some friend up in the admissions office that worked right hard on getting me in and all ready for the spring semester. And I was real proud. But I was also real sad because weren't no way I could afford to get outta here and go. I was so close to escaping Momma and Ricky and all my mistakes I could damn near taste it. But math, it don't lie. My scholarships would cover half. My canning and going to the markets, they'd get me through another fourth after I paid my living expenses. But that left a big ole chunk, a hole I didn't have no way to fill up. Didn't make no sense to come outta school with all sorts a' loans when you'd be doing the same job either way.

So I was gonna go online. It were right much cheaper. I could stay at Graham and Khaki's, keep you and Alex and Grace and pay my own way.

I am going to get an education. I was trying to be real positive. Girls like me, we didn't get that kind of opportunity all too often.

But I found myself looking up to heaven anyhow. You know, just in case. "Lord, if you find it fit, I sure would like to get outta here and go to college."

Graham and Khaki, they'd have paid my way. But I wouldn't let 'em. Ain't no way.

I got to breathing in all that fresh, freezing air on my way to the mailbox, feeling right selfish for wanting more and not counting my blessings. I sat on the curb, real sprawled out with the mail all over tarnation.

Right there, in the stack, was a big manila envelope addressed to me. I held it away, all scared, like a postal worker in an anthrax scare. I weren't real sure I wanted to know what was in that package. ECU, they couldn't just take back my acceptance letter, could they? I breathed in real deep, ripped the top open, and there it was. The answer to my prayer, the best early Christmas present a girl could imagine. Right there was a big, thick contract for my cookbook. I unfolded a note from Patrick that said, *You're the only woman in the developed world who doesn't have e-mail. The entire board loves the cookbook. We'd like to publish it. Congrats! Two more of these checks will be coming—one when we finish the edits and one when the book comes out. Royalty information is enclosed. P.S. If we're going to work together you have to get an e-mail account!!*

I flipped over that other thin, narrow piece of paper. It had my name on it right there in black ink. I got to gaspin' and feeling like I might pass out right on the curb. It was three thousand dollars. And I was gonna get two more a' them checks too.

Ask and ye shall receive. It'd been that easy. The advance check that Patrick weren't even sure I'd get had arrived. And so had I.

I cain't tell you how long I sat on that curb, bathing in the light of the sun, the way it warms you right through the cold, my eyes burnin' a hole in that check I stared at it so hard. I ain't never got one check that big in my entire life. It musta got to be five o'clock because Buddy drove by in that big, old diesel truck, honking the horn and rolling down the window. He put her into park. You could just leave your truck in the middle of the street because nobody ever came down the road anyhow.

"Whatcha doing there, girly?" he asked. He threw out the sprig of Lord only knows what that he'd plucked from the field and been chewing on.

I looked up at him real serious.

Then I whispered, "I asked God to help me go to college. He put this right in the mail." I stood up and showed him my check.

Buddy whistled. But you could tell somethin' in his face, it had changed. It were like the teeny shift in the color of a green bean that lets you know it's been preserved. He turned to look at me, putting his hands on my shoulders, real dangerous like he might kiss me or something. But he just said, "Oh, Jodi. I'm so proud of you."

Then I did something I ain't never done sober. I stood on my tiptoes, threw my arms around Buddy's neck, and kissed him right on the lips. And it wasn't like a first kiss, neither. None a' that awkwardness of whose lips go where and clankin' teeth. It was like that amazing second kiss, deep and slow and real passionate. I cain't tell you exactly how long it lasted, but it weren't like any kiss I'd ever had. It felt pure and sweet coming off his lips. It were right near, something like, well, love.

I give his hands a real tight squeeze, then I let go and started backing away toward the house.

"Hey, wait," Buddy said. "Do you think—" He stuffed his hands in the pockets of his blue jeans and looked down at his boots, real fidgety. "Do you think I could maybe take you to dinner sometime once you get all settled in?"

Buddy, he was as nervous as a preschooler on his first day. But me, I was calm, cool, and collected. I put my hands in my back pockets. I had to bite my lip to keep the smile from ripping my face clean in two. "I think I'd like that."

Then I turned real quick. And I got to tell you, baby girl, it's one of the best damn feelings in the world to have a man watch you walk away and know, deep in your heart, that he'd never let you wander too far.

Khaki

SYNCHRONICITY

My boss, Anna, is always letting a younger associate pick paint colors or find a white linen for a couch. But I've never been too good at trusting anyone but myself.

Standing in Charlie and Greg's yard that afternoon, on a scarily warm January day, everyone lightheartedly crediting global warming, your birth momma squeezed my hand and said, "Can you believe she's one?" And I realized that everything I had been through over the past several years had been an exercise in trust. Trusting God, trusting Graham, trusting Jodi. And, though it hadn't seemed like it at the time, it had been exactly what I needed.

I looked over at my sister, her fiancé Fletcher, and her Hershey's Kiss–sized diamond. She had announced her engagement to the entire family earlier that day, all of us gathered at Charlie and Greg's gorgeously remodeled home celebrating two other marvelous events: your first birthday and your birth mother's official send-off to college. Anyone who could count could realize that it was way past your birthday. We made the excuse that we were traveling and that we didn't want your birthday to get lost in the holiday celebrations. But the truth of the matter was, after the wrapping paper was cleared and the champagne drunk, this day, for your daddy and me, was a celebration that the dreaded statute of limitations year had passed. Come addiction claims or petitions for reversal or pleas of insanity, for the rest of our lives, no one could argue that you were our little girl.

Scott, Clive, Stacey, Joe, Bunny, and even Daniel had flown in for the occasion, to watch you, in your hand-smocked bubble with the birthday cakes, blow out that teeny candle and smash those gorgeous fingers into a mound of icing. You giggled, so did we, and, in that moment, standing between Graham and Daddy, watching Pauline and Benny fret over the birthday girl, I knew that everything I'd ever been through in my life, every heartbreaking event, bad decision, impenetrable loss had led to this one moment. I had my family and my health, and, in reality, that was all a girl could ask for.

Graham's arm appeared around my waist as if from nowhere, and he kissed my forehead. "Another one of our babies is already one."

I could feel the tears springing to my eyes. I laid my head on his shoulder. "Where does the time go?" I whispered. I felt that familiar longing to be with my babies every second, to not let a moment pass. "When I close my eyes I feel like I just met you, lost in the fields, on the way to that pool party." I lifted my head to kiss my husband's lips and heard Scott say, "Okay, guys. This is getting out of hand. Five more minutes, and you're going to look like Stacey again."

"Five minutes?" Graham asked. "Dude, give me a little credit."

Everyone laughed, and I looked over at my friend, her five-months-pregnant belly roughly the same size as her husband Joe's. Stacey was, without a doubt, the most beautiful pregnant woman I had ever seen. She was the woman that "pregnant glow" was named for. Maybe it was all the yoga and green juice, but she was most in her element, most alive when she was pregnant. I shrugged. "Now that Anna bought the store, I do have a little more time on my hands."

Graham winked at me, and Scott interrupted. "Since this is a day of grand celebration, we have a little news of our own."

Clive and Scott smiled at one another and Clive said, pointing to Scott, "One of us is going to be a stay-at-home dad in a few weeks!"

I gasped, feeling, I'll admit to you, a little panicked. Scott had picked out everything I'd worn for the past decade. But, of course, I was thrilled for them. "Details!"

Scott smiled. "Clive was going on and on about a documentary about Ethiopian orphanages he saw, and I looked into it. Very, very long, convoluted, emotional story short, there's a little girl there waiting for us to pick her up."

Stacey, with her hand on her belly, said, "I'll warn you, when you get there and see all those children, you'll want to bring about a dozen more home with you."

"Please, God, don't bring one to us," Graham said, and everyone laughed.

But then he turned to me and raised his eyebrows. I shrugged. We'd played around with the idea of adopting again.

Jodi's friend Marlene appeared at my side and whispered, "Thanks so much for the donation."

I smiled, even though it irritated me that she was always trying to steal my husband. Not that I felt threatened in the least, but still. It was the principle. I might not have been on board with Marlene, but what I was on board with was her new job at the pregnancy crisis management center. She wasn't too good at selling tangibles, but, after she convinced your birth mother to have you, Marlene realized that she'd finally found her calling. I put my arm around her—she was harmless, after all—and said, "Those girls are lucky to have you." And I meant it.

Jodi appeared through the back door and said, "Well, guys, I hate to leave the party, but I think I better get going."

She had driven back and forth to Greenville for her first few classes that semester so she could tie up some loose ends on the farm before she moved. Secretly, I hoped that she would be content with commuting and would change her mind about leaving us. But no such luck.

We had packed all of Jodi's things from her room upstairs into the old camp trunks Mother still had in her attic. That room that had been so full of Jodi's warmth and love felt so cold and empty now. And she'd sold that trailer—and its bad memories—to one of Graham's farmhands to help cover the last of her tuition. That little patch of land that had been her home for a short while was back to just a patch—but that row of red flowers would still come up every spring, waving in the breeze, an unlikely memorial. That square of land, the one Graham couldn't get a thing to grow on had, in the end, grown the most important thing of all: you.

I could feel the tears springing to my eyes yet again, realizing that I wasn't going to see Jodi every morning at the breakfast table in her pajamas and socks. I wanted to say so many things, but, to avoid looking like a total spaz at my child's birthday party, all I said was, "Are you sure you don't want us to drive you?"

Jodi shaded her eyes and said, "Buddy will get me all moved in just fine."

I tried to imagine Jodi, so wise and unnecessarily seasoned, moving into a dorm room with some spoiled eighteen-year-old who had no idea how the real world worked. When Jodi kissed you good-bye, I swear it was like the day she told us we could adopt you all over again. It damn near ripped my heart out to watch her walk away. I gave her a hard hug and kiss standing outside the running truck. "Come on now, Khaki," Buddy said. "Don't get yourself all worked up. She's only a half hour away."

"I know," I said, wiping my eyes. "I just love her, is all."

Jodi squeezed me again, looked deep into my

eyes, and said, "I'm gonna say this real quick so it all comes out without too much carrying on." She smiled. "I know you're barely older than me, but I swear you've been the momma I never had."

I could feel the tears running down my cheeks because I was so happy that Jodi was finally getting a chance that she deserved. I *was* a little like a proud momma. She put her hands on my shoulders and said, "I don't know how you do what you do, but I hope and pray that one day I can be half the woman you are."

She cleared her throat and pointed back up at the house. "You and Graham, you coulda just took Carolina and walked away. But you didn't. You made me a part of a real family. And, even better, you did that for Carolina. And there ain't nothing that will ever in my whole life mean more than that." She gave me a real quick, hard hug, and, the tears finally escaping from her eyes, said, "And that's why it's so dern hard to leave."

Needless to say, I was a mess at that point. So I blew her a kiss, slammed the door, and did my sobbing on the way back up to Charlie's. She met me at the door with a hug and said, "I don't want to be around when one of your kids goes off to college."

I shook my head. "They aren't going. They're going to live with me forever."

"Oh, okay," she said. Then she added, "Khak, this house is absolutely resplendent."

I took a moment to admire the massive silver orb in the entrance hall. The few modern touches in the classic home—the contemporary lighting, the abstract art, an unexpected accessory here and there—were what transformed it from Graham's momma to Charlie and Greg. It was my greatest decorating masterpiece to date. But then again, I say that about all my projects. And thank goodness. Who would want to work at anything if they didn't keep getting better as they went along?

"Frances," a shrill Bunny shouted through the entrance hall. "Now that I've been here, I don't think you really applied yourself on my penthouse. I think we need to remodel."

I sighed and flopped dramatically into a reproduction spindle chair that could take the sudden thud. I thought about the hours upon hours upon hours I had spent not a year ago finishing Bunny's new town house. "You asked for glamour and mirrors and chandeliers," I said. "This place has more of a hunty, farmy, rustic air to it."

Bunny crossed her arms. "So what you're saying is that we need a country house?"

I put my finger up. "No, I . . ." But before I could say anything she was off, yelling, "Honey!"

I shook my head. "He's going to be thrilled with me."

Graham came in and handed you to me, saying, "She's doing something with her hands, but I don't know what."

You were signing almost violently for straw-berries. "She just wants strawberries," I said to your daddy like he was dense.

He nodded. "Honey, I think it's great for you to teach the kids sign language. But if you don't teach it to me too, it doesn't do a lot of good." Then he added, "I guess it's a good thing Jodi talked me into that hothouse. No way I could keep you girls in fruit all year round without it."

Charlie and your daddy left to rustle up some strawberries for the birthday girl, and you leaned your head on my chest snuggling up so close I could smell the icing on your breath. I took a mental Polaroid, savoring each second of this sweet, unlikely time alone like it was a long-awaited apology from a slow-to-concede friend.

You sat up, gave me your biggest, goofiest grin, and signed "I love you," laying your head back down on my chest.

I kissed the sweet top of that head and said, "Oh baby girl, I love you too." I rested my cheek on yours and said, "You can't even imagine."

It was so easy and so right that I couldn't conceive of what I had ever done without it. I think it was that moment that gave me the strength to let go. To let go of Alex's biological daddy. To let go of the life I had with him. To let go of New York. And I think it's the most shocked I've ever seen your daddy when he walked out of the kitchen with that plate of strawberries, and I said, "Let's sell the New York apartment."

It struck me, the synchronicity of that moment, Jodi leaving Kinston for the first time, and me, after years of feeling torn in half, living a life in two different worlds, finally feeling like it was right to say that I wanted to come back home.

Graham licked the strawberry juice from his finger, squatted down in front of us in the chair, and said, "Are you sure about this, babydoll? You love New York."

I smiled and shook my head. "No. I love my children. I love you." I shrugged. "Besides, we can still visit all the time. It looks like Bunny's getting a country house, so there will be plenty of room for all of us."

Graham smiled and squeezed my shoulder. "So you know you'll have at least one more New York design project. And, for what we were spending on that apartment, we can travel there in high style whenever you want."

I nodded. "I think all of this other stuff—the store, the books, the magazine articles, the rushing and pushing to be better and bigger—has gotten in the way of the pure love of the designing." I thought about that open field and Graham and the kids again and shrugged. "I just want to get back to being that girl with her sketchbook and her swatches. Back to basics."

I think in that instant I grew up and settled down all at once. It was like I had handed Jodi my wings when she walked out the door and, finally, after all this time, I couldn't have been happier to be grounded.

Jodi

BOOKENDS

I always get real nervous 'bout preparing seeds for plantin' and plowin' the dirt after a crop. That's 'cause I ain't never been too good at beginnings or endings. That's why it all made a lotta sense that your momma was the first person to hold you in the hospital. And that's why I couldn't tell you good-bye when I said your momma and daddy could adopt you. I don't never know the right things to do or say. And I always get to thinking on what shoulda been different. So, between you and me, I stick with the middle. Once you're in the middle, it's nice and comfortable. The butterflies of the beginning are over but you ain't had all them tears at the end.

But even the middle ain't without its heartache. I'm getting to know that right good. Sometimes my visits with you make my heart sing and spill over with joy. But sometimes they near rip that same heart in two. And I cain't figure how I could ever have give you up.

Them days I think it was harder the way I did it, giving you up after I had you for a while. I start thinking it woulda been easier if I never even seen you once you were born. But then I woulda spent my whole life wondering where you were, what you were doing, if every little girl I passed on the street was you. And I don't have to do that. 'Cause you're right there, on the same farm, growin' and gigglin' and happier than a chick peckin' at the ground. And that's all a momma really needs in life, to know that her child is happy.

There's gotta be a lotta things a lot of women standing where I am would want to say to their youngens. But all I need to tell you, baby girl, all you gotta know, is this one thing: You are loved. There ain't no day too hard, no mistake too big, no mountain too tall that will ever make a dern difference in that love. Cain't nothin' take it away.

It's real simple. But at the end a' the day, it's the only thing in this great big ole world that makes a smidge a' difference.

It took me right near twenty-one years to realize that, to know that there's people in this world who love me so good that they wouldn't never let nothing happen to me. I'm thinking, looking over at him sitting beside me, him grinnin' like his kid's winning the Little League tournament, that Buddy just might be one of them. He's here with me today at the Kinston farmer's market, the place it all began. "I'm just gonna bring my biology textbook," I told Buddy. "Might as well get some studying done for my exam, 'cause it ain't like I'm gonna be busy here."

Buddy smiled. "You might be surprised at how many people wanna come get them books signed by you."

I got all my cans and jams lined up on this here table. But I also got my brand-new book, all glossy-covered and me smiling with my hair fixed. Khaki and Graham and Buddy, they wanted to have me some big fancy party at the country club for my book launch. But that ain't me. This place, right here under the big green awning, with the air fresh and the other farmers around me, this is where I got to getting my life back together, the place that made me remember there's something I'm right good at after all. It gets me choked up to see the line of my regulars, all waiting to buy my book. And to tell me that I actually taught *them* something.

It makes me think a' my grandma, how she shown me that, even when everyone on this green, wide earth lets you down, the ground, it won't never disappoint you. It just keeps on givin' in ways you never could've expected.

And I feel real blessed because, even though

I'm not the one that's spending all my days makin' sure you grow up right, I get to teach you that. You and me and Alex and Grace, we go out into that little plot a' soil that your daddy tilled up just for us and you dig in that dirt with them chubby fingers, and, even though you can't talk real good yet, I know you get that same feelin' as me. That bright smile and happy laugh and joy over the digging and raking and pulling—well, that's from me. And, of all the things I could've give you, I sure am glad that's the thing you got.

Some days it gets real hard, but loving you like I do, getting to watch you grow and learn and change, it's the best damn thing that's ever happened to a girl like me. And, you know what? It makes me so happy, I'm thinking that I might could make it right by being a mother to a youngen who don't have one, just like Khaki is to you. Well, you know, one of these days when I actually take Buddy up on his offer to get married. But me and Buddy, we both know that me finishing college is the most important thing right now.

Them voices, they still creep in that I shouldn't have done what I done, that I don't deserve another chance. But them voices, they're getting quieter. And you never know when God'll put that second chance right in your path.

So that's all. The whole story. The truth. Maybe it's 'cause I already lived it, I fought the battle and got out alive. Maybe that's why I ain't as nervous 'bout them bookends that mean it's over—and something else is starting up. 'Cause this, baby girl, for you and for me, is only the beginning.

Khaki

NUMBERS

I've always thought the crux of my life, the great symbol when I looked back, would be beautiful design. Instead, looking around at your birthday party that day, I realized it was numbers. I had suffered one monumental loss, had two great loves, three perfect children, and four best friends.

Deciding to give up the big-city life that I'd dreamed of for so long would have been impossible without the support of those people. I'd spent too long worrying about all those voices in my head, those ghosts of my childhood that ridiculed my ambition and doubted my dreams. And now, the only people I had to prove anything to were the ones around me, the ones that mattered: my family.

I don't think I've ever done anything particularly right or great to deserve the life that I'm living now. When I think back, I can't imagine that I have paid enough dues to have gotten this amazingly lucky, had it all fall into place like it did. But Pauline always tells me you can't think about it that way. She says, "Baby girl, whenever you start to feeling guilty, you drop to your knees and thank the Good Lord up above for everything He give you."

Tonight, especially, feels like a gift. You and your brother and sister are asleep and your daddy and I, as we do every so often, pop a bottle of champagne, and, with the video of our wedding streaming on the TV in the background, get out those little scrapbooks.

"We need to put down that Grace rolled over today," I say, and we clink glasses and take a sip.

"And Carolina did a somersault at Little Gym," Graham says.

I take another sip and say, wide-eyed, "She did not!"

He nods, and I let a wave of sadness mixed with guilt that I wasn't there wash right on through me like y'all crawling through the tunnel at the park. Instead of ruminating, I add, "Alex hit his first home run at T-ball tonight."

Another sip, and Graham forces a manly burp, making us both laugh, and says, "That's my boy."

I make little notes in each book and then scoot to lean my back on the couch and snuggle up under my husband's bare arm. I can't help but smile looking at me looking at Graham saying those wedding vows. I lay my head on his shoulder and say, "Oh my Lord, we were so young."

Your daddy kisses my head and says, "Sweetheart, it was only five years ago. We look exactly the same."

"Maybe," I say. But I don't feel sure about anything.

This has been my first week of full-time motherhood—with a little bit of design thrown in during naps and preschool. No flying to New York. No store. And I know without hesitation that I have worked harder, slept less, and been more exhausted than ever before in my life. But, as I run my finger over the monograms on those books again, I feel the ecstatic tears spring to my eyes that make me know that I've never, ever been happier.

Some moments those voices creep in again, the ones that tell me I'm not living up to my potential. The ones that whisper that they knew I couldn't make it long-term. But when I look into the faces of my children, I know that those voices don't mean anything anymore. Because I'm right where I need to be.

I'll probably start working more when we find a great nanny. Graham and I might move away. We might even have another baby. But, for now, we're content to let the chips fall where they may.

As I watch us run down the aisle of the church for probably the hundredth time, I have a wonderful thought: It might be the end of the wedding, but, for this new chapter of our scrapbook, it's only the beginning.

Center Point Large Print
600 Brooks Road / PO Box 1
Thorndike, ME 04986-0001 USA

(207) 568-3717

US & Canada:
1 800 929-9108
www.centerpointlargeprint.com